T0413650

EDWARD RAMIREZ

DEATH COUNT

This book is dedicated to the Peacekeepers (law enforcement, fire department, rescue, and the unknown heroes of our country.) and the Men and Women of the Armed Forces.

Copyright 2024

All rights reserved. This book or any portion thereof may not be reproduced or used in any manner whatsoever without the express written permission of the publisher except for the use of brief quotations in a book review.

ISBN: 979-8-35096-619-0 (print)
ISBN: 979-8-35096-620-6 (eBook)

Start of a New Era.

This book is not for the light-hearted.

Just because we *can* do it, does not mean we *should* do it.

The California sun was high in the sky. The air was hot and the smell of the Pacific Ocean was overwhelming. A lone young gentleman walked the dock of the rich yacht club. He looked at the private boats, sail boats, and yachts, then he looked down off the dock into the clear ocean water. He looked around at the dock numbers and saw a large truck being loaded with metallic plastic rectangle boxes. The crew were taking extra care with the coffin shaped boxes. The guard waved at the young man, then wiped sweat from his forehead. "Can I help you?" "Hello, Sir. What are those coffin-like things?" "Science equipment." "Well, I have a job interview here. I posted my physicals to the company." The guard smiled and looked at the list. "Let me check. It will be a hot one today. In the hundreds. Oh, you are going to see my boss. What is your name?" "Sir, my name is Todd Miller. I am here trying out for the job to help the scientist." The guard walked to the podium. "Yes, your name is here. You are the last one on the list. The other guys did not show. Better for you. I will open the gate. Go to the last mega yacht. I will call ahead. Be careful of the workers. They are moving fragile scientific equipment." Todd walked to the gate and the guard packed his things.

He buzzed him in. "Todd good luck. They will take you. It's your last interview." "Thank you." "Oh, everyone that came here today and it was their last interview, they got the job. You got this." Todd walked down the dock to the last yacht. All the other yachts looked like small military ships. He saw the yacht and it was massive. He saw the work crew taking off from the yacht four metallic plastic shaped coffin boxes. He heard someone calling him. "Are you Todd?" He looked up from the dock. "Yes, Sir, I am." The well-dressed man smiled. "Hi, Todd. Come upstairs to the back of the ship. I cannot wait to meet you." Todd ran up the custom wooden stairs. He walked into a large richly decorated bar room, and walked up to the bar. The man in the suit stood behind the bar. "Hello, Sir." The man smiled. "Hi, Todd. Want something to drink? It is hot here. I am happy you are dressed as we asked. Ready to travel? Want a beer?" Todd replied, "I do not drink." The man looked him over. "Do you smoke or use drugs? Sleep around? How many partners? I ask because this ship will be going around, and we do not need a guy running around starting trouble." "I do not smoke, drink, or use drugs, and I do not sleep around. My test shows that. I hate that stuff. I do not want to say it, but I have not been with anyone yet. I would like to get married someday. I like to be clean."

The suit smiled. "Good, very good. We were watching you. If you did you would not be here. You're a health nut. Not full of himself." "Thank you, Sir. Love to exercise and eat right." "So, Todd. New York, Florida, Texas, Idaho. Nice. You will meet the big boss. Here's a bottle of water." Todd snapped open the bottle of water and drank. "The boss handpicked you. He will be happy that you showed up. I hope the plane ride was to your liking. First class, and the hotel, did you call for any fun to your room? Like the ladies of the night? Like whores?" Todd shook his head. "I do not do that." The man watched Todd finish drinking the water. "He wanted you. The six did not show and three were lies. He wants you. Oh, the cameras on the dock are on loop. No one knows you are here." Todd looked at him strangely. "What type of interview is this?" Then he heard a woman scream and someone collapsed. Todd jumped away from the bar, but his legs were jelly. He collapsed to the ground as the guard walked in. One of the workers ran in. The guard looked at him. "I am the boss. I will kill you all myself. Close the doors. You idiots! Get me the medical staff." The Suit walked around the bar. "We had to kill the three liars. Boss, we took them out to sea and through the bodies overboard." "Good." The worker ran out and closed the doors. Todd tried to get up but felt weaker. He looked at the bottle and saw a mark on the side of it.

The suit looked down at him. "Yes, Todd, we drugged you. You told your mom and dad you were here. Sorry, you are not here. You should have looked at the numbers better and the cameras are on a loop. No one will find you. The hotel has no one staying there by your name and there is no hotel by that name. The plane ticket has been changed to another state. By the way, you are the experiment." Todd's head hit the floor and he was too weak to raise his head. He watched them put a metallic plastic coffin next to him and opened it. The medical team was plugging him up to fluid bags and a machine. They got him ready for something. The Boss walked out talking to his worker. They put him in the coffin. The suit leaned over and said, "They want you alive Todd and the others. Oh, you are the experiment. They will test you. Load him up and ship him out. The next three are on the way here and keep the doors closed. We do not want anyone hearing what we are doing." They put a breathing mask on him, and he watched them close the coffin. Todd's eye lids got heavy and before he knew it, he fell asleep. The boss looked at the suit. "We only got one male. He will have to do. The Nine other are a waste. Men, handle him with special care. We have no time to look for more men. We are already overdue." "Lucky guy." "No, I would not want to be him."

Lab in Nebraska

A young lady danced in the lab as the other ladies laughed.

Sharon: "Mila, I am so happy you and Doctor Zoyo are working with me in bioengineering and biotechnology."

Mila: "Sharon, I am happy to work with you. We have to get these containers locked."

Zoyo: "It was a lot of fun. We have to get ready for tomorrow's flight."

Mila closed a container: "Will all those drugs work?"

Sharon leaned back in a chair: "Yes, hundred percent. I worked on them over ten years."

Zoyo closed a container: "Do not forget the loved ones."

Sharon: "My two angels. I have to leave them behind. I will be back. We will go to the island lab and do our jobs, then I will go home to them. Mila, how many do you have?"

Mila: "I have no one. Look at me. I'm a small round person."

Zoyo looked Mila up and down: "What is wrong with your beautiful body. You are a lady a beautiful lady. I will find you a good Russian man to chase you around. He will marry you and give you babies. I do know this guy. You met him and he likes you. When we are done here. You'll see! You are very cute. If I was a man, I would marry you. I would want your round, cute lady body all over my body, Mila."

Mila smiled and looked at Zoyo: "Thank you. Sharon, all those drugs. When they get put together and put it in a person what happens?"

Sharon: "The human will die or mutate. Hundred percent the human will die. I do not know what will happen if the person lives. I know the super soldier is designed to mutate the human body. That is abuse. That is against human rights laws. We did not make drugs for that. The drugs are for farm animals and plants. The super soldier will have animals in it."

Zoyo walked over to the windows and looked out: "The truck is here for the containers for the lab. Let's go and have fun. No drinking after that for forty-eight hours. Let's have fun."

Office building.

The uncomfortable heat and humidity in the office space made it unbearable for everyone in the office. The small fans did not work but push the heat around. The window in the building made things worse because they did not open. A well dressed man took off his suit jacket and looked at the lady walking into his office. The man sat down and said. "Sorry, I had you, twenty ladies waiting in the Arizona heat. Ladies, here is ice cold water bottles. I had these twenty metallic plastic coffin boxes here with the scientific equipment. Drink up ladies. All of you are scientists?"

New York

A lady walked into her boss's office. A well dress man wiped the sweat from his brow with his handkerchief.

Boss: "Heidi, did I say your name right? I am sorry the A/C is not working in this summer heat. It is very hot in here. I bought you that ice cold bottled water. Are the ladies drinking there water outside?"

Heidi: "Yes, they are."

Boss: "Oh, that metallic plastic box back there in the other storage office has the computer stuff in it. Drink up. I know it is hot. The A/C will be fixed." The man smiled as Heidi drank from the water bottle that was marked.

Pacific Ocean

A large helicopter flew out of South America over the Pacific Ocean. It flew south over the islands. Sharon looked down at the huge private island.

Pilot: "Ma'am, your friends are on the island. You wanted to know. The island is over ten miles long and it is seven miles wide at its widest point. It was a Russian space rocket test site and a super cargo ship building site. This island was a lab and for storage. It is experimental farming now. They sold it after the cold war. No one has used it for some years. The big man wants it."

Sharon: "Who is he?" Pilot looked around in the sky then at the landing pad. "Sorry, Ma'am, I do not know his name. I hope you like your stay. Look at the cargo ship there. It is unloading the lab equipment. I do not know what the metallic plastic coffins are. I bet it is the lab equipment. The big boss is here. His plane is there." Sharon counted twenty metal boxes. The crew was handling a metallic plastic coffin with special care. Pilot: "Ma'am, we will be landing by the building at the end of the island. They build the buildings there so the hole island can be easily accessed."

The main building.

Sharon walked into a huge room with windows around it. There were thirty beds in the room. Mila's head was against the table and Zoyo's head was looking back at the ceiling. Sharon finished her water bottle and began to feel funny as she asked, "What is wrong with you two?" She watched some-one wheel in a metallic plastic coffin. It was followed by a medical crew and a business tycoon. Sharon fell to her knees and felt weak. Sharon looked at the business tycoon. "I do not work for you, Ethan Quinn." Ethen replied, "Hi, Sharon. I am the boss and you do work for me. How are you?" Sharon saw his people put Mila and Zoyo on the floor. Ethen continued, "They are okay. They drank the water like you did. I wanted you to see what you have created with Doctor Drex. You remember him. You helped throw him out of the industry. He wanted to make super soldiers by forcing a woman and a man to have the child. Yes, the super soldier will kill the parents. You and the others reported me for human rights violations. I need the super soldier to make billions. Put those on the floor in the room over there. I want them to watch. I made sure your drink was not that drugged. You and your friends will mutate and help make super soldiers." Doctor Drex walked out and back in with one of Sharon's crates.

Ethen smiled and said, "He changed it a little and it works on humans. You showed him how to put everything together. One side of the vials are for females and the other is for males." He pointed at her, and two men grabbed her and put her in a chair. "Watch. I want you to watch. Bring him in and take him out." Two people rolled a metallic table, then they brought in the special coffin and opened it. There was a blue gel on top. They reached in and pulled out Todd. Todd tried to open his eyes, but they would just roll back into his head. They placed him on the table and hosed him down clean. They took off his breathing mask. The gel deteriorated his clothing. His clothing and sneakers washed off his body. They put his body on a bed and strapped him down as Sharon cried as she saw her creation used for evil and she screamed out, "No! No! Stop! That is not for humans! It is for farming!"

Ethen looked at her and said, "The doctor here with his billions of dollars crew made it for that. They took the animals I had studied for their best qualities in survival and combat. Oh, this is Todd. We already did tests on him. See, his skin has changed color. We made it work with your DNA. We know it works on humans. We tested it on him and some others. Oh, in time they will die, but before that they will give me my billion-dollar super soldiers." Sharon was too weak to speak because the drugs made her weak. They covered up Todd with sheets. Ethen pointed at Sharon and said, "Oh, she is next. Get her drugs ready. I found out it will hurt like hell." The lab tech took vials of blood that had Todd's name on them and put them with the drugs Sharon made. Then, they walked to her, cut the right arm of her shirt off, and took blood from her.

Sharon thought to herself, *I hope this kills me and the others. I do not want to give them a child. A super soldier, a monster. Poor child.* A doctor walked over to Ethen and said, "Sir, this will work even with the sedation drug." Sharon heard in horror. Ethen smiled and replied, "Good, I want her to know all of them and herself get drugged." Todd moved slowly. Sharon watched in horror as they took her blood and put it in with Todd's blood. Then, they took Todd's blood and put it in all the ladies' blood. Ethen looked at Sharon. "You are my best, but I no longer need you to work for me. This is going to be beautiful. Put her on the metal table." They carried her and placed her weak body on the table. They cut her clothing off of her and put her on a bed. They covered her with sheets. Doctor Drex walked over to Ethen and said, "He will be Alpha. We are ready now." Ethen replied, "Doctor, use up all these drugs on them. I mean all of it. Nothing to chance." Doctor Drex "Yes, Sir."

The Doctor clapped his hands, "Open them up. Get them all ready for me." The other metallic plastic coffins were opened. They were now cleaning every-one up and putting them in their own beds. Sharon thought to herself, *God Forgive me! What have I done?!* The medical teams connected tubes to their bodies. She watched in horror as they worked on Todd and injected him with all the male drugs. Todd's body shook as he tried to get out. Sharon watched in horror as Todd bled from his skin and all other parts of his body. Then, he stopped moving. She looked at the machine he was plugged into. He was still alive. His skin got rock hard. They moved him to a bed. His skin changed again. They cleaned the sheets and moved him to a special room. They locked the door. She saw him through the window shaking. They walked to her and began injecting her with the drugs. Her blood ran hot and cold like fire and ice throughout her body and her skin felt like it wanted to jump off of her body. Her brain felt like hellfire one second then artic cold the next. Her body shook violently, and she lost her eyesight. Her bones felt like they were all breaking individually and turning into ash and her inners felt like they were liquefying and exploding. Her heart felt as if it was tearing itself apart.

She wanted to scream in pain but she could only hear herself. Sharon shook out of control as Ethen looked on and smiled as he looked at her in pain.

The cage rooms

Ethen looked at the man in the suit. He looked at the specially made reinforced super plexiglass, super metallic bars, the super doors, and the room cages all about one side of the room. "Mark, watch over them. Keep the cameras on them. No one, I mean no one is to do anything to them except food, water, and change the sheets. Oh, and clean their cages. The scientists are to study them. I will be back. Oh, and if there is some hurricane on its way evacuate the island but leave a security team here."

Cage

Todd tried to open his eyes and saw a white blur. He had a horrible headache. He could not hear. It felt as if someone ripped his eyes from his head and he was growing new ones. He had pain all over his body. Someone was sticking something into his arm. His muscles felt like they ripped off the broken shattered bones. Everything in his body felt as if it exploded or ripped open. He felt his body on fire one second and the next it was ice cold. Then, he saw blackness. He felt as if someone ripped him open and his teeth fell out of his mouth. He felt like he was bleeding all in and out of his body.

Washington DC

The head FBI agent walked through the office and pointed at his best man: "Paul, what are you doing?"

Paul: "Sir, me? Helping everyone with their cases."

Head FBI agent: "Bring your man and come with me, now!"

Paul looked at his man: "You heard him, David." The two men walked into the head office.

Head FBI agent: "A missing persons case has turned into a nightmare. Hundreds of scientists, doctors, and men and women from around the world have gone missing. That is not the bad part. This case is over six months late. It's yours. I hope you know languages. Countries are looking into this and their embassies are calling us. There are twenty-one people missing from other countries. They went missing here in the United States. The Russian government wants answers, as well as other big countries. There was twenty of them who went to dock thirty-one. Dock thirty-one was ripped apart and under construction for over two years. And they went missing at the yacht club. The club says there is no dock thirty-one. There are three doctors or scientists, who went to the pacific. Their container's lab equipment went to the Atlantic and it is missing with them. One company is behind this, and it never existed. The CIA and NSA are calling us for help. They should have called earlier. This is big. The water is so hot now that the President is involved. We have to find those containers and the people. Oh, it is one guy and ten women, plus the scientists and doctors. I want this guy found. Todd is his name. Here is the file. Re-interview everyone."

Paul opened the file: "I have something."

Head FBI agent looked at him: "Go."

Paul: "The company called Global. That was Ethen Quinn's company. It was a bio company for farming. It was closed over fifteen years ago."

Head FBI agent: "Well look into it. Get me answers. Before my boss's boss, the President, comes after me. I will send him after you. Get me answers."

David looked at him: "What is going on?"

Head FBI agent: "The war they say may start. Europe or the world had enough with World War Two. No one wants that. Forget it and get me answers. This may help stop that from happening. Oh, I need you to look into the guy in the Texas desert. Now get out of my office. I have to tell my boss you are on it."

Island

Ethen looked at the caretakers: "What is wrong with them? I have government officials and countries wanting this. They want to make a war so they can make money. They are the money. These things need to move in their cages."

The Manager of the Cage rooms stepped forward: "Sir, they come out and in of this comatose state. We do not know what is going on with them."

Mark: "Sir, I do not think it was wise to kill all the medical staff, lab personal, and scientists."

Ethen: "Where is Sharon's container lab? Find the note books."

A handler walked forward: "It is with the other containers in storage. I think the drugs should have been given in doses."

Ethen looked at Mark: "They want to start their war. I am selling weapons and told them I will have super soldiers. Many of the countries paid for this. Find out what is going on. I will be back. Call me if there are changes."

The handler: "Sir, there is changes."

Ethen looked at him: "Tell me!"

The handler handed a tablet to Ethen: "They are all growing in inches. Their skin shed. Remember, putting all the animals with the strongest skin. Their bones and blood are changing. We do not know what is in there."

Ethen: "Money! Super soldiers are in there. Keep me informed." Ethen walked out of the room.

Mark looked at the handler: "You are an idiot. Everyone, get back to work." Mark walked out of the room.

The handler looked at the manager: "This is taken out of a horror film. Like the one with the dinosaurs. The movie where the dinosaurs broke out and ate the people. What did we not learn from that? I am terrified of the people in the cages. We made a new human. They can make us extinct. Wipe us off the face of the Earth. These things are dangerous."

The manager looked at him: "Man, you are going to get me killed. Shut up. There is ten of us left from the two hundred people. We take care of them, get paid, and go home. Forget this place. This island is weird. I cannot wait to get paid and get out of here."

Todd and the others began to hear again.

Manager: "I cannot wait to get out of here and get home."

The handler looked around: "Man, they are growing their hair back on their heads and they are growing tails. Their teeth are growing back and nails. You have to see them. I know you are scared like me. I am going to double lock their cages from now on. You should see their eyes and their pointy ears. It's like out of a horror film. Man, like I said, I want this to be over now."

The main breaker switch was turned off in the cage building. Todd smelled the air and heard echoes through the halls. He smelled the guards and heard them quietly walking about through the closed doors. They were mainly watching the cage room.

Sharon spoke up: "I need to know how many names. I need to know how many people are here." She heard twenty-nine lady names, plus she made thirty.

Amber: "Hi, I am Amber. I know biotechnology. I cannot see but I can hear. I know how far the walls and doors are." Sharon ran the numbers through her head. "There are thirty ladies here. I smell a man. Why do you not say anything?"

Todd: "I am Todd. What did they put into us? What did they put us in? I can barely see. I know I can see in the dark now."

Sharon smelled the air and heard the guards walking around outside and in the halls. She smelled the fear in the air: "Todd, you will be the first to see and stand. You have to control your body. Control yourself."

Todd heard a guard tapping his foot to music. It helped him draw an echo map of the building. "I know what you are talking about. I have an attraction to you ladies. I can control myself and I will control myself. The children that will come from us will kill them all or the children will control them. You know they will lose control of this, and they will try to kill us. I can smell the rain and hear the storm about five miles away."

Camila: "Hi, I am Camila. My friend is not here with the other ladies. We have science degrees. I know some of the ladies were into construction and engineering. What will happen after we change? You know we must escape and undo this."

Sharon can smell the grass outside: "Well, we have toddler bodies now and we are growing into our new bodies. Todd, they gave you all the male shots. You are going to have to escape and get them away from us till we can escape."

Todd tried to look out the large view window: "So, we have limited everything till we are adults again."

Sharon: "Yes."

Todd: "Well, I know what I have to do. I will get them away from here."

Florida

The FBIs walked around the shipping yard. Paul picked up the phone at the shipping office. "Hello, Sir. The container lab went to South America, then to the Pacific. I just talked with the Mexican officials. There were over two hundred dead who washed up on shore. They all had the company markings on them. The company that does not exist. Oh, Sir, an agent of a South America country called me. He has a retired Seal and other special forces teams from the USA down there. They went in and did a sting on a human trafficking ring. They found out there was a person buying women of certain ages. We have thirty-three missing. The Mexicans say there could be more women missing. Yes, Sir. I know. I will find out the real number of missing women."

Island

Todd felt them put a tube down his throat. The handler looked to his crew: "Hurry up. Hurry up."

Assistant handler: "What is wrong he is out. He is not awake."

The handler: "Just Hurry Up. I do not want to come in these cages anymore."

Second assistant handler: "Well, we are done. Okay."

Mark stood in the hallway and picked up the phone: "Hello, Sir. More news. Three more inches. Todd was five ten when he got here. He is six four. We cannot put the needle in his arm. They are moving around in their beds. They may wake up any day now. Yes, I know it has been over six months. Yes, I know we are way behind. We need new cameras for the cages. The ones we got are the wrong ones. Yes, we need a major upgrade. They cannot see in a pitch-black room. We believe they are moving in their beds a lot at night, and we cannot see them. Will do. Goodbye." Mark looked at the crew. "New cameras are on their way. Boss just has to get them off the shelf. What is wrong with that handler now? Stop acting so scared. We have full control. Those people are all strapped in." The staff turned off the lights and Todd opened his eyes and looked through the dark as it was day. No one saw his eyes glowing light yellow.

Security tower.

The guards laughed as they drank their coffee and one said, "This is the easiest money I will ever get. Sunning and sitting around like a vacation."

The Chief of security walked out of his office and looked at the cameras: "You guys are over there not watching the cameras. What is wrong with the cameras in the cages? They are all off."

Guard: "They cannot be off. They do not work in the dark and they sit behind three inches of steel housing."

Chief of security: "Come here and look."

One guard looked at the tv screens and saw static noise: "That was not like that a minute ago."

The Chief grabbed his pistol: "Let's take a look." Five guards walked with him to the cage building. They walked into the main cage room and one of the guards turned on the lights. The Chief and the guards saw the lights out in the cages. The chief went to look closer but jumped back in fear and screamed out. "Close the door! Lock down this building!" They all saw predator eyes looking at them from within the cages. "Close the Vault doors to the room! Wake the boss!" They aimed their guns at the cages as they retreated back. There were claw marks on the windows of the cages and the cameras were ripped apart. The three-inch housing was ripped and crushed from the ceiling that was fifteen feet up.

Guard: "Sir, he is asleep and gave orders."

The Chief screamed: "I do not care what time it is! Wake him!" The door to the room slammed shut and massive doors closed behind them.

Mark ran down and looked through the security camera first before entering the cage room: "They cannot get out. They are weak. They need a drug to help them move. We did not give them that drug. How did they get up to the ceiling to rip down the cameras?"

They saw Todd and the others made a makeshift living area on the ground. Todd placed the mattress on the floor and behind him. The sheets were covering his whole body.

A guard walked to Mark: "Sir, the walls and steel bed are just like the window." The concrete wall was damaged with claw marks, and it looked like someone used their fists against it. The Lab bed that was steel was ripped apart.

Another guard walked over: "The same thing in the women's room."

Mark smiled: "One of you guards call the boss. He will want to know this. Wake the handlers. Leave them more sheets and have them fed well."

The Chief pointed at the floor: "What is that?"

Mark looked at the hair, teeth, and skin: "I am happy. We designed these cages. Get the caretakers to get that out. You can barely see his eyes. His eyes are scary. The lights are broken in there. That means their eyes are still changing. We can use light against them. Lock the vault doors on the cage rooms. I want the video of the room. I will see them in the morning. Turn off the lights. They're still too weak. Make sure the handlers and caretakers take care of them." Mark went to walk out and stopped at the door. "What is that tapping? Have someone look into it later."

California

David watched the video with Paul. Paul: "See the man on the bicycle in the back ground. Find him. The guard here says he bikes by here every day. Also, the security company for the cameras at the yacht club. Get me the cameras from the next-door repair yard, gas station for boats, and the building on the hill that overlooks the yacht club. The security film we just watched five times was a loop. The same thing is repeating. Let us get to work people."

FBI office

Paul looked at all the agents working at their desk, and he picked up the phone: "Hello, Sir. The CIA and NSA were very helpful. We found out there was an abandoned hotel opened then closed. There are more dead. There are labor workers, security officers, guards, doctors, scientists, lab techs, drivers, handlers for animals and people, caretakers, and hotel workers. There are over three hundred dead. The people who are missing all came to America. Something big is going on. They disappeared and everything points to the Pacific. We are checking private islands right now. One name came up, Ethen Quinn. Sir, I know the money he has and the political contacts he has. I have to go. Some new information came in." Paul looked at the FBI agent at the door as he put down the phone.

FBI agent: "You have to talk to this guy. We found a lab that got destroyed." They walked down the hall to a meeting room. Paul walked in and saw a middle age man.

Paul: "Hello, Sir. The other agent wanted you to come in to talk to me."

Middle aged man: "Yes. I am scared. My family and I are hiding like my other workers. I am a lab technician. I have a private office. The guy hired me to do a study on feces. This happened before the building burned and blew up. I have the camera footage. It went to another building I have. Lucky no one was there that day."

Paul: "Why wasn't there any one there?"

Middle aged man: "Well, my father died, and he worked at the lab. So, every-one went to the funeral. I am scared right now. They say they found the guy who did this, and he is dead and the other guy who killed him is dead too. I have a police friend who told me this. I brought these studies home of the DNA. They are in this book." He handed the book to Paul. "These are three DNA samples here. Look, I went to college with a lady friend, and she is nice. They had us all take each other's DNA. Her name is Irina. Her family told me she is missing. I checked the FBI records. She is one of the missing."

Paul looked at the agent: "You have her file?"

FBI agent: "Yes, right here."

Paul: "Who did she work for?"

FBI agent looked at the file: "A lab company in the west. Well, you want to read this." He handed it to Paul. "She made a human rights complaint. She was not taken seriously."

Paul looked it over: "The name here is Ethen Quinn. So, what is in the book?"

FBI agent, "Well, the paperwork in that book says she is alive. There are two other women in there. Oh, I have the guy's card who wanted the work done."

Paul looked at the card and saw the company logo: "I need a full interview with him. I want him to have protection. Do you think all three are alive."

Middle aged man: "Yes, the samples were two to three days old." The FBI agents smiled. "Sir, there is something strange. There are animals mixed in and a guy mixed in it. They are very healthy and muscular. Irina hated working out hard. She just walked, ran, or did yoga." The FBI looked at him. Paul opened the other files and read them.

Island

Todd heard them turn off the lights: "What ladies? I do not know how long we are in here."

Mila: "I think it is a month or two. I am taller."

Kira: "It has to be longer than that. We sleep a lot. My tail is growing longer."

Sharon: "I wish I was taking notes. I am getting stronger."

Ava: "I have a question. You put this together, Sharon."

Sharon: "Yes, but not like this, not all of this. They changed my work. This was for farm animals. There was a scientist in here that was arrested by the FBI for illegal bio experiments. Doctor Drex."

Natacia: "Well, I saw five of them in here. I read about the FBI arresting them."

Aera: "We all have to find out what they did. I can hear the wind. It is snowing outside."

Brandy: "There is a ship at the port here. There is a storm outside, where do you think we are?"

Sharon: "I do not know. We get out. We will find out. Todd, you asleep?"

Todd smiled: "Yes, I am asleep."

Sharon: "How are you talking?"

Todd: "I am sleep talking, you should try it some time."

Sharon: "Todd."

Todd: "Okay, Okay. I was asleep. You ladies got me up."

Amber: "People are leaving. I can hear forty people going to the ship. There is no one getting off the ship."

Kira: "There are twenty on base."

Sharon: "Todd."

Todd: "Stop! I know. I have to get out."

Sharon: "Why are you not doing anything?"

Todd: "Well, there has to be thousands of people here. They are moving people off this island. I say we wait. There is a tunnel that connects the buildings. They leave the doors open once in a while. So, we hear what is in those buildings. There are less and less people. Even the guard team is getting smaller. So, we wait."

Security tower

The Chief looked at his men: "There are fifteen of us. This will be easy. The handlers and caretakers will keep the records at the lab. Lock the vault doors and all the gates. This is a nasty storm down here at the bottom of South America. This will be easy. We stay in the building and walk through the tunnels."

Cage room

Emily: "There is livestock on this island past the second fens. The wind is going around the bridge, building, wall, and the fences."

Heidi: "There are caves out there."

Todd: "Stop, I can hear it too. Ladies, there are other fences past the second bridge."

Kaori: "You know we are trying to help each other make a map."

Todd: "Yes."

Zoyo: "My grandfather was a rocket scientist like my father. This is the island they worked on. We were not supposed to be on this island. It was a space study and storage base. This base closed over twenty years ago."

Sharon: "Flying here I saw an island two or three miles from here. We can swim to it."

Todd laughed: "Sorry ladies we cannot. Have any of you swam the ocean?"

Sharon: "Todd, no we are not swimmers."

Todd: "We have to hide first. Have you looked at yourselves? We are going to walk to someone and ask for help? They will be horrified. They will kill us. We have to find a place to hide until we reverse this. Remember, they are going to hunt us."

California

The FBI walked the yacht club. Paul looked at the guard: "You say there was a truck here and wrote in the log book. The truck was here but none on the cameras. This guy and girl ride their bike by every day."

The guard looked at them: "Yes, those two do. I saw the truck and wrote it down."

Paul: "The day the cameras were on a loop. You wrote in the log book. The cameras are acting funny and the numbers on the floor moved."

Guard: "Yes, Sir. I saw on the camera as they got off the bikes, but they were in front of me. There was something weird. Well, a lot of weird."

Paul: "What was weird?"

Guard: "The same cab driver kept coming back and dropping people off on top of the hill. Never saw where they went and as I said never saw the truck until it left."

Paul: "Thank you." Paul walked to his car and picked up the phone. "Hi, Sir. Found the people on the bike. They told me someone was fixing the back gate. So, they had to ride around, and they said the numbers were changed for the day. We found the cab driver dead, and the cab was burned. Fake cab company. I had agents check an office building. They just reported someone set up a fake company there. Global. I talked to Ethen Quinn. He said the company was closed for years and does not know what I am talking about. He also said he just bought an island in the South Pacific. He said there should be no one there. He has plans for it, but he has not finished making the plans. He does not know we have his flight logs from the FAA. He has gone down to South America many times and his plains beacon gets turned off down there. The Island is down there. Sir, I need warrants to get on the island. Thank you for your help there. As you do that, I am going to a ranch to ask about Sharon. We already talked to people about the other ladies."

Island

The handler put the empty hampers by the doors of the cages. Then he put extra sheets and blankets under the door.

Handler: "You think they understand us, and they made clothes?"

The caretaker looked at him: "You not counting?"

Handler: "No, why?"

The caretaker looked at the cage: "You have to count and track everything. You said this feels like a horror film."

Handler: "Yes, it feels that way."

The handler jumped back as he looked into the cage room. He pointed up: "She is on the ceiling looking at me!"

The caretaker ran over to the cage and looked in: "Where'd she go?!"

The handler looked at her name: "Rachel. She jumped down. She made clothes from the sheets. She has a tail, and she has to be six feet."

The Manager looked at him: "What does she look like?"

Handler: "Head to toe, covered with sheets. Her eyes are eagle and cat like."

The manager looked around: "That tapping again." They heard something by Todd's cage. Five of them watched Todd grab the reinforced tube bar in his cage. He crushed the metallic tube. Then he moved further back into the cage. The five men ran for their lives, closing and locking the doors behind them.

The Chief stormed over in the hallway: "What? What is it?"

The handler pointed: "Sir, he crushed a bar!"

The Chief opened the control panel for the cages and hit a button that erected an extra cage surrounding the cages. "There you can go in now. It has been three months since they have been awake. They are not getting out. They need a drug. You are safe."

Handler: "They do not need that drug anymore. Their body is making every-thing their body needs from the food we give them."

Chief looked at him. "You and your movies. We are safe."

Wyoming

Paul read the medical records and picked up the phone: "Sir, they were hand-picked. They are all health nuts. Ate right, exercised, and they are athletes. No drugs, no smoking, and no sleeping around. Sir, we found the person hiring the lab techs. Yes, he is dead, and he was a lab tech. He had a friend help out. The guy wants protection. He said his friend, the lab tech, left samples in his house. The lab tech had files on Todd. Yes, Todd is a live. There is something weird about the samples. We have the samples, and our lab is doing the studies. Okay, so we will give him protection."

Island

The Chief looked out the window of the command room in the security tower at the snow falling and saw the sun was setting. "Lock everything down." The handlers and the caretakers walked into the cage room. The security locked three doors and the doors in the hallway. The Chief looked at his security staff now armed. "This building, we will secure. The cage room is secured, and we will leave it alone. I want everyone watching the cameras. We have the new ones." The phone rang and the Chief picked it up. "Sir, we are going to move to the building at the dock. You want us to stay in the security tower. The boat will be here in two days. Sir, we just found out. They are playing us. Sarge told us they are talking to each other in Morse code. Yes, the one who always works outside, and he stays inside the base during the winter months. They are destroying their cages. One of them was drawing on the reinforced Plexi glass. There was one drawing in the concrete. The male crushed the bar. Yes, Sir. We set up the feed system. Yes, we will wait in the security building not the cage building. Have a good night." The Chief hung up the phone and looked at the handler. "You are right. This feels like a horror movie. Two days. There will be only three people down here for maintenance for the winter months. The beaches have the sonic and ultrasonic weapons up. We do have sonic shields up. We have to leave the island in two days. The storms get really bad down here during the winter."

The manager looked out the window: "Well, they will be fine with food and heat. We have to leave in two days. It will feel like forever."

The handler looked at them: "This is a horror nightmare. They will rip out of there in minutes and not days. They are waiting on this day. They were testing us. They will kill us and wait for the boat. They will do what they want to our planet. We have to kill them, Now!"

The Chief looked at his guards and security officers: "That is a lot of money in those cages. You need to calm down. I will not kill them. Put the sonic shields on the buildings. Get the emergency building ready. Put the sonic shields on the two bridges. We will use the third bridge. There is a bridge to the dock, and it is two hundred yards to cross. We will raise it in an emergency. And you, handler, you need to calm down. We have more than enough ways to stop them."

One of the guards looked at the handler: "Calm down. You watch too many movies. All the vault doors are closed. They are not getting out."

In the air.

Paul listened to the airplane engines. He looked at the information the lab sent him. He picked up the phone. "Sir, you see what I sent you? This lab report does not make sense. The hair sample and skin sample does not match the other samples. The lab said these people changed their bodies or mutated into something. Yes, Sir, this sounds like a Syfy horror movie. We know they are all alive but in what condition? What is being done to them? I have to go out to the ranch. The father said Sharon made a complaint about an old company before she went to work for this farming company. Yes, the company that does not exist. I still want to bring in Ethen Quinn for more questions. Sir, we do know the lab containers went to South America, but it did not get there. Sir, when I get more information. I will call." He thought to himself, *I need to find out how Ethen Quinn got in the middle of all this and what is going on.*

Island

The Chief smiled: "We have some hours left for the boat. You made sure they have everything?"

The manager leaned back in his chair: "Yes, I told the handler he was over reacting. They have everything."

The Chief picked up the phone: "Hello, Sir. Just reporting in. We are ready to get off this island. We moved the last of the things to the dock. Yes, the storms are coming in heavier and heavier every time." Everyone heard a loud noise of metal being ripped apart and the noise came from the mics in the Cage room. Everyone looked in horror into the direction of the lab. The Chief looked at the guards glued to the cameras view screens.

Chief screamed out: "What was that?!"

Guard: "Checking!"

Chief: "Sir, something happened in the cage room. I do not know what that sound was. Mark, I will call you back. I do not know what is going on." He hung up the phone. The guard studied the cameras.

Guard: "Chief. I am looking at the cameras of the cage room. The male ripped the doors off his room and threw it across the room."

Chief: "There were three steel doors. I wanted to see him walk, jump, or run around, but now I want to get away from him." The cameras just started to go down and the radio mic came to life.

Sarge: "This is Sarge. I am in the lab building doing routine patrols. I have seven security officers with me. We will check out the cage room."

The handler ran over: "Get them out of there."

The chief looked at him: "Calm down. This is no horror movie."

The chief looked at the Manager: "How strong is a human man?"

Manager: "I do not know. Why ask me?"

Chief: "Great."

Cage building

The Sarge looked down the hall: "Who opened the vault door and the doors to the cage room?"

Guard: "They would need a combination to open it from the inside. The sonic shields are up in the hallway."

Sarge: "They are smart. They watched us test the doors and open them from the inside. Careful everyone. Stun weapons at the ready. We want him alive. We move as one to the room and watch everything." They walked to the lab with their stun rifles at the ready. The Chief listened to the mic. One of the guards looked into the room.

Guard: "The lights are on."

Sarge waved his hand forward: "Move in carefully." The guards walked into the lab and looked around. One guard stood by the door as the other guards walked around the room and looked around. The guard closed the door to the cage room and walked away from the door to help with the search. The Chief watched through the camera from the hallway. He saw Todd's hand appear above the door and he opened the door slowly. The Chief screamed over the mic, "He is on the wall above the door!"

They all turned and saw Todd looking at them. He was upside down holding the wall. Todd jumped down and rolled out the door. He threw a part of the metal bed into the sonic shield device. The device threw sparks everywhere. One guard screamed out, "He is fast!" The Chief watched Todd run into the hall and through the building. The sonic shield devices began to get destroyed. Todd ran by a second vault door that said "Cage Room Two" and he turned. He saw "Cage Room Three." Chief watch Todd run to the back of the building as he knew his way around the building taking out the sonic fields.

The guard looked at the cameras: "Wow! We got to get off this island!"

Chief: "Put the sonic shields on maximum!" The Chief keyed the mic, "He is running to the back of the building. He is taking out the sonic shields. That thing is opening doors." Todd opened the outside door and destroyed the sonic shields. He ran by some jeeps and snowmobiles. The guards chased him. The Chief looked at the two guards in the command room. "You two are snipers. On the roof. That thing is outside. It is minus thirty-five and overcast. Get ready." The Chief picked up the phone. "Mark, what did you guys make? The male named Todd is outside and running. I do not care. This thing is faster than us and my men are chasing it outside."

The team ran outside into the cold night as it snowed. The guards got on the special vehicles and gave chase. The Sarge pointed and screamed out, "You can see him through this storm! He is over there. He is running." The drivers pushed down on the accelerator. Sarge keyed the mic, "Chief, this is Sarge. You still got us on cameras?"

Chief: "Yes, I do."

Sarge: "He is fast, but we will have him. He is running at thirty miles an hour. We caught up with him. We have him."

Chief: "Good."

Todd looked at the vehicles around him. He took off running at top speed on all fours. The Sarge screamed, "What happened?! He is faster. Driver, what do you mean he is running at fifty? Chief, he is running on all fours." Todd smashed through the electrical fence. Electrical sparks flew everywhere as Todd jumped to his feet. He ran and jumped over a ravine. All the security vehicles stopped. Sarge keyed his mic, "He jumped a hundred feet easy. What is that thing?"

Guard: "Sarge, the dart gun." Todd stood at the other side of the ravine. Sarge aimed and fired the dart. He was amazed as Todd caught the dart and threw it down. Todd ran into the jungle.

Sarge pointed: "The number one bridge. We go across there."

The Chief saw four guards running to him: "I need you four guards to go down and lock the cage room and close the doors. Lock all doors. Go now!" The four guards ran out of the security room.

Security tower.

Two guards looked through their scopes on the roof. The guards looked around in the distance.

Guard 1: "This is not good."

Guard 2: "You are right. He needs to call everyone back."

The Chief looked through the binoculars and the radio came to life.

Guard: "This is the roof guards. We have a problem."

The Chief looked at the handler: "Do not say anything."

Handler: "I told you. He is still learning. Then he will kill. He will get the ladies out and they will help him. We do not know what he can do or the ladies."

The Chief keyed his mic: "This is the Chief, go."

Guard: "Sir, we are the roof guards. He is up here with us."

Chief: "Impossible. He would have to run around us at forty for us not to see him." He remembered. "Get out of there! Get off the roof!" The chief looked at the handler, "We forgot to put the sonic shields in an area to prevent them running around us. Handler! Go to the manager and tell him to get his crew to the emergency building and raise the big bridge and leave the small one down. My men and I will use the small one to get across. You can easily see him trying to get across the small one. Raise it if you do not hear from me or my men giving reports on what is happening on the island, or you hear us dying. He may get to the building. If you hide there, they will not find you. Now go."

Security tower roof

Todd sat there watching the two snipers. The guards looked at each other. Then they looked at their guns. Todd looked at them. "Do not go for the guns." The guards moved to a control council. He looked at them, then looked at the side of the roof and saw eight disc shaped devices on the roof. He dove off the roof as the guards turned on the sonic shields. The Chief ran to the window as something flew past it.

Guard: "This is the roof guards. He is gone. He is close to seven feet tall. What you say? The other guard is talking, hold. He is looking over the edge. He is down there. What do you mean he is not? He jumped down forty feet. He is gone! Where did he go! We are getting off the roof."

The Chief screamed over the radio: "Everyone outside, come into the main building! Then work your way to the security tower!"

Cage room.

The guards walked into the cage room and saw themselves looking at thirty ladies that stood over six feet three inches tall out of their cages looking at them. The bars of the cages were mangled and ripped apart. The guards looked at each other and then they ran for dear life. They ran into the hall as one of the guards raised his rifle and opened fire behind him. The ladies disappeared from sight as he shot into the room. The other guard hit the emergency button and the vault doors closed and locked. Sharon screamed out, "Ladies, we have to hit that door hard!" All the ladies charged the door. The guards smiled until all the ladies hit the massive doors at once. The vault door ripped from its hinges and hit the floor. The guards ran and fired their rifles behind them.

Security Tower

The Chief jumped as he heard gun fire. The work crew ran down the stairs to the third bridge. The handler hit the button to the building. The sonic shields came to life. They heard screams behind them. They turned and saw three ladies over six feet tall run back to the lab holding their ears. They hit the emergency button on the bridge. The number three draw bridge rose. The vault door on the emergency building closed.

The Manager looked out the window: "This is a horror." The Chief looked around outside the big window as the roof guards ran to him.

Guard: "The roof is locked, and shields are on."

Chief kept looking out the window. "Turn on the sonic and ultrasonic shields. Turn them on, Now!"

The guard at the control desk looked at the controls. "Which ones?"

Chief: "All of them!"

Field beyond the last gate.

Sarge's team drove back over the first bridge and through the fence. Sarge: "Chief, we did not find him. We are on our way back."

The Chief keyed his mic: "Go to the dock emergency building and turn on all emergencies. We will be there." The crew stopped in a clear field. One of the guards looked at Sarge.

Guard: "What do the red and yellow lights mean?"

Sarge walked over to his vehicle as the driver of the vehicle got out for a smoke. Sarge: "I do not know. I do not know what is going on. There is no fire." They heard gun fire coming from the cage building. Then, Todd ran out of nowhere and grabbed Sarge's jeep with one arm. He threw it ten feet away and ran into the night. Everyone jumped into the other vehicles and drove at top speed back to the base.

Guard looked at Sarge. "Sarge, where did he come from!"

Sarge looked at the guard: "I do not know. You were looking in the same direction I was." They drove past the cage building. They drove around the corner of the security tower and found the Chief and his men running from the security building.

The Chief waved to them: "Let's go." They heard a scream come from behind them. They turned and saw Todd holding his ears. He was forty feet from them, and he turned and ran away. Everyone jumped out of the vehicles.

Sarge looked at the Chief: "Why does the sonic device not work on us?"

Chief: "We have the equipment on." The chief pointed at the emergency building at the end of the dock. They ran over the small bridge. Sarge hit the button and the small bridge rose up. They worked frantically to chain up and lock up the bridge. The handler opened the vault door to the emergency building. The manager turned on the power. The guards set up the sonic shields.

The Chief looked at the guards: "Lock the door and put the furniture in front of the doors. Get the rifles ready. Load up. Leave the lights off in the building and use night vision."

Sarge pointed at the camera: "The females are still in the cage building. They are throwing things out of the building to hit the sonic shields."

Outside

Todd looked at the cage building and could not get in because it was locked down. He looked around and saw cables on the ground. He smelled the air and listened for the generator. There was a sonic shield around the generator building. He ran to another building and ripped the metal door off. He used the door as a shield against the sonic sound and got to the building. Todd could not get to the door of the building, so he ripped through the building wall. There was a sonic shield in the building. He looked through the door at the sonic shield dish. He through a piece of the cylinder block wall at it and destroyed it. He walked into the building and looked at the fire door to the generator room. He ripped the fire door off the hinges and used it as a shield against the sonic machine. He reached around and unplugged it. The sonic devices turned off throughout the island. Todd walked over to the generator and powered it down to normal power.

Emergency building.

Chief looked out the building: "Who turned off the sonic shields and the ultrasonic shields on the island? Someone get me the phone and see if it works."

Sarge pointed out the small window: "The male is moving around over there. He is being careful."

Chief looked at the handler: "The only sonic shields that work are in this building."

Sarge: "This is bad. This is worse than a horror film. It is a nightmare."

Chief raised the phone to his ear: "Ethen Quinn, they took the island. Yes, Sir they have control of the island. They just ripped out their cages. There is just a hand full of us and we cannot get them. The male got out first. He gave time for the ladies to get out on their own. Yes, on their own. They can run on all four or on two legs. They are faster than our vehicles and can jump long distances or dive from high up. That is impossible for a normal man. I have no time to get data or do studies. You can ask them to do it again when you are here. My men and I were running for our lives. You can come down here and talk with them and get the studies. They want out. They threw a jeep. We had on the shields, and they got to the generator room and turned it off. I think you are not hearing me. You can come over and turn it on. Oh, yea! What? I do not care if you are my boss! You can fire me if you like. You can come down here and ask them to get in their cages. I will not order anyone out there. They threw a car ten feet and climbed a tower and they dove off it for the fun of it. There was no water on the bottom. Yea, they landed safely on the ground below and ran away. Look, they ripped from the hinges off the vault door. I do not know how heavy the vault door is. That did not hold them in. The vault doors were locked but they learned how to open them from the inside. Yes, we have no control. No one is dead for now. How long till the boat gets to us? What? The morning?! Wake the guy up and send him here. We will not last a second with these things. They out smarted the men and they can crawl on walls and ceilings. We will try to hold until the early morning. The boat is at max speed, good. Thank you." Chief hung up the phone.

Sarge walked to him: "The male was watching us, and he is gone now. He knows we are in here. He was looking at us at the end of the dock behind us."

Chief looked out the small window. "What?! How did he get behind us? He had to swim around us. You know how cold that water is. Wow. This is not good. We have to wait."

The handler walked to them: "So, what will happen?"

Chief: "He is sending his personal army here to get them."

Handler looked at him: "They do not know these things and what they can do. They have no idea what they made."

Chief: "Look, we just have to hold on till that boat gets here. Everyone make sure everything is locked down."

Outside.

Todd ran to the cage room. He walked into the building as the ladies were opening the other vaults and found more women in them.

Sharon pointed: "Ladies, like Todd told us before, we may get the island then it will be a matter of time before they take it back. Ladies get food, medical supplies, and blankets. We will come back for more. First, we have to make a base on the island we can hide in until we change this." She looked at names on a list. "Todd, you are the only guy here. There are two hundred women here. They were going to artificially inseminate us. They tried test tubes, but the children died. You know test tube babies have no human bond and they are very dangerous. They have been outlawed. Ethen covered all areas like science and studies in farming here. He wants to make sure no one knows."

Todd looked at everyone: "There are woods over a mile from here. There is an abandoned base past the gate. It is two miles from the gate. There is a lot of equipment there. The base is locked down. Then the caves are past that."

Some of the ladies walked the hallways. They ripped through doors looking for anything they can use. They found log books and paperwork.

Emergency building

The Chief watched through the binoculars at the new species of human walk out the back end of the building carrying things to the woods. They watched Todd run around the outside of the buildings as the ladies ran away to the woods.

Sarge looked at the Chief: "This building has its own power station. This building also controls the sonic weapons on the beaches. They are not getting off this island."

The handler pointed as he held a rifle: "The lights to the main building" The lights flickered then they heard an explosion and sparks shot up into the night sky. The lights turned off.

Chief looked about: "What are they carrying?"

Guard looked out the small window. "They found the base on the island and took out its sonic shields and power locks."

Chief: "Are the phones working?"

One of the guards looked at the computer: "Phones out but the radio works. The second the boat comes over the horizon we will be able to call them. They took out the main power building. When does the ship get here?"

Supply building

Julia smiled: "That will keep them busy."

Mila looked at Sharon: "I have some laptops and they got power. One of the ladies found emergency portable generators. She is carrying two of them."

Sharon smiled: "Good, we make a small base in the woods. How cold is it out here? Anyone cold? It feels like it is in the low seventies."

Natacia carried the two four hundred pound generators: "I always wanted to be stronger but not like this. One of the other ladies is carrying the emergency batteries and soler panels."

Dalisay: "There is a bridge. The woods are on the other side."

Orit: "There is snow on the ground, and we are not cold. The last time I was around snow I was freezing and it had to be in the thirties."

Sharon remembered she saw someone put in the super soldier drug an internal cooling and heater drug. "Ladies, let's get to the caves. Anyone know how to make a fire?"

Brandy waved her hand: "There are ten of us. I know how. I do. My family loves camping. I also lived on a farm."

Hana: "I lived on a farm too. We can use those bulls and make a wagon to move things."

Sharon looked at the cattle in the field. "Good idea."

Nebraska

Paul picked up the phone, "Hello, Sir. I found a Russian FSK agent working on this. He gave me everything he found or has on the case. He was talking to Sharon's father. Her father said the same thing but I noticed she made a complaint about a company. Many of the ladies made the same complaint about the same company. I had that company checked out. I found out the women who made the complaints are on the missing list. The complaints are about human rights violations. The company is into everything. The father showed me this fitness expo. Todd's name came up with every lady that is missing but we still do not know the number of women that are missing. Todd did a part time job at the expo. The business tycoon we are after. Yes, it is Ethen Quinn. The Russian agent told me Ethen Quinn owns two of the islands in the Pacific. No, not the island we thought. It is closer to the South Pole. I will get back to you when I have more information."

Island

The Manager pointed at the horizon. "The ship is coming." Then the radio came to life. "This is vessel Sandra. Anyone there?"

Manager: "We are happy to see you. We will be on the dock. Emergency escape."

Captain: "This is the captain, and we hear you loud and clear."

The Chief looked at everyone: "They will send a team to the island to get these things. We only bring our personal items. The ship will not tie on. The ship will open its side door and we will all get on as fast as we can." Everyone ran out the emergency building.

The ship pulled up to the dock and everyone stormed to the end of the dock. The ship touched the dock, and everyone jumped on pointing their guns at the beaches. The ship crew also had the weapons aimed at the island. The ship pulled away and the captain asked. "You guys, okay?" The Chief looked at him and replied, "Get us out of here." The ship sailed away as the Sarge pointed and said, "They will get into the emergency building."

Captain: "Let them have the island for now."

The handler looked at them: "We have to destroy them."

Chief looked at the island. "The Boss wants them. That is money there."

Main building

They saw Todd standing on top of the roof on the main building watching them leave. Todd smelled the cold morning air as the ship vanished over the horizon. He jumped down and walked to the woods.

Sharon looked at the ladies: "We need a plan. We need to find the containers and get a lab set up and running."

Akemi: "We need to scout the island for anything we need."

Todd walked into a cave the ladies made into a temporary base and he sat down. He took off his head scarf and mask.

Emily looked at his face: "Do we all look like that? Pointy ears, fangs, and an appearance like a mix between a cat, a dog, and a bear?"

Aera: "Yes, we do look like the animal wolverines but humanoid and without the snout. We still have our human structure, but we are muscular. Todd, did they leave?"

Todd looked at them: "They left six hours ago. I was exploring the caves and the rocket base. It is in good shape. I found caves that lead to a dry dock with huge container ships. They have to be one thousand seven hundred meters long. So, what is the plan?" None of the ladies had a plan.

Todd: "I think we need to move deeper into the cave."

Neith looked at her hands: "I love cats but never wanted to have them as a part of me. I study the weather. We have to find out where we are. One of the log books says it is September, October, or November. We are south somewhere. There is no island north like this. We are nowhere near Alaska. The USA or Russia would be here by now. I am with Todd, we move in more inside the cave. If we are south, it will get too minus seventy to eighty."

Sharon looked at them: "I do not know where we are. Some of the ladies are walking through the caves. We do need a map."

Todd: "Well, I know where there is a map of the world and maps of the island. We need a plan fast."

Bian: "Why?"

Todd looked at her: "There are laws against this. I saw five people they were looking for. They did Bio laws against super soldiers. I remember everything I read." The ladies started to walk toward them.

Katie: "He is right. We have to reverse this, and the nations of the world agreed on these laws."

Aila: "We reverse this and they will still hunt us."

Sharon: "I am thinking."

Todd pointed at Sophia: "What do you see in the dry hangers?"

Sharon looked at him: "What are you doing?"

Todd looked at Sharon: "You cannot think of everything."

Sharon: "Let me plan."

Todd: "No. We let you plan. We would still be in the cages or fighting a full security force."

Sharon: "What? I was trying to help."

Todd: "Okay, but we need something now. They will drop nuclear weapons on us. These ladies have strengths we can use. All of you have engineering degrees or work experiences."

Sharon: "Wait, some of us speak languages we do not understand."

Todd: "We will all learn from the other. Sharon, you are a chemist. You also have a chemical engineering degree. We have rocket scientists here. We can stay by Mars till they want us back or they find a way to kill us."

Sharon: "I have two kids. I will not leave them."

Todd stood up: "You have to. To save their lives. They will hunt you and destroy or kill everything around you. Even if you reverse this, they will still hunt you and kill you."

Mila: "Listen to him. We have to work together now."

Grace: "Look Sharon, many of us have children. How long will it take them to hurt our children? Or one of us have children. We can get pregnant by normal humans. If one of us started fighting how many people would we need to kill to get them to let us live?"

Sharon: "We stay around Mars. So, how do we make gravity and how do we get there?"

Todd: "I have a Plan. We have sea dragon engines and other engines. We have some ladies who got the gravity wells working. It is Mars. We need every inch of this island explored. We also need the containers looked at."

Sharon: "I need ten ladies. I will go through the containers."

Todd: "You need more help than that. You have not seen how many are down there. The manifest is down there at the first containers. There are thousands of containers."

New York

Paul picked up the phone, "Sir, I am sending an agent to look at the crashed plane. I am following every lead. We found a dead scientist that was coming up on charges over illegal bio engineering of super soldier and human bio animals. We talked to Ethen Quinn again. He was no help. I know he is hiding something. I know this investigation is over in a few years. Yes, I know. The plane that crashed does not exist and the people who died worked for a company that does not exist. Yes, yes, I will look into it. Have a good night."

Island

Todd walked into the base, and he looked at the ladies. "We need a design. This ship and others like it need to be put together. Some of you are working on the rocket sea dragons and Ion engines, other chemicals we need, and some on the gravity wells. We are working on three ships. We already built working robots and some of the ladies found some industrial robots. We have everything we need. This guy who owns the island was getting into the space program. One of us can do the work of a hundred people. So, let's do this. Oh, no one is to walk outside. We want them to think we left."

Louis: "I am working with you. Todd, do you want the hull on the front ten feet thick, sides five feet thick and rear four feet thick?"

Todd: "Yes and the front shield twenty feet. The ship will have to be three thousand meters long and a thousand meters wide. Some are working on life support systems and new rocket engines. Let's get to work."

Louis: "You have a design? Where will we get all the materials?"

Todd pointed at the island: "There is a ship junk yard over there with four cargo ships that are easily a thousand seven hundred meters long, and six that are a thousand meters. Hangers full of rocket materials and farm equipment. Yes, I have a design, but I want to see everyone's ideas. Let's get to work."

Esther looked at him: "How will we launch that?"

Todd pointed: "The ship launch ramp is at twenty degrees. We need to make it forty-five degrees."

Zuri pointed at the side of the massive steep hill: "What about that? The hill looks sixty degrees."

Todd looked: "Good Idea. Let's get to work." They worked quickly and smart.

Caves

Aremi walked to Sharon: "This is a better place in the caves. We need more copper and carbon-carbon. We also need to make that graphene you made."

Sharon looked up from her workstation: "They found a map of where we are. It will get between minus eighty and minus one hundred here in the winter. These fires in the cave must stay on. We have rubber and materials to make super rubber. They found metals down here. We have to dig up. the carbon-carbon we have to make it. Wow, he is right we are smarter."

Orit: "Yes, he is right. We are faster and stronger. We are getting more work done in a day. Oh, you see the industrial robots?"

Sharon: "How many robots do they have?"

Juliette: "They have over a few hundred with the ten monster robots. They are working on a Nova one rocket. They are upgrading it. They can make it work. They are working on the programming of the new computers they made. We found oil."

Base

Heather walked to Todd working on the launch site: "I need sand from the beach and oil."

Todd looked at her: "The sonic machines are turned off all over the island. There are some ladies on the beach getting sand. The oil is in the pumps or tanks. There might be someone there checking on how much oil we have. Are you making the super glass?"

Heather: "Yes, we are waiting for the graphene and other materials."

Vered "We all are. I am going to help Sharon make materials."

Petra: "The next forty-eight hours we will easily have the materials we need. Sharon has us making some robots. The machines are working now."

Todd: "That is good. We are going to have a thousand machines helping. Vered, you can go and help there but we really need you here helping with the small four-hundred-meter ship. We need the ship first. It goes inside the main ship."

Vered: "I will help with the ship."

Caves

Mila walked to Sharon: "There is a massive snow storm outside. We brought the animals into the caves. They will be warm there. We have feed for them for years. They have a lot of food. We found the hanger where they kept more animals. They were going to move the animals to the holding areas, but we got out. We found a store house of food for hundreds of millions of people. We dug up more rocks and made that foil paper and found sand stuff for Titanium. There is a lot of junk on this island for us to use. We made the fire proof insulation. We also pumped more oil and made some from plants like you asked."

Zoyo: "The materials will be ready faster now. Todd sent help. The super paint is ready too."

Sharon looked at the computer in the lab: "Todd wants us take apart the buildings to the base and the base we were in. He wants to use everything here."

Reachel: "We started taking them apart. All the animals have been moved to the caves. Both bases do not look as they were. We have all the sonic weapons and fencing. We moved the massive generator here. We took them apart, upgraded them, and rebuilt them."

Launch site

Sharon walked onto the ship: "Todd, how wide is this ship and how long? This is too big."

Todd smiled as he put down the tool bag: "Thousand meters wide and high and three thousand meters long. It has four sea dragon rocket plasma ion engines. Each engine is two hundred meters long and gives over five million thrust. Then we got the smaller rocket pulse engines. The engine room is seven hundred meters long. It has these new reactors, nuclear fusion. More than enough power."

She looked at the deck: "You got in the new decks we made. So, how will we stop when we get into space? Have you thought about that?"

Todd looked around: "Yea, um, I did."

Sharon: "I hope you did. I do not want to find out we are on the other side of the galaxy trying to find our way home."

Todd: "I did. We put in the decks."

Sharon walked upstairs and saw massive doors: "The floor to ceiling? The fuel is ready and the paint. The outer four doors work?"

Todd: "Yes, there are four hulls in the living area and three to the hole ship. Ceiling to floor will be about ten feet after everything is in. Some places will be fifteen feet. Storage is twenty feet high ceilings. Emergency all around. Just in case."

Sharon looked at everything and smiled: "It looks good."

Todd: "It has almost been a year. No one came looking."

Sharon looked at Todd: "They are looking for missing persons who do not look like us. They will find us like this. They will kill us like you said. You know there are massive storms outside."

Todd embraced her: "Calm. It will be okay."

California

Ethen looked at his staff in the meeting room. Ethen: "The FBI is all over us. I know the creatures are loose on the island. I want one of you to find the one that did not get on the plane you crashed. He took a train. Find him before he makes it to the US. We have to get back to the island. We left the wrong people there. The people there panicked and did not follow orders. They did do something right. They left on the sonic weapons. General, what is your plan?"

The general put the map of the island on the meeting table: "This is what has to be done to get back these humans without hurting them."

Island

They worked together as a team and moved the four-hundred-meter ship into the main ship. They fixed it into place. They moved the eight-hundred-meter ship and placed it on top of the main ship. Then they submerged all three ships. Sharon heard on the radio.

Yuval: "This is a good idea. You said you heard they did this during World War 2. There is no water in the four-hundred-meter ship. We are looking."

Heidi: "No water in the eight-hundred-meter ship. We are looking."

Daphne: "There is no water in the three-thousand-meter ship. We need to name these three ships."

Nergui: "These space suits are working nice."

Emma: "The suits are nice. There are no air bubbles. This new welding works."

Ava: "The life support is working in all three ships."

Rosa: "Nosotras estamos arreglando danos menores menores en el motor."

Todd: "I am glad we all taught each other languages." He keyed the mic. "Arreglarlo estare alli. Hoka no chiiki mo chekku-chudesu. Hanggang sa muli. I hope I said that right."

Cristina: "Vocedisse certo."

Todd: "Good I am learning ladies."

Ara: "Unlineun mun-eul gochigo iss-eo"

Todd: "Naneun geogi iss-eul geos-ida. Prochainement. Yanindan gecmek. Wow, how many languages did we learn?"

Bolormaa: "Every language on the planet."

Todd: "Okay, ladies. Let us get the work done. I will be moving from ship to ship. See you all soon."

Hours Later

Todd opened the dam to let out the water after a hundred hours of the ships being under water. Heidi smiled and opened the outer doors: "We started working on everything that needs repairs and upgrades."

Emily: "We need to start putting in more sensors and computers."

Todd looked at the ship: "Put in the outer shielding and cover up the two ships. All three engine rooms have been finished."

Sharon looked at the ships. "Let's paint."

Bian looked at Todd: "The work pods are working. We got eight working and they are moving buildings."

Florida

Paul looked at the file in the FBI office. He drank coffee and looked at the airport log books. Paul: "One man missed his flight, or he did not want to take it. He saw the same person take a train up from the bottom of South America, then a ship from Brazil into Maimi, Florida. Why did he go that way? He lives in Colorado." The agents thought it was odd. Paul: "The person's plane ticket was paid for by the company that does not exist. Why didn't he take the plane that crashed? There was a ship destroyed and the ship's crew is dead. We have more dead and more questions." He looked out the office window into Maimi. "This person ran to New York. Why? He ran from New York to Pennsylvania. David, find him."

David: "I will find him. I am on it."

Washington D.C.

The Airforce Colonel sat in front of Paul.

Paul: "Thank you for meeting with me Colonel. What do you have for me?"

Colonel: "You asked for this. We sent a drone by that island. We did take pictures. The Russian old space rocket base is gone and the buildings on the base to the east end are also gone. It appears the ten buildings on this side of the island are gone. They are doing a major remodeling on the island. The cargo ships are gone with all the other junk that was there. There is no construction equipment anywhere. They could have moved it before we sent the drone. Remember, it was years before we sent a drone down there. Livestock have been moved and they are not there." The colonel handed pictures to Paul. "Look at this. These are the old pictures." Paul looked at the old pictures and then he looked at the new ones. The colonel pointed at the pictures and explained, "These two pictures are over two years apart. You can see in one there are people walking around and there are over ten buildings. The other one there is no one there. There could be underground tunnels. There is a huge cave opening here but we cannot look into it. I do not know what you are looking for, but the new pictures do not make sense."

Paul: "What you mean?"

Colonel: "This hill has moved. Trees are missing. The large beaches are gone." The colonel put a picture in front of Paul and the picture showed a shadow in a cave. It showed someone looking up at the drone. "We measured that person. That person is six to six three and a muscular person."

Paul: "Can I take these pictures?"

Colonel: "Yes."

Paul: "Thank you for your time."

The colonel handed the pictures to Paul: "You can have them. I hope you find them."

Paul: "I will find them. We just have to get to them. Thank you once again, Colonel."

Island

Sharon pointed: "We made the computers work better than the ones we had."

Zoyo: "We are now putting dirt and grass and trees in the three ships. The bridges are ready."

Amri: "The medical bay is ready. Did you know we made a lake? And the labs are ready."

Grace smiled: "The living conditions are nice. The green houses are up and working. Do you know why all of this was on the container ships?"

Sharon looked at them: "The guy who did this to us was crazy. He also had a fear of the third world war or apocalypse."

Launch site

Bandy looked at Todd: "Everything checks out. We almost got all the live-stock and the other animals on the ship. We got the fish on. The green house is one hundred percent."

Todd smiled: "We are almost done. How long have we been doing this?"

Yuval: "Well over two years, I think."

Freja: "You think the FBI is asking this Ethen guy questions and holding him up?"

Todd: "Well, I think they are looking for us."

Texas

Paul looked at the pictures with the shadow. He then read the lab report and looked at the laws. He looked out the window at the Dallas night skyline. He opened the door of the car and climbed out. Paul keyed his radio. "All agents hold your positions. I am going in." He looked around the dark desert and walked into the truck stop. Paul looked around at the people there and walked to the bus agent. "Hi, when is the last bus?"

Bus agent: "We got one going to Dallas, Texas. Nine P.M. One hour from now."

Paul put his badge on the counter: "Do not board anyone until I give the go ahead. I do have someone I am looking for. I will be back."

The lady looked at him: "Yes, Sir. I will let the Manager know."

Paul walked across the truck stop and into the diner. He looked around and saw a bar through the window. He ran across the parking lot of the truck stop to the bar. He walked in and saw a man sitting in the back watching everyone carefully eating a burger. He pulled a picture from his pocket and looked at it.

Paul walked up to the guy watching everyone and sat across from him. "Sir, I am FBI. Do not go for your weapon. I heard about the shoot-out. This is my badge. I am here for your help."

The man looked at him: "I cannot help you FBI. No, I do not know of any shoot out."

Paul looked at him: "You need protection. I need help. Your nickname is Sarge. You did not get on the plane. I know why you are running."

Sarge looked around: "I cannot help you."

Paul: "You hiked out here. You have plans to backtrack. We can help. You have plans to hide in the desert. We can hide you better. You can help us find a hundred and one people."

Sarge looked at him: "You want to leave that island alone and leave them there. If you are the government blow that island out of existence. One of those things gets off and it is over for the human race and your number is wrong."

Paul looked into Sarge's terrorized eyes: "If I do not bring you in, they will find you. Three shoot outs in three deferent states. They will find you. I need your help. They are waiting for you at the airport. Mark is dead in Florida. You know anything?"

Sarge: "He was dead when I got there. I left really quick." Sarge looked around. "Okay, look, I want a good place to hide. I will help. I have stuff to get help."

Paul: "What stuff?"

Sarge: "The people on the island. The things they did to them. You have to make sure none of them get off. They are really smart, strong, and super-fast. One of them could easily take out one hundred people."

Paul: "I want to know what is happening on that island and what they did to the people. I want to know how many people they did this to." Paul keyed his mic. "I am in the bar. All agents come to me. I need one agent to go to the bus agent to release the bus." Everyone watched the FBI SWAT personnel come into the bar with their weapons ready. Paul walked onto the armored truck with Sarge.

Paul: "Let's go. We are going to the AirForce base."

Sarge fixed himself in the seat: "Here is a file."

Island

Sharon looked at Todd and the ladies: "This is nice. This lab will help. I can do a lot of work here. The hospital is nice too."

Todd looked about: "We got these ships working. We got the trench dug. We can get the ship ready to be in a seventy degree for launch. The radio will be ready in the hour."

Sharon looked at the fields outside: "I think we should wait."

Todd: "We can do that."

Sharon: "No one has come for us. We should stay until they do."

Air base

They walked into a meeting room and Paul sat across from Sarge.

Paul: "I need to know everything." He put pictures on the table and files.

Sarge looked up from the wooden table at him: "I was there from the beginning. Your number is wrong. The building of the Island base. The kidnapping of the people. I had no way of calling off the island without them hearing. He found me looking for work over ten years ago. I was living in the street or going from friend's house to friend's house."

Paul opened the folder and saw Sarge looking at the pictures. He looked at the picture that had the shadow. "They are still alive? What is the number?"

Sarge: "Two hundred and one. I feel sorry for one lady who came to help. Rosa did not know. She found out and tried hard to free them, but she was caught up in it. They turned her into one of those things."

Paul: "Hundred more women?"

Sarge: "Yes, they have been taken from their families and homes. I wanted to help but I was on the island, and could not call or get off."

Paul: "Can you ID them?"

Sarge: "The ladies. A human smuggler brought them in, and I do not know what all of them look like. They spoke languages of the world."

Paul leaned back in his seat and knew Sarge was telling the truth. He could see it in his eyes. "Okay, we will have to call around and look into this more."

Sarge: "They are all alive. We should leave them alone or kill them off."

Paul looked at the picture with the shadow and moved it to Sarge: "Sir, what do you know of them?"

Sarge: "I was with them for a year. You read the file I gave you?"

Paul: "Yes, I did but I need everything."

Sarge: "They mutated them and killed everyone who knew how to make the drugs. The books were lost in a fire. I burned the books when I saw Todd do his thing. The picture has two of them in that picture not one. They were looking at your drone. They have eagle-cat-like eyes. They run at thirty but on all four at seventy miles an hour."

Sarge looked at the pictures: "They work fast. Todd threw a security jeep ten feet. They can move a thousand pounds. I felt sorry for them. No one should ever have that done to them. I know they learned morse code in under a day. I should have said something then. They are extremely dangerous. I remember when the drone went over two or three years ago. They are doing something on that island, and we left them there. The only thing I can think of is defense." Paul put pictures of people in front of Sarge. Sarge looked at him and explained, "All those people are dead. Mark kept files on the island about them. They were all there. All of them are dead. All the pictures you are showing me, they are buried on the island or dead somewhere on this planet. I see the stacks of pictures and folders of people. This is money for some sick new human that will kill us all." Sarge looked at everyone in the meeting room. "Like I said they were all there. You have over three thousand dead and want to know why. The money for a super soldier. They checked everything before you left. They checked all the buildings. They never checked the emergency building at the dock, and they left it to me." Sarge put four small flat boxes on the table. "I just gave you a file with a little information. They used to leave me on the island alone during the winter. I knew I would need them. I set up my own cameras." David entered the room with a laptop and took the four hard drives. He plugged them in.

Paul looked at Sarge: "We will talk more. Give us time. I will house you in a secured location on this base. Thank you."

Twenty-four hours later

Sarge sat down in a room full of people. Paul moved a TV screen over to him. "These metal coffins here that look like equipment containers. Is this how they moved the people?"

Sarge: "Yes, that is how they moved them. You can also see everyone there that you are looking for. Also, there is Rosa with her red bow and the other ladies."

Paul: "Rosa was your friend?"

Sarge: "Yes, and I warned her and told her not to help them and for her to leave. She did not listen. She thought she was helping these ladies make money for working for a modeling and film crew. She loved the money she was getting when she brought them ladies. When she found out she was helping ladies being smuggled it broke her heart." Sarge pointed at the hard drives. "These videos have everything and more. I do not understand, what did he think?"

Paul: "Who?"

Sarge: "Ethen Quinn! They will kill me for giving you this. You see that massive party he had on the island for very power full people of the world were there. Those are the ones pushing for this crazy war."

Paul: "Okay, let us talk about the end. Before you got on the boat or ship? You saw Todd on the roof. How did you know it was him?"

Sarge smiled: "Look at the videos. Look at his height and frame. He walked through the buildings. Before I left with the hard drives the ladies left through the back of the building. I do know Ethen wanted to make money off this."

The Head Agent of the FBI looked at Paul: "You need to get down there now to find out what is going on. I mean now. The general of this base has a jet waiting. Gear up."

Paul: "Sir, I do not want to go down there."

Head Agent: "Paul. You are the one who found all this. I want you down there. You are the best. The President wants you to go."

Paul thought to himself. *They're crazy. They want me to go down there and take on these things. They are hiding something.*

David walked over to him: "Better you than me."

South Pacific

A United States Cruiser sailed south as a navy helicopter landed on the aft deck. Paul climbed out of the helicopter, and he felt the cold air on his face. He was escorted to his room.

Paul looked at the seaman: "Hey, when do I meet the captain?"

Seaman looked into his room: "Sir, when you are ready. I was told to bring you to your quarters and let you put your stuff here."

Paul: "Okay, let's go." He was escorted to the bridge. The captain was looking through some high-power binoculars. He saw Paul walking onto the bridge.

Captain: "We have company." He pointed to the port windows. "A Russian cruiser on the horizon. How was your flight to Chile?"

Paul looked at the captain: "The flight to Chile and the embassy was good. The Russians are looking for their people. They know what we know."

The Captain sat down: "We sent a scout drone up. The Russians did the same. They are on the same course. We are going to the island. Communications, call the Russians."

Communications: "Sir, The Russians are calling us."

The captain looked about: "I knew they would call. Let them come closer."

Paul looked out the window: "Captain. Ask if there is an FSK agent on there. The name is Adrei."

The captain picked up the phone: "Hello, how are you doing Captain?"

Russian Cruiser

Russian Captain: "I am doing well, Captain. We meet again. FBI agent Paul wants to talk to the FSK agent Adrei. The phone is for you."

Adrei picked up the phone: "Hello, Paul. Yes, it is me. I see you took my advice. My government also wants to talk with them. No one was ever successful at this madness. My government was thinking the same. It is not their fault. We were thinking of reversing this. Hold on. I have to go." He looked at the captain as he hung up the phone. "You cannot let them on the island. Even if it means you destroy the island with the monsters on it."

American Cruiser

Paul hung up the phone and looked at the captain: "We cannot let them on the island. Even if it means you destroy the island with the monsters on it."

Captain: "Sir, there appears to be three unknown ships by the island."

The captain looked at the lieutenant: "Report."

Lieutenant: "Sir, the drone sees three ships with military boats on the beach. They are not from any country."

Paul looked at the drone view screen: "Ethen Quinn has a private Navy and an Army. Those are his boats. They are all around the world. The marking on the side is his."

The captain looked at helm: "Full ahead. The Russians see this?"

Lieutenant: "Yes, Sir, their drone is out there. Sir, the biggest ship has guns firing into the island. They have people running from the island forest."

The overhead speaker came to life. "I am giving warning! Leave us alone! We will kill you all! Leave!" They heard a roar over the speaker. It ran fear through their bodies.

Lieutenant: "Sir, we can see the island now. We just went over the horizon. We can see the fighting from here. They are shooting out of the island at the ships. Sir, the drone just made it to the island with the Russian drone. The drone found people dead on the island. None of them are Ethen Quinn's people."

Paul pointed at the screen: "They are the other groups that Ethen Quinn hired."

Lieutenant: "Sir, the people who attacked them are losing bad."

The captain picked up the phone: "Hello, the one giving warning. Who are you and do you know who is attacking you?"

Russian Cruiser

They heard it over the radio in Russian and English. "We do not know who attacked us. They tried to get one of us but we attacked back. There are over three hundred of them dead now."

Adrei ran to the window to see Ethen's large ship with guns get hit by heavy cannon and gun fire from the island. Adrei: "I told you they are highly intelligent. They made their own weapons."

Missiles flew from the island and slammed into the large ship, and it burned uncontrollably. The ship began to sink. They heard a lady's voice. "No one is getting on this island without our permission. This is our island. This is our home." They watched as the drones made it over the island and saw a massive warship burning out of control on the other side of the island. There was a smaller ship sinking.

The Captain looked through the binoculars: "Bozhe Moy!" He pointed. "Look there!" Something climbed out of the water onto a large ship. "Get me the American Captain!" The creature climbed onto the ship and ripped through a steel door of the ship. It threw the door through the deck. The creature began destroying the ship and began killing everyone on board. Then more creatures jumped over a hundred feet up onto the ships and boats. The creatures began to massacre everyone on board.

American Cruiser

The captain picked up the phone: "I agree! We will go no closer. It is too dangerous. We are also getting targeted by the island. We see fifty ships of all sizes by the island. We will stay by the horizon. We are getting their SOS. They are not hiding themselves." The radio came to life. "Please! We need help! SOS! We need help! Some creatures are attacking us! We need help! AAA!"

Captain: "Yes, I am watching. I do not know what they are, and you say you do not know either." Paul overheard, "This is Sharon. We see you on the horizon. Do not get closer or try a rescue. We are only protecting ourselves."

Lieutenant: "Sir, the creatures are retreating back to the forest."

Paul walked up to the Captain: "Sir, that was Sharon and I think Rachel. We can try to talk to them."

The Captain pointed at the view screen: "You see that there? They had air cover from the carrier that is now sinking. Where did Ethen Quinn get a carrier and an army that size? There are new fighters that are destroyed and I have no clue what they are. Comms call Washington! I want to nuke that island."

Paul: "You cannot do that!"

Captain: "The Russians are doing the same. I put my money on it."

They heard Adrei's voice come over the radio. "Captains please think about this! Do not nuke that island."

Paul picked up the radio: "I agree. Captains come on now."

They both heard from the Captains. "The governments give the order and we will both do it at the same time. Those things are Super Dangerous!"

Paul: "Sir, there are ten more ships on the other side of the island. The Russians are looking to the ships on the other side of the island. The ships are burning and sinking. The computer counts over a thousand dead. There was a fight on the other side of the island."

Russian Cruiser

Adrei got on the radio: "Rachel or Sharon is that you by the caves?"

The captain pointed at the view screen: "What is that there on the screen? That weird looking ship at thirty degrees. I know the Americans see this."

Sharon came back over the radio: "The ones by the cave are part of my group. We do not want a fight, leave us to this island." Rachel spoke in Russian and said the same. Sharon keyed the mic. "Yes, the two hundred and one of us are the creatures you see. We do not want this. We never wanted this. They did this to us."

American Cruiser

The Captain spun in his chair as he heard from the Commander. "Sir, missiles fired, not by the Russians. It will go by us."

Captain: "By Who?"

Commander: "Sir, it came out of nowhere."

Captain: "Missiles do not come out of nowhere."

Commander: "Sir, it is a sub shadowing us."

Captain: "Why and who's sub?"

Paul looked at the captain: "Not the Russians. Someone is trying to start a war with us and the Russians and the creatures on that island. Hoping they shoot at us. Ethen Quinn has more dealings than anyone knows. We have to look into it. I want to know where he got a military this size and the aircraft carrier fleet."

Captain: "Me too."

The Russian and American cruisers defenses turned on and the cruisers destroyed the missiles flying by them.

Russian Cruiser

Russian Captain: "It is military, and it is not the Americans or ours. Who's is it?"

Adrei looked at the screen: "Ethen Quinn's. How did he get a military this size? We all never saw this. He played us all."

Captain Lieutenant: "Sir. It had to be fired from some kind of new sub."

Russian Captain: "Find It! We will work with the Americans. Call our government and give a fast report just in case so the Americans do not start shooting at us or we at them. I know the Americans are giving their report."

American Cruiser

The Captain turned to look out the windows as he heard.

Commander: "Sir, more ships of the same markings. Three more from the other side. They are getting ready to attack."

Paul looked through the binoculars: "Someone is watching this from a satellite. They want people to see this."

Captain: "This is some sick show of how their new weapons work."

The commander ran to the science stations as he saw a red light shine above the station: "Sir, Ethen Quinn's satellites are overhead with the Russians and ours. Water temperature around the island is up by ten percent to thirty percent and rising."

Lieutenant commander: "Sir two missiles hit the island from the other side. Huge explosions. The missiles came from submarines."

The captain looked at the Russian cruiser: "Call them. We are moving away."

Lieutenant: "Sir, the Russians Captain is doing the same. He asked if you saw the steam coming out of the caves. He asked do you see Todd pointing at the cave and all the creatures now running back to the caves."

Paul looked at the view screen: "Todd was the only male that was kidnapped."

The captain looked through the binoculars: "You think all those scientists they kidnapped made a rocket ship?"

Paul: "Many of them on the list are part of space programs."

Russian Cruiser

The Russian Captain picked up the phone: "Hello Captain. Yes, the submarine went by us and on its way to the island. I do agree not to send any helicopters up to look for the subs and yes, they made a rocket ship of some kind. We can see it on the view screen. The rocket ship has a mushroom head. We are giving more distance. I believe we should stay just over the horizon. We also have two drones up. We called our government. The sea dragon rocket is the world's largest rocket, but like you, I believe they made a larger rocket. I do not know where they will go. Maybe one of the scientists helped find something up in space they have not told the public about."

American Cruiser

The Captain ran to the window with binoculars in hand: "Paul, my mission was the same as the Russians. I was to make contact and see if they were a threat and leave the island. We were to stay down here to make sure they did not leave that island. They have limited food and water. So, if they did have children, they could not have a lot of them. We know the caves and the underground caverns go down a mile."

Paul looked out the window and at the view screen as the temperature was rising. "They know the international law. They know they are a new species. They also know we will not let them live. Yes, I would build a rocket ship if I had a chance."

The Earth shook around them as fire and steam came out of the caves and steam shot into the air. The Earth shook the hill apart exposing the rocket ship. They watched the hole island disappear in a cloud of steam, black smoke, and fire. They knew many of Ethen Quinn's troops were caught in the opening. The Captain grabbed the key from around his neck. "Commander, to your station. Ready for nuke launch. Overhead mic, open to the Russian cruiser only, Comms."

Lieutenant: "Comms Open, Sir."

Captain: "Captain, do you hear me?"

Russian Captain: "Yes, captain. I agree, we cannot let them leave. What are they calling them?"

Paul: "The Forbidden Ones."

Captain: "Target the rocket ship and the island for full nuclear destruction. All twenty small nuclear cruise weapons. Emergency Code NCD001. Launch, launch, launch. Turn keys."

The Captains looked at their commanders. They inserted their keys and turned them. The missile pod tops popped off exposing the nuclear cruise missiles. The small nuclear cruise missiles shot out of the launch tubes. They shot into the sky and raced for their targets.

"Sir, the water is at a hundred degrees around the island and rising and the submarines are coming out of the water."

The captain looked out the window toward the island. Captain: "Captain, our weapons are free. We have, targeted the ship and the island."

Russian Captain: "Yes, Captain. We have weapons free. We targeted the rocket ship and the island. Now, we wait for impact. One minute."

They watched fire and smoke rise into the air. Then they saw the top of the massive rocket ship rip through the top of the white smoke. It began to pick up speed.

Island

The dams exploded and the Pacific Ocean flooded the caves. The middle of the rocket ship sunk under the water. The rocket's engines ignited, and the steam shot up into the sky and engulfed the whole island. Todd locked the last of the air tight doors and he climbed to the bridge as the ship began to shake. He screamed out, "Do not wait for me! Start the count down!" Amder hit buttons and everyone did the cross on their chest and a kiss to the sky.

Zoyo: "10, 9, 8, 7, 6, 5, 4, 3, 2, 1, 0! Launch!" The rocket ship was now fully under the water as Todd buckled in. Everyone worked on their computers and started the small rocket engines. They ignited.

Eloise: "We have lift off. We are moving." The ship began to shake violently, and the flames made it form a blueish white light around the ship as the flames and steam engulfed the outside of the ship. The two cruisers watched flames come out of the caves. The rocket ship shook as the island erupted into fire and turned into lava.

American Cruiser

The captain called out, "Everyone put on your face and ear protection!" The two cruisers were over three miles away from the island and everyone heard the roar of the rocket engines as it was right next to them.

Ark

The rocket ship began to lift up into the sky. "4, 3, 2" The cruisers launched their cruise missiles and anti-ship missiles at the rocket. "1" Maria hit a button. The four huge monster upgraded sea dragon Ion plasma rocket engines ignited in the air and the rocket ship super accelerated. The ship turned white and looked like a shooting star leaving from under the ocean. Everything burst into flames for two miles. The people who attacked the Forbidden Ones never had a chance to scream. Everything turned to ash. Ethen Quinn's ships melted under the water and above it. His troops in it turned to ash. The island was melting and the molten rock exploded with extreme forces. It created a shock wave that took out the entire island. Everyone on the nearby island could hear the rocket ship. They felt the shock wave and felt the heat ten miles away. All the people looked to the sky in fear. The shock wave forced the missiles fired by the cruisers to hit the two submarines, and it hit the warships three miles from the island. The submarines and warships exploded and melted. The nuclear cruise missiles melted before they hit the island. The bridge windows of the two cruisers shattered by the force of the shock wave. The front ends of the cruisers were forced out of the water, and they crashed back into the sea. The crew covered their faces and took cover behind shielding and their instruments console as they watched the shock wave come from the island and impact them.

Amber: "We are at Mach two and counting."

Aera: "We are now at Mach five and counting."

Todd: "I have the controls. She is starting to spin. It is normal." The two cruisers fired their hypersonic missiles. The Forbidden Ones felt their bodies sink into their seats.

Hana: "We are at Mach seven and counting. We will be in space in no time."

Akemi: "We are now at Mach nine. Wow, we are fast. Mach fifteen is faster. Mach twenty-five is coming down from space not up. We just launched the largest ship to space."

Zoyo: "We are now at Mach sixteen. We are accelerating. We are still in Earth's atmosphere."

Sharon looked at the speed and looked out into space from the window. She looked at the white light that surrounded them. "We are at Mach twenty-seven. You think we used too many rockets? We go any faster we will blow up."

Todd: "No talk like that! We have stopped and are staying at Mach thirty." The chasing missiles ran out of fuel and fell back to Earth to the destroyed island.

Ava: "The gravity wells have activated. We are in space. True space. Like outer space." The sky turned from blue to black with stars.

Bain: "We flew past the international space station. We are moving. Everyone knows of us now." The ship stopped shaking and shot into space.

Todd looked down at the computer: "Wow, we left the Earth at Mach 30. Check the ship for damage. Ladies check yourselves. Is everyone okay? The rockets are now out of fuel. The engines will run for five hours."

Irina: "Some of the ladies are sick. Plus, me. I never want to do that again. The ion engines are ready and working."

Island

Hours later, Paul walked over what was left of the ten-mile island as Adrei walked over to him.

Paul: "Sailor, what you mean there is only one eighth of a mile left of the island? This island was over ten miles in length. This is not even a city block." "Sir, Like I said. The Russian tested a super-fast torpedo. It heats the water around and makes a heat shield for itself. So, it can go very fast in the water. The ship they made did the same but it works different and uses a different science. The rocket ship destroyed the island."

Adrei: "That rocket ship did destroy the island. It went faster than Mach twenty."

Paul: "This ground is cold to the touch. The ocean cooled it. Call the Captain and tell him I am coming back. There is nothing here. I need to get to the carrier and get on a plane. I need to get to Nasa. Everyone saw this."

Adrei looked around and saw what was left of the island. "I will meet you there."

Paul: "Good see you there. Oh, thank you. Tell your Captain thank you as well."

Adrie looked around and thought, *There is nothing here. Time to leave.*

Space

Todd looked out the window: "Okay, we under estimated the power of the rockets we made."

Sharon looked at him: "We talked about this."

Todd: "Yes, we did. Okay, three hours."

Sharon: "What does that mean?"

Todd: "I am no rocket scientist. They are. Ladies, how fast are we going?"

Sharon: "Todd!"

Todd: "Ladies, what day of the month do you think we are in?" Everyone looked at each other as they passed the moon.

Sharon looked out the small window at the moon: "You!"

Todd: "Hey. We still do not know the month, year, day, or second. Forgive me if we F up. You know what? I am not supposed to be seven feet but I am. Ladies Help."

Brendy: "No one went this fast before. Sharon, calm down."

Dayana hit buttons on her computer: "We will get to Mars in two months at this speed. I think we made a new form of speed like a semi warp. We have to slow down. Okay, we are not sure if we are right. Mars can be on the other side of the sun from us. Okay, we have to work at refueling the rockets to slow us down, then we can work on finding Mars."

Mila: "Wait, no one did Mars in six months and the moon in ten hours. We did the moon in three hours with new fuel and rockets."

Todd looked at the ladies: "We can trade technology."

Sharon looked at the cameras: "The paint held. Everything is one hundred percent."

Todd: "Mila, you take first watch. The rest of us will check out all three ships. Suits on and grab a radio. We will be back."

Earth

A navy fighter launched off the carrier. Paul sat in the back seat and looked out of the canopy. "Pilot, the fastest you can take her. I need to get to the states."

The pilot accelerated to Mach speed. "We should be at the next carrier in one hour. You will get a plane to the states."

Three hours later

Paul climbed into an AirForce fighter jet in Panama. The pilot climbed in. The canopy closed and the jet shot off the runway. "Sir, I will get you there fast. There is a car waiting for you. The President is waiting for your call."

Nebraska

The jet fighter landed. Paul climbed out quickly and ran to the waiting car. The car siren came to life as his door closed. The convoy of cars drove off the base as Paul picked up the phone. "Hello, Mr. President. I am going to the Nasa facility as you ordered. Sir, what you mean we are at war? We or the Russians did not shoot or destroy any Navy ships of any country. There were six large warships and submarines that did not ID themselves. We fired at the Forbidden Ones' rocket ship. The rocket ship they made is nothing we have ever seen before. Ethen Quinn's people attacked the island and were losing. They were also attacked by unknown forces. Yes, Sir. I will get you information. Yes, the island is totally destroyed, and we found nothing we can use. Good bye, Sir." He looked out the window, then at a manifest Sarge had given them on the island. He saw Sarge was on the island for months at a time, unsupervised. "Politicians are always hiding something. If they do not get their way they always get mad and make you the fall guy when you cannot get it for them, I mean steal it. They left them three new warships, farms, materials, equipment, weapons and space programs. This place was a hidden supply base. Driver, get all the cars faster. We need to get to Sharon's father's ranch. David has the other families that want to talk to their loved ones."

Washington D.C.

The President put the phone down. "He does not know."

Senior advisor: "The evidence is destroyed, and we are happy about this. We can use this to our advantage. We make this war to make money like Ethen Quinn said. How did he get a military force?"

President: "The world gave it to him. We all can see we need him to make us billions of dollars. Where is he?"

Senior advisor: "Ethen is on one of his islands."

President: "Have him call his people and make a good war. It will make us a lot of money."

Vice president: "I wish his guy got us something from the island we can use."

President: "That is okay. The rich and powerful want this. We will all make money from this war."

Senior advisor: "When do you think we should stop it?"

President: "I do not know. Ten years like the others. We have full control of this."

Vice president: "It will be funny if we lose control."

President: "Do not talk like that. We easily control all the small wars. This one is just bigger. We have control."

Nebraska

Paul ran up to the farm house. Sharon's father walked out of the house and said, "What is going on? The President says we are at war. To tell you the truth, I never voted for that guy. He is not too smart. We should start talking not shooting. On the news there was something about an illegal rocket launch and some Forbidden Ones started the fight. They destroyed a fleet of ships."

Paul: "Sir, your daughter Sharon is alive."

Sharon's father: "Bring her home."

Paul: "It is not that easy. Where are her children? I need you and her mother."

Sharon's father looked at him: "The news lied again. Thats not what happened on the news is it? Is my daughter a Forbidden One? My wife is at the Dairy farm where she works part time, and the kids are at school."

Paul: "You did not hear it from me. I will get into a lot of trouble. Whatever the news said, that is not what happened. They were attacked. Yes, your daughter is a Forbidden One and she is on that ship. Sir, we need you. We are hoping they stop and stay by the moon or Mars. I am hoping for Mars. Please get in the car."

Sharon's father looked at the agent: "I will help." He gathered his things and got into the car.

Town

The boss walked out with Sharon's mother and said, "Tell me what you find out. Good Luck."

Four cars pulled up with their lights flashing and Paul jumped out. "Ma'am, I am Paul from the FBI. We talked before."

Sharon's mother: "Yes, I remember."

Paul: "Can you get in? Please?" She looked into the car. She saw her husband in the car and climbed in. The cars drove off the company grounds.

Elementary School

The FBI convoy drove onto the school grounds. Paul jumped out and Sharon's mother went to get out.

Paul: "Ma'am, stay here. We will get the children. We have a warrant for them." Paul ran into the school with the other agents.

Sharon's mother: "What is going on?"

Sharon's father: "Sharon is a Forbidden One. They lied on the news about them. She will be okay." They grabbed each other's hands. Her husband looked into her eyes and looked up. Sharon's mother looked up and she prayed with her husband. The agents came out with the children.

Sharon's mother: "Wow, that was fast. It normally takes over an hour."

Paul: "We called ahead and had agents come to the school." The kids climbed in with the agents.

Paul "I have you all. We found Sharon and we need your help. We also called the other families to help. You need to get her to say where they are going." The children's grandparents put on their seat belts. The Kids were excited to see they were running red lights and there was a full state trooper escort through the large town.

Sharon's father looked about: "The airport is the other way. Why are we not taking a plane to where you are taking us?"

Paul: "It will take us too long to get on the plane, get clearance, and land again. We do not know what they are doing."

Sharon's father put his hand on his wife's hand: "This will be okay." He put his hand on his grandkid's hands. "We are going to talk with your mom. She flew into space, okay? Everything is okay."

Sharon's mother looked at Paul: "What if we need anything?"

Paul: "I will make sure we take care of everything. If you need anything just ask."

Sharon's father looked at him and whispered: "I do not trust the government. Like Reagan said, if the government says I'm here to help, runaway, runaway as fast as you can go."

Paul leaned over: "I like Reagan. I will help you. Not the government. We need your help, and they need your help."

Sharon's father: "I do not like the government."

Paul: "I do not like the government either. That is why I am helping you more."

Sharon's mother: "Men, I do not like the government, but I trust you, Paul, and the Russian guy. Will he be there?"

Paul: "Yes, Ma'am. He will be there."

Hour later.

The FBI cars stopped in a hanger bay. The AirForce General opened the door. Paul stepped out and said, "This is the family. I need them with passes. The children need bathrooms. They have to stay the night with the other families."

The General looked at them and waved a hand: "We have that covered. The nurses will take you to the bathroom. If you have a bag at home you want us to get for you or want us to take you back by helicopter to get anything, just ask tonight. You have a Russian agent here."

Paul: "Yes, he is with me."

General: "Lieutenant, take them to the quarters. Then bring the families and the agent to NASA command center."

NASA command

Paul followed the General to a table as Adrei walked in.

General: "I can tell you two what we know. You were both there. What do you want to know?"

Paul looked out the large windows at the massive view screens: "What happen to the ships and submarines?"

General: "The Forbidden Ones' rocket was the thing that destroyed them and the island. We have video from the satellite. We watched through infrared. They had caves and caverns all through the island and over a mile down. They dug out the island."

Adrei looked at the screen: "General, how fast where they going."

General: "You see the view screen. They look like a shooting star. They left at Mach thirty. The flame from the ship was a quarter mile long. They left the pad or the launch bay at Mach two. That was before the two hundred meter long rockets the sea dragon rockets ignited. They were only ten feet off the island when the other rockets or engines turned on and those flames went over a mile. Then, the shock wave from the blast of the rockets started. It was felt ten miles away."

Paul pointed at the screen: "The missiles and hypersonic missiles."

The General looked at him: "The missiles went Mach six or seven. They went Mach fifteen."

Adrei looked at them: "You want their technology."

The General looked at him and smiled: "And the Russians do not?"

Adrei: "Okay, we do."

The General waved his hand and they watched the families walk over. "I apologize. We just want you to talk to your family members. We need to know where they are going and where are they now."

Paul pointed at a symbol on the screen: "What is that?"

General: "That is their ship flying through space."

Paul: "General, they passed the moon. Hold on. You are telling me they passed the moon? It took me over twenty-four hours to get here. They shouldn't be getting to the moon."

The General looked at them: "They are not normal humans anymore. We need open talks. They passed the moon in three hours or more. They will be at Mars in three months. We need you all to talk now with your loved ones on that ship."

Adrei looked at the screen: "You got that new communications array working good."

General: "What are you talking about?"

Adrei: "The Communications array. Makes talking in space faster. Mars has two. Moon has one and Earth has one." The General watched the families take their seats before he started talking.

General: "How do you know of this?"

Adrei: "General, we helped you put it up there."

The General looked at the view screens: "I remember those times. Yes, they are up and working and yes, it makes talking faster."

Adrei: "General, I read the reports. It is better to have more than two around a planet."

General: "Yes, that is what it says. Now let us begin."

Ark

Camila looked at Mila as the radio came to life. "This is the General of the AirForce. Can I talk to the ship that left the Earth?"

Mila: "This is that ship. Hi."

Russian General: "This is the General of the Russian Federation AirForce."

The US General looked at his staff: "Is there any way we can make this private?"

Russian General: "Please General, we do not want to go there."

US General: "You will do it will you not?"

Russian General: "I already tried."

A Colonel looked up from the computer screen: "No, Sir. They have to do that from the rocket ship."

Mila picked up the internal radio: "Todd, get up here. They are calling from Earth."

US General: "This is the US general. How are you people doing? So, where are you going?"

Heidi: "Hi, we will go to Mars and stay there."

Paul: "This is FBI Agent Paul. I need your names. How many people do you have up there? Why Mars?"

Todd: "Thank you for calling. This is Todd. We are going to stay on Mars until we can reverse this. There are two hundred and one of us here. I will let you talk to them all. I will send you a list of names."

Paul: "Are you the leader, Todd?"

Todd: "No, we all made this choice. The biochemical laws. We did not want this."

Adrei: "This is FSK agent Adrie. If you are not the leader, Todd, then why did the ladies call for you to talk?"

Sharon: "This is Sharon. We chose him to be our leader."

Todd: "Well, the ladies chose me to be a leader."

Adrei: "This is Adrei."

Paul: "Hey, this is Paul. The Russians said they will listen in. We will give the Russians a chance to talk. We have three months."

Todd: "Hold on. Stop ladies. Let them fight. We now only have each other. We have to work together. Thank you, ladies. Okay, I will ask. We will trade technology for supplies. We all have questions. There is a ship of some kind. A UFO sitting on the dark side of the Moon. What is it?"

The Generals looked at each other through the TV camera view screen. "We do not know. We will look into that."

Natacia: "Natacia here. We have work to do."

Todd: "The ladies would like to talk to their families. If you can."

Paul: "We have them here."

Todd: "We have a different mic so everyone can talk."

General: "We did the same. Remember, everyone is listening in."

Airman: "You can talk Sir. This is Sharon's father."

Sharon: "Hi, Dad. This is Sharon. I am sorry. I never knew what they did with my work until it was too late."

The ladies cried as they talked with their families and Todd talked with his. Paul and Adrie walked together and whispered to each other.

Paul: "You feel your government is up to something?"

Adrei: "Yes. Like yours. You know that piece of equipment we can use to find where people are talking?"

Paul: "Yes. I know it. They are using it here."

Adrei: "What do you think they are planning?"

Paul: "I do not know."

The two Generals picked up phones.

Russian General: "I have to speak to my government."

US General "As I. This is dangerous. We have to plan this out. Four months flight."

Russian General: "Yes, let everyone get comfortable. We can do anything to them out there and say a number of any accidents."

US General: "Yes, I agree. I will start talking to my government."

Sharon's mother: "This is Sharon's mother. I spoke to the other mothers, and we are all talking. All of you watch over each other. Todd, watch over the ladies and my little girl, Sharon. Bye for now. The kids are tired. We will talk more tomorrow. The Agents want answers."

Sharon: "Mom, Dad. I am sorry."

Sharon's father: "This is not your fault. This is a sick man's plan."

Todd: "Ma'am. I will watch over everyone. They will watch over me."

Sharon: "Dad, you and Mom are good at this. The ladies want you all to stay together."

Sharon's father: "We will. All the families are now together and talking. Good bye for now."

Three Months later

Paul slammed the phone down and Adrei looked at him.

Adrei: "What is it?"

Paul: "They say Ethen Quinn is dead. His whole crew is dead too. They said they just killed themselves."

Adrei: "That is a lie. This war is getting out of hand as we speak."

Paul: "The US and Russia are allies in this. Something is telling me he is alive. You know the rich and powerful wanted this and spoke about this as a sick game of some kind."

Adrei: "I would like to talk to the Forbidden Ones. The governments will want them dead. They know they are dangerous. They say if one comes down it will become dangerous. I saw twenty of them destroy about five hundred soldiers. Todd can take out that group himself."

Paul: "The Generals are planning something. They give the order, and they can launch nukes at them. We have to find a way to talk with them where no one hears us so we can warn them."

Sharon's son was hiding behind the couch where he held his candy bars, he got from the vending machines. He listened in on the agent's conversation. He heard the agents walk out of the room and he snuck down the hallway. He leaned against a door of the command room and looked around. There was no one walking in the hallways. He heard two men talking. "Did you hear?" "Yes, they fired them months ago. The nukes will hit their mark. Forbidden Ones no more."

Hours later.

Todd pointed at the view screen: "Bian said we can make our own communications array. She looked it over. They are back on the ship. We can monitor one of them."

Zoyo pointed: "The ladies say we are sending our signal through the satellites. I say we stay at one of the moons of Mars."

Sharon screamed out: "What are you saying?!" The security staff of NASA struggled with the families. Todd ran to Sharon and she hit the overhead speakers, and all the ladies ran to the bridge. The radio was alive with noise of fighting. Paul and Adrei helped Sharon's son. He keyed the mic for everyone to hear.

Sharon's son: "Mom! They shot nukes at you. You have to run!" She heard her daughter.

Sharon's daughter: "Mom! They lied. They fired the nukes three months ago. They are tracking you."

The families screamed out: "We love you!"

The General and his staff cheered as the nukes exploded. "We got them!"

The families looked at each other and were about to cry when everyone heard Todd.

Todd: "General, you missed! You hit the communications array satellite site one. We are somewhere by communications array two. We are sending our communications through the satellites."

The General looked at the screen: "Your species will never be allowed on the Earth. We will stop you."

Todd: "General, we are human. Those people who wanted this wants this to be cleaned up. Well, you missed. We all thought of this. We hear the radio and knew World War Three is getting out of hand. We know of the war the governments wanted. They wanted to start playing God. Do you know how much we can hear from up here? General, two cities have been nuked and you are worried about us? This war they made is out of hand. Ethen Quinn's people said he is dead. Oh, he is alive, and we heard him on a satellite phone talking to his men. General, you need to hunt down the man who did this to us and give us a chance to reverse this. Let us come home in peace."

General: "No! We know what we are doing. We know what you are. You will never set foot on Earth. We will hunt you to the end of the galaxy if we have to."

Todd: "Good luck, General. You have a massive war on your hands and no real space program. We hear everything up here through the satellites."

The General and his staff walked out of the room. The families looked at the screens in the control room. Todd looked at Ava running to the radar. She looked at the computer and said, "Radar shows a ship chasing. It will hit one of the communication satellites."

Todd: "They are shooting in the wind and hoping to hit us." They watched a satellite blow up in a nuclear explosion.

Ava: "How did we not see that?"

Todd: "No one is watching the radar."

Ava: "We all have to start watching."

Todd keyed the radio: "We are still here. You missed again."

Adrei walked to the mic: "They left. They have no control over the missiles they launched after you. We did not fire it from here. Todd, run to Pluto. They cannot target you there or find you. We will try to help."

Tanya looked at the screen: "We have four more. They are going after the old communications satellites."

Todd looked at Heather: "You, on helm. Fire the rockets! Let's get out of here."

Sharon: "This is Sharon to the families. We love you. To my family, I love you. We will try to call."

The rockets ignited and they watched Mars disappear into space behind them. They saw more nuclear explosions around Mars.

Six months later.

The war on Earth roared out of control and missiles shot up at the satellites in space around Earth. The satellites exploded and crashed into Earth. Missiles launched off the ground, flew up, and flew down blowing up every city on

Earth. Planes fell out of the sky as rain. The human race went backward, not forward in intellect and peace as humans died. Cities burned with the lands around them as the massive Army and Navy fought each other to the death. The leaders for the world cried out but died in their madness they had created. Countries were ripped apart into civil wars. The whole planet was now in chaos and burned out of control as it fought war with itself. The Earth was in true chaos and people moved underground and made underground greenhouse farms cities to survive World War Three. The Earth cried out to God to stop the chaos. There was no end in sight of the madness of war. Children marched to war with their parents and loved ones. Billions died in the fighting. The wealthy died along with the average people in the streets. The ones who wanted the war cried out for it to stop but they died with no one hearing them. No one could see an end to the war.

The Ark

Kira looked at the view screen: "We should have seen Pluto by now. We passed it. How?"

Fatima: "I did the calculations. We passed it over six months ago."

Durga looked at the space map: "We have to talk to Todd. We can turn back or get to that planet we found."

Chepi looked at the map: "Where is Todd?"

Khadija: "Working on something or comforting one of the ladies."

Zoyo looked at Sharon: "What is wrong with you?"

Sharon looked at her: "What? I am okay."

Zoyo: "Why are you leaning forward, and your top is loose?"

Zoyo looked at Julia: "You are a doctor. She is not standing straight up."

Julia looked at them: "She is not the only one leaning forward and has a lose shirt on."

She walked over to Sharon: "Call Todd to the Bridge. I need to give you ladies a test."

Brandy walked in: "Mia, she is sick. I took her to the hospital. Why are they all glowing? Just like Mia?"

Sharon looked at them: "We are feeling lonely at night so many of us are looking for Todd."

Julia looked at them: "I know. I do the same. That is why I will give you a test."

Sharon: "What test?!"

Julia: "Pregnancy Test. You all have animal instincts. They gave us drugs to make it stronger amongst us. Call Todd to the bridge now. He has been with us all. Let's go ladies."

Sharon stood straight up, and everyone saw a small bump coming from her stomach pressing against her shirt.

Sharon: "We are going for the planet."

Brandy: "Which one?"

Kira: "The one that looks like Earth. The one over thirty years from us. You know we cannot reverse this. We did all the tests. You know why they put our blood with his and his blood with ours. So, we want him, and he wants us. I want my kids to never have to worry about fighting for their lives and live in peace. Julia, we have different bodies than human women. We have four breasts."

Julia looked at her: "Let's go. I have been studying our bodies. I know. Our bodies will yearn for his body. That is the animal they have put into us. I also know the ship of ladies need to take this test. I know we are all going to have children. We may have three or four children. I feel sorry for Todd."

Sharon looked at her: "What you mean? Why him?"

Julia: "You ladies are taking advantage of him. We, ladies, are opposed to support and comfort each other and stay away from him. We are supposed to reverse this. He is staying away from us. We are looking for him."

Sharon: "How do you know we are doing this?"

Julia: "Because I am doing it as well. I see all you ladies doing this and we look for him. I do not know how many children we will have at once. I see how you ladies are looking at me. I need the test myself."

Two years later

Paul held his AR30 rifle and looked up at the night sky. He walked into a back yard. It was a cold night. Adrei held his AK40 rifle and followed him. They walked into a destroyed back yard of a rich man's yard. They looked into the distance and saw a city on fire. They walked onto a boat dock and looked at a sunken massive yacht. A man stood at the end of the dock and looked at his dead children and said, "I did not know this war would get out of hand this fast. We thought we could control it and make money from it. In the 1990s and early 2000s they warned us that no one could control World War Three, but we wanted to make money." He looked at the burning house and continued, "This War is out of control. Our families are gone." He looked at the water and looked at the bodies floating in the water.

Paul looked at him: "Ethen Quinn, they wanted this. You wanted this. World War Three can never be controlled."

Adrei looked at Ethen: "Tell me about the Forbidden Ones."

Ethen: "The ones in space. The ones having babies now. The world powers wanted their slaves. They wanted to control the world. They wanted to know if it could get done. We made a new species that is lost in space now. They wanted to play God. The house had many of the powerful people in it and someone blew it up with them in it."

Ethen looked at the burning forest: "They say more than two billion will die or more."

Paul looked at Ethen: "Tell me about the ones in space."

Ethen: "We took the people who spoke out against us. I never knew it would get this far. We were going to push for peace. One of us said many or all of the world leaders are dead."

The agents saw the gun in his hand. They heard military tanks and personnel carriers rumble by and fighters fly overhead. They heard gun fire and fighting in the distance. Ethen began to cry over his dead family. "This is America. We are not supposed to fight here or many places on Earth and they are fighting there." He looked at the agents. "We wanted power. Absolute Power. They say there is no such thing. They are right. God can only hold and have Absolute Power." Ethen looked at the gun in his hand. "I am an untouchable. That is funny. I joined that group. It is over." He brought the gun up to his head. "This mess is because of the rich and powerful and world leaders thinking we can control everything. We cannot control ourselves, let alone control other people. I cannot live in this world." Ethen pulled the trigger and his lifeless body hit the ground.

Paul looked at Adrei: "Let's get out of here. We will go to Texas."

Adrei: "Texas?"

Paul: "Yes, the guy I arrested."

Adrei smiled: "He can get me home and back? The one steeling airplane parts. The place the Forbidden Ones families went to live to save their children?"

Paul: "Yes, him. Let's get out of here before we become part of that fight out there."

Into the Stars

The wind blew sand across the dirt runway. The hot morning sun came over the Texas desert as the father came out of the small mountainside bunker and looked up at the clear morning sky. His daughter came walking up behind him. "Dad, why can we not wait? It will be easier at the end of the week. This is a bad idea. We can have a crew go up with you. I can go with you." His niece walked up to them. "Those government people are coming. Edward, listen to Victoria." Edward looked out over the hot morning desert and turned to look at his family. "No, Christina. This must be done. We are in World War Three. Thousands of cities were destroyed, about three billion are dead now, and we are still fighting over ten years later. From 2020 to 2034 everyone used up their defense systems, so there are no more nukes. There are whole civilizations massacred because of these weapons of mass destruction. What we are doing can help unite the planet in a new space program. We must find a way to stop the killing and unite the people. We must unite the Earth. We must find a common peace."

The American government NSA agent walked over to them and said, "You want to start early? I had no time to call anyone."

The Russian government SVR agent walked over and said, "I have to call my government if your country will not let you back in. You can land there in Russia."

Edward looked at the American FBI Paul, Russian FSK Adrei, and American CIA agents walking toward them. "It has to be done now. No one is expecting this. Well, if you have to call. Call now. I will be in the air in ten minutes."

Paul looked at him: "Well, I am going to get fired but I will not arrest you this time for working with foreign powers. You did not work with America first with this. You did this on your own. I have to call the President."

The FSK agent Adrei walked over: "I have to call the Russian President. We will help pay for this. My President wants to see this."

One of the ground crew walked over from the shuttle: "We are fueled and ready."

Victoria: "Dad, I love you. Do not do anything crazy. We know these shuttles work. We tested them multiple times. Fly up and back down, okay? We will be in the command room. Remember how we designed the shuttle." Victoria and Christina embraced Edward.

Edward: "See you when I get back."

Victoria: "Dad, be careful."

Christina: "Ed, listen to Victoria. Do not do anything crazy. I love you."

The CIA agent walked over: "Remember, you will fly by the space station and a ship that was under construction. It was made for a flight to Mars. Fly by and check on them, then come back down. I have to call off the military."

Victoria and Christina walked Edward to the shuttle and embraced him. The shuttle design came from an old B1 lancer bomber. It was redesigned.

The belly was flat, the engines were above the wings and next to the body. The wings were solid to the body, it had two rudders, and no tail horizontal stabilizer. It was upgraded to carry two new rockets on its back and two new engines. Edward put on his space suit and climbed into the shuttle. The ground crew strapped him in and closed the hatch. They all walked out of the hanger and over to the command center. Victoria walked into the command center and heard, "We see you and hear you. 5 by 5," as she walked into the bunker.

Christina and Victoria put on their headsets and looked at the massive twenty-foot long and ten foot high television view screen. There was a hanging chair at the end of a crane arm. It swung across the front of the screen. The command center had people working everywhere on the computers. "Dad, we see you. Remember, you are sixty and there will be no way to get to you for three days if there is an emergency. That is why we built the emergency pod. To get you home. We did make a second shuttle to get to you. Chair, start checklist and then count down."

Edward's friend, Richard, went down the ten-page checklist: "This is the chair. Clear the hanger. Engine warm-up good. Everything looks good." The shuttle drove out of the hanger and rolled onto the ten-acre long dirt road. Albert looked at the screen. "This is nuts, but we are doing it, dude. Ready, last chance." They all heard the words. "F-it." The shuttle engines roared to life and the shuttle raced across the runway and shot into the air.

Victoria sat down and then jumped to her feet. She screamed out, "What is he doing?! He did not let us do the count down."

Richard looked at her: "That is your father. He gets done what has to get done and he waits for no one." The shuttle rose into the air and the wheels retracted. The shuttle flew through the air. One of the people in the command center looked at their radar and computer screens. "The Air force sent up fighters. We did not get clearance to be in the air. They will force him to land." The SVR agent looked at the massive screen. "That is if they can catch him."

CIA agent looked at the screen as he put the phone to his ear. "General call off the birds."

Air Force General: "No, you know there is a war going on still. I sent up the new fighters and they go Mach three. The President said no one in the air until they make it safe. The enemy will send a hypersonic missile. I want him back on the ground. Now!"

Paul looked at everyone in the room. He saw Sharon's son and daughter watching. "Mr. President, please, he is in the air now. He did not want to wait. Call off the military. Yes, the Russians are here. No, Sir, I had no idea. They have this open to the internet and everyone can see it."

President: "What was your job, agent?! NO! General! He does not turn around shoot him down. I gave you agents' orders, and this is what I see getting done."

Adrei looked at the view screen: "Ten thousand feet. US government does it again with their company's backed government. I did tell him to do it from Russia."

Christina looked at the screen: "May God be with you Uncle."

The Air Force next seven gen fighter caught up with him. Edward looked through his two helmet space suit. He looked to his right and left and saw the fighters. "I am Air Force, and you will get back to the ground or I will shoot you out of the sky. The two rockets on the side of your fuselage will not help you outrun us. Turn around now. Last warning or we shoot you out of the air."

Albert looked at his computer screens: "You did not tell them of the new engines we made. Ion Plasma engines."

Edward looked at the pilots in the Air Force fighters: "I have no time for this!" He pulled the throttle back and the shuttle shot forward. The two next gen fighters could not keep up.

The air force pilot keyed his mic: "We lost him. He has to be going Mach 5, easy. Out of range to lock weapons."

CIA looked at the screen: "General."

General: "Yes!"

CIA: "He is going Mach three and he can go faster."

General: "I can see he is out running our birds. What engines is he using?"

CIA: "I did not learn about this engine until now."

General: "Did the Russians know of this?"

SVR agent smiled: "No, yes. We helped him get the money, but you know, how you say it? Deniability."

The NSA looked at him: "Great. What are you people not telling us? The rockets are what?"

Victoria looked at him: "My father planned on this and what all countries may do. It is one of the experimental engines the US made, and they threw it away. He just took it from the junkyards and advanced it. The rockets are new solid propulsion rocket engines. They can be easily started cold in space."

The NSA agent looked at her: "What is its main ingredient for rocket fuel?"

Christina looked at him and giggled: "The Germans used it in World War Two. What is in all the fields outside? That fuels the rockets and we made two Ion thruster plasma engines. The engines make a hypersonic plasma. There are two engine that are arc jet and if all fails. Two rocket jet engines. That will help him get to the ground. Oh, its heat shield is called Adept and it is spider weave. We just found out it make the body of the shuttle stronger. It covers the shuttle."

NSA: "You mean what I cleaned off my shoe this morning? No! It cannot be."

Christina: "Yes, I was surprised but it was smart. We also used more of the bison and other things that are easy to get and make."

NSA: "Where did he get the aircraft fuel?"

Christina: "You drank some last night."

NSA: "What?!"

Christina: "Where do you think we get the drinks? More than three-quarters of the planet is destroyed and is trying to rebuild in this war. We grow it from more than one plant. Oh, everything is super redundant and safe."

Paul: "Thank you, Mr. President. Call them off."

One of the people in the room screamed out, "Oh, God! I know the enemy is all but lost in this war. We have a new problem. The hypersonic missile in the air. It will take one minute till it gets to the shuttle!"

Victoria: "Dad did you hear that?!"

Edward: "Yes, I did." Edward looked at his controls and pulled the throttle forward and he was now at Mach two.

CIA: "The enemy missile has a booster."

Victoria screamed out, "Dad, faster or do that maneuver thing!"

Albert looked at the large screen and laughed: "No, it will miss him."

Victoria looked at him and pointed at the view screen: "What?! The enemy missile is going Mach seven."

Albert pointed at the view screen: "The missile cannot maneuver in space."

Victoria looked at the screen: "What?" Everyone looked at the screen and saw the missile fly aimlessly into space. The shuttle was still flying at the outer edge of the atmosphere.

SVR agent looked up at the screen: "That is why we call him the Grand Admiral. He got the thing to think he was much higher and there is no air at that height."

Edward watched the missile fly by the shuttle over fifty feet away. "Okay, let us start this. Speed is at nine hundred miles an hour. Count down for rockets. Leaving Earth."

Victoria: "Dad! Be careful. Count now. 10, 9, 8, 7, 6, 5, 4, 3, 2, 1, 0, rocket on. Now." Edward turned on one of the rockets and flew out of the orbit of the Earth.

Victoria: "Dad, do not go past the space station." The rocket shut down as the shuttle flew up to the space station and passed it.

Edward: "Sorry, I came up here to do the impossible and make history."

Albert looked at the screen: "I am your friend, and we did talk about this. No mission to the moon or fly around it. Come on, you hear me."

Edward: "Do the math. I can be there in under eight hours then fly back."

Albert: "That is a flight of sixteen hours."

Edward: "F- it. I drove trucks in my younger days. I drove twenty hours. We did the test many times. I easily flew that many times over. Just days back."

Albert: "That was a test! No! We were just moving things to the bunker."

Edward: "It will bring back the space programs."

Albert: "No, Edward. You are going to do it anyway. See you when you get back."

Richard smiled and shook his head: "Like old times." The rocket turned on high and the shuttle sword through space to the moon.

Victoria: "Dad, I told you this is a bad Idea. I knew you were going to do this. Dad, I love you. If anything happens you know what to do. We are getting the other shuttle ready just in case. You have the communication and video satellites. Launch them, one by one. Make sure you drop two before the dark side of the moon. You have five."

Edward: "I will do so. Oh, the space station looks good, and the ship is good."

Albert looked at the computer: "He will be flying by the moon in six hours. Watch him. He still has one rocket which is full of fuel." The shuttle rocket ignited, and the shuttle flew toward the moon.

Montana.

Senior advisor: "Mr. President. I have no idea he invited the Russians. Edward is a war hero and he freed many states the enemy took control of. He made his own space force. He said in 1982 or 83 that he wanted Russia in it. Well, it would help with world peace if we worked with them. We are not enemies."

The President looked at the television: "When everyone forgets about this get him arrested on something. The other aerospace companies never wanted him up there. How did the Russians know of this? How did he get them involved? And how did we not know of any of this! Get me a plane down there. The Russian President is on his way there."

Eight hours later.

Victoria: "Dad, the rocket engine one is empty. Drop second satellite now."

Edward: "I dropped second communication satellite." The cargo hatch opened, and the satellite flew out and the hatch closed again. "Wow, you should see the moon closer. Wow, look at the Earth. It is beautiful. Coming up to the moon now. Going to the dark side and dropping the third satellite now. What is that?"

Richard looked at the screen: "He launched the satellite, but we cannot see him or hear him. Satellite up. What is that?" Everyone looked at the main view screen in shock. Victoria ran to the hanging chair.

She looked at the person in the command chair: "Get out of the chair! I want the chair! That is an alien ship, or the governments of the world never told us they made a new ship of some kind. That is an alien ship. It is just sitting there. Dad, do you hear us?" She climbed into the hanging chair in front of the screen and worked on the computer.

Edward: "Yes, I hear you! This answers the question. Are we alone in the universe. You see this? It looks about seventy-five meters long and a trireme ship with wings and metallic. It is not moving. It is just sitting here." The shuttle flew to the alien ship. "I am slowing myself down."

Victoria: "Dad, again, that is not a good idea. Get out of there." The alien ship began to move, and its running lights turned on. "Dad, get out of there. It is moving." They heard the radio come to life.

Albert looked at the computer screen: "They are calling you?"

Edward looked at the radio: "Yes, they are."

Alien ship: "Human ship, do you hear us? We hear you."

Victoria moved around in the command chair. Her fingers danced across the keyboard. "Do not say anything."

Richard looked at her: "They hear us. That means they heard you." The alien ship moved and stopped in front of the shuttle.

Alien ship: "Human ship or shuttle, you do hear us. Who am I talking to?"

Edward: "This is Edward. Who are you?"

Alien ship: "We are the Siogai. I am Ambassador Ronan. We are not here to take sides. We know you are in a Third World War. We did not hear from any government on the Earth for some time. So, we came into your star system hoping to talk to your governments and we hope no one shoots at us. We know of your laws of aliens on your world."

Edward: "What do you mean talk to our governments? What do you mean by laws on aliens? What? Wait? How long have you been talking to our governments?"

Alien ship: "You did not know? We thought you came up to talk with us and the government sent you. We were asked not to call down to your world."

Edward: "No." Everyone in the command room looked at each other.

NSA agent looked at the screen: "Well, no one here knows of this. I guess the old governments of the world hid this. They are all dead now, because they started this war, and they never knew this war would get out of control. Now they are all dead."

Edward looked at the alien ship: "How long did you talk to our governments?"

Alien ship: "Our satellite crashed into your planet in your 1950s. Then we left your world alone. Then, we came over after your 1960s when you went to space. You flew a crew to the moon to talk with us. We started talks after that. We met and negotiated on the moon."

Victoria: "Dad, do you know how long that is? You know everyone on the Earth sees this."

Edward: "Yes. How can I help you?"

Victoria: "Hold on."

Paul looked at the screen: "Our President has no idea about this. The last government was wiped out five years into the war, way before we restarted this new government. He is having someone investigate this now."

FSB agent looked at him: "We are also looking into this."

The Siogai ship was now moving in front of the small forty-four-meter-long shuttle: "We are hoping to help you clean your world."

Edward: "For what? I mean cost."

Alien ship: "For trade and hope to get you humans into space."

The CIA agent looked at the screen: "Tell him no."

Richard looked at him: "What? No! You think he will listen to us? Oh, you also forgot we are in America. You know that is a rough neck up there. He is an American. He is a war hero. He helped command the forces from the east coast to the west coast after the destruction of the leaders in this country. He helped push the enemy out of this country. That alien ship is coming down here."

Edward looked at the Alien ship: "Come down with me."

Alien ship: "We are not fighting a war for you. We are not taking sides."

Edward: "No. I am inviting you. This war is about over."

Alien ship: "Your world has a law where they will kill any alien that comes into your world."

Edward: "I would like you to come. Trust me. No one wants war anymore. That was the last government. We all had to restart the governments after ten years of fighting. There are new governments now. Come with me."

Alien ship: "We will come with you to Texas."

Edward: "You know our states and countries? You also know our language?"

Alien ship: "Yes, we studied you for a long time. The old governments know the Siogai language." The shuttle flew past the Siogai ship, then the alien ship turned and followed the shuttle back to Earth.

Airfield

The President looked at the aid: "Damn the old governments and what they did. Damn them to hell. We needed to unite back then. We need the military there now. Get me the Russian President. We need to talk."

Senior advisor: "Yes, Sir."

President: "Forget about what I said. We cannot get him on treason, because the shuttle he was made from a 1970s bomber and from junk he bought. The Russians have that tech as well as we do. I want that shuttle. Get me Europe and the other leaders of the world."

Senior advisor: "Sir, is there anything you want to talk to them about?"

President: "Yes, emergency meetings. Start them today. Start them now. Tell the Russians we want to work on this with them. Get me all the generals and admirals. I want the command staff as well. I want an emergency meeting here. Everyone sees this on the computer or TV. You say he made a space force in 1983. I want that program up and running. I want him in charge of the program. We are not alone and that is dangerous to the human race. We have to work together on this fast. We will have peace."

Senior advisor: "Sir, may I say this? Let us not distrust anymore. This is how we got here."

The President looked at him: "Yes, you are right. We will share technology. Humanity will need us to be better."

A second aid ran over to the President: "Sir, the enemy saw what we saw and now accepted the unconditional surrender. We did take out the leaders three months back. The war is over."

The President smiled: "That is good news. The war is over. Get me the Russian President. Get me the ambassador we just had a meeting with. I want him on a plane down to the Air Force base down there then put him on a helicopter. I want him down there now."

Texas desert.

Victoria looked around and saw the military was setting up.

Victoria: "Do we need the military? It has been six hours. I do not think they came here for a fight with a ship that size."

The army General looked at her: "We do not know."

Christina looked around: "This is not needed. They said they want to trade."

General: "Like I said. We do not know. This can be very dangerous."

Victoria pointed: "They are landing." The shuttle wheels hit the ground and rolled across the runway. The Siogai ship hovered over the runway and landed. Edward opened the side hatch and climbed down the ladder of the shuttle. He took off his two helmets and walked to the Siogai ship.

The General looked at Edward: "Do not go to the alien ship and come back here."

Albert looked at the General: "You have no idea. We are in America."

Edward looked at them and walked over to the alien ship. A ramp lowered and everyone heard the Siogai calling out from inside the Siogai ship. "I am the Ambassador Ronan." Edward looked up the ramp into the Siogai ship at Ronan.

Ronan: "No one will shoot me?"

Edward: "Please come down. No, we do not want to shoot you. We do not want an interstellar war. Come down."

A cloaked person walked down the ramp. Edward raised his hand out as a sign of peace. The Ambassador lowered his head cloak, and everyone looked at him. Edward shook the hand of Ambassador Ronan.

Edward: "You look human, but your ears and eyes look different. Your eyes iris glows and your ears are pointy."

Ronan: "Yes, we do look a little alike. Did your species bring an ambassador?"

Edward: "That means we almost have close to the same worlds. I know the governments of the world will send ambassadors."

Ronan: "Yes, they will." They heard a helicopter coming in the distance.

New Earth headquarters

The United States President raised his hand: "Let us start."

Russian President: "Everyone Quiet. Let us begin this. We all start with peace talks."

US President: "Thank you, and thank you to all who are here. Our old governments never told us the truth. We learned it the hard way. We must make peace."

China President raised his hand: "Yes, borders back to normal."

The Russian President raised his hand: "No. Hon Kong President will argue that with Taiwan President and Mongolian President. We help get that land back. Remember, there are Aliens out there wanting this world. They will want us all dead. Not one of us will live if we do not find peace and stand together. Like the US President said."

China President: "Fine, we want peace. Ten billion people on this planet before the war and after this war more than three billion dead. Peace. Hong Kong is the size of Alabama because of the British, Filipino, Vietnamese, and Japanese. They will stay that way. We recognize these countries and respect them."

United States President: "We give back Mexico and all South American countries. Is that okay China?"

China President: "Yes, we make that trade."

Russian President raised his hand: "I give back part of China and European countries we took during the war."

The Israeli President raised his hand and the Egyptian President jumped to his feet: "NO! We have peace. Israel will be Israel let it be. I am sick and tired of terrorists that need to learn the truth and history. Not just letting someone tell them it is bad and not look into it. Arab countries join me." All Arab countries raised their hand. Egyptian President: "See, Israel, we all help you in the war. Let them be gone in history. Israel was there before Christianity and Islam. We now all stand with you. We stand together."

Israeli President: "Thank you. We want peace."

Saudi Arabia Prince raised his hand: "Israel, my family would be dead if it was not for you. I say we rebuild Iran."

US President: "Yes, I agree." All countries of the world began to give back countries. Peace and common ground were found. They began talks about the aliens and technologies. They all voted for the new Earth Defense Force.

British Chancellor raised his hand: "Does anyone know when this war started?"

Afghani President: "I know the old governments and leaders died the first five years into the war. We need to look into this. When did World War Three start? Who started this madness and why?"

The News.

The news, helping tell the history by reporting real news people want to know or do not know. That helps the people know by letting people choose and decide for themselves.

"You never want to repeat history that is why we learn history."

2035

The human race and Earth find true peace for the first time in history. Full peace talks work, and the humans make peace with themselves and start their climb into space. Humanity will never see war with itself ever again. They still hold their borders and keep world leaders. Everyone on Earth voted for their first diplomats to the new galaxy positions. Humanity cleans their planet with technology and the people of the Earth work together. The birth rate climbs massively on Earth to help rebuild the loss of life in the last war. No one knows the number of humans on Earth, so the new census starts. The humans start a massive investigation into the old governments. They find horrifying information that the old governments hid from the world. The earth's people gain massive new advances in medicine and technology.

The cities of Earth are now being rebuilt and people are moving back to the abandoned cities. They find there are billions of children born in underground cities. Underground cities on Earth empty out. Humans are happy to be outside and no one is scared to be shot by someone in the war or get sick from radiation. The humans make the Space Force work for a better tomorrow. Some humans believe an unknown super soldier program known as the Forbidden Ones started World War Three in 2020. Some say the war started in 2010, and somehow, they escaped the Earth. The Russians and Americans make a strong alliance before the war to stop super soldier programs. After the Third World War information was leaked about the Forbidden Ones program. Massive investigations start looking into the old governments and when World War Three started.

2036.

The humans begin their climb back into space. The people of Earth make thousands of launch sites. Thousands of rocket ships flew today. The ships will be going to the Moon and to the International Space Station. The Earth forces are taking apart the International Space Station and building Earth's first Star Base. Folks, we just found out our star system is the Terran system. The Star Base is called Terran1. The Star base is ten times bigger than the space station. The Star Base will be finished in the year 2040. Humans will be landing back on the Moon in the next month and will be going to Mars this year. There is talk about colonizing the whole star system. We, humanity, is ready to return to the stars.

2037.

Earth's new materials, warp drive engines, and space engines were put to use today. The human race finds out the old governments were hiding a lot of new technology for some kind of sick control over the human race. Massive improvements have been made on the warp engines that were invented in the early 2000s and other engines like the ion drive and plasma drive. Space technology has massively improved. We have warp one technology and we can now travel our star system, Terran, in one day. Humans have now doubled their numbers with a massive growth in the birth of children. Everyone on Earth and other colonies in the Terran star system are having ten children by all natural childbirth with the help of technology and robot nurses'.

2039.

Humans build their first star base over Earth and explore and colonize every planet in its solar system. Humans now trade with two new alien races. The Siogai and the Torldor. The three species make border rules and determine how far from their home world belongs to them. One light year from any home world, which means at warp one in twenty-four hours. A very young cat-like alien race crashed on Earth and wanted to make peace with the human race. The Earth people thought it was an invasion at first but learned quickly it was not. The humans helped them get back to their home world.

2040

The Earth's first Star Base opened today and will be open to the public in days. The humans built a massive star base called Terran 1 and they built a star base over Pluto called Terran 2. Earth reaches warp two technology. Russia and America love the new spaceship designs, and the Typhoon, Alfa, and Seawolf class submarine will help with its designs of the new spaceship class. They will be called Independence, Vostok 1, and Freedom 1. There will also be ships called Gagarin and Shepard. All of the nations of Earth help in the designs and naming of the ships. The new exploration class spaceships are now flying through space. The governments of Earth form the Earth Defense Force and it is known to the humans as the EDF. New Military space warships, vehicles, equipment, and fighters are made for the defense of the home world. Billions join.

2041

The Siogai tell the human race where to find the Forbidden Ones new home world. The humans find out the Forbidden Ones were in space for forty years before they took control of their home world. Humans ready themselves for the hunt and fight ahead.

2050

Humans begin fixing their history books and find out World War Three started in 2010 and ended in 2035. The horrifying truth comes out for all to see. Over three billion dead, and every city, town, and village was destroyed. Countries were wiped out. The new leaders of the world have rebuilt these countries and help rebuild the cities, towns, and villages. A new peace comes over Earth. Humans join forces to become better for their children.

2070

The human race sends two hundred thousand troops to hunt down and destroy the Forbidden Ones, only to find out there was one million Forbidden Ones soldiers. They find out Todd is their leader. The humans find out the Forbidden Ones' home world has a population in the billions. The whole of the human forces is now missing. The humans believe their military forces have been massacred by this animal-like race. We found out many alien species made loyal super soldiers they could not control and never wanted, and they were sent to the same world of the Forbidden Ones. The Forbidden One were made to be loyal super soldiers but they are some kind of new animal and were sent to a planet for safety reasons. Later on, we found out many of the Forbidden Ones families joined the military and snuck onto the expedition with civilians. They helped the Forbidden Ones and helped the humans lose. The children of Sharon are the leaders of the group, and they were helped by the retired FBI agent, Paul Taylor, and retired FSK, Ardie Ivanov. They are all now with the Forbidden ones.

2070.

Edward Franklin War hero of World War Three. The man who flew around the moon in a space plane. The man who helped restart the Earth and founder of the new Space Force. The one who helped make peaceful relations with four alien races died today at a hundred.

2099-2117, First space war.

Humans win against the far more superior advanced bully alien race, Aquilae. Most of the fighting was in the Black Rose nebula.

2100, Star system M9 was found.

The star system asteroids move to block any ship from entering the system. The military was called in to help find a way in. The star system was explored, and they found ancient ruins of a very advanced civilization who died out hundreds of years ago. Planet M9 can be explored. Planet M793 cannot be explored safely, and new means will have to be found. Planet M793 is a very scary and prehistoric nightmare of a planet. The planet is super extremely dangerous, and its environment is unstable. Planet M793 has extreme storms, and its gravity forces constantly change. The planet is extremely mysterious. M793 disappeared in some kind of space cloud and reappeared out of the cloud. Planet M9 is being explored but we were forced to leave because of some kind of defense the ancient civilization put in place. It will have to be explored more carefully. The other planet in the system has some kind of force fields around it and we are trying to learn how to turn them off. All species have put up warnings around the star system to stay away and out of the M9 star system. The system is very dangerous.

2110

An unknown warrior alien race the Siogai call, Wolf Cats, have attacked them. They saw the Wolf Cats appear in space for the first time and they land on a peaceful Siogai colony. The Wolf Cats attack the colony without warning. The survivors of the colony said they left without saying why they attacked the colony. They do not know who the Wolf Cats are or where their home world is. The Wolf Cats ship looks to have a hammerhead and forward swept wings. Other aliens have also said they were attacked by this warrior race.

2117

Many of the alien worlds see the need for a rescue force of some kind in space. None of the planet's governments can agree on one rescue force and many of them have to make their own. Many of the alien worlds do not trust the other. The alien worlds wish to govern their own space. The human race, with many of their allies, make a new force called the Peacekeepers.

2119 Pirates wars

Space will always be lawless. Pirate activity is on the uprise and no one can get ahold of it or stop it. No one knows where these lawless pirates come from. They are many different alien species and they are robbing ships and making them into homemade warships. No alien race trusts another species to put their true trust in any other race to protect them. Many species think they need to protect themselves first before helping the other. Many feel someone is planning to rob all their resources and extinguish their species. Large space militaries are made to protect their space and the space around them. Many of the species help others to protect themselves. Many alien races argue over planets and resources outside their space.

Many of them make unified colonies to show they all can make peace with the other species despite their mistrust of each other. They are willing to make peace. The humans started a massive war against the pirates. All pirates' ships now avoid human ships entirely. The humans enjoy hunting down the pirates. The humans defeat massive numbers of pirate fleets and forces with smaller numbers of forces. After the major defeat of the pirates at Klangdagg, all the alien species want to know how to make their own human Marines, especially the Devil Dogs and Black Death. Humans never give up their secret.

Three hundred Marines took a pirate base of five thousand pirate forces. Marines have minimal casualties but the pirates lose three thousand and there is a thousand missing. The pirate prisoners describe it as a massacre of their forces. They describe it as unbelievable acts by the humans. They never believed how small of a number the human forces were. Pirate forces surrender to the humans after the defeat at Dorlat. The only force to defeat the pirates was the humans' forces and their Marines. Alien forces now want to make peace with the humans. Pirate wars end by the human hands but there will always be pirates and lawless space. The aliens learn human history and a new fear starts against the humans, but the humans ensure them of peace.

2120

A Siogai lost ship was returned to them by the humans. It was found in the year 2070. The humans learn and use their technology to help win the war against the Aquilae. The Siogai Ambassador was not too happy because the humans held this information from them and held onto their ship for many years. The Siogai are happy the humans respected their dead crew and returned them to their families. The Siogai say the humans are very flexible, resilient, and should be respected. Humanity has now reached warp seven technology.

2130-2148 Robo war.

A large experiment with a new A.I. in the star system Sag24. The A.I. became self-aware and must be stopped. The A.I. kills billions and took over its star system. Many aliens got together and formed a new Alliance. The machine AI was defeated by the Alliance.

2150-2157 War with the Lykoi.

The warrior race, Lykoi, started war with the Alliance. After first contact with the new species they started war. After the Alliance obtained much detail of their ships, they determined they were Hammerhead wing ships. The Lykoi is known to be the Wolf Cat race who attack many species around them. The Alliance stands against the warrior race, Lykoi. A Neutral Zone and an unsettling peace was formed.

2161-2170 Alliance against the Ittors.

The Alliance breaks into a civil war. A new Alliance forms and fights with the Ittors. The Alliance goes to war with the Ittors and their allies. The Alliance defeated the mad Emperor of the Ittors. They had to fight the Ittors and the unknown cyborg race all the way to their home world and the Ittors signed an unconditional surrender. There was a planet in the Ittors star system that was overly protected. Only the Ittors were allowed to go to this planet. This unknown planet appears to be very toxic and dangerous.

2171-2173 War with the Lykoi.

The warrior race, Lykoi, attacks across the Neutral Zone and is forced back by the Alliance. A stalemate occurs and new talks start for peace. Both sides stop shooting.

2175-2180

War with the Forbidden Ones starts. Some say the surrounding systems started the war with the Forbidden Ones. The Alliance fights to hold back the Forbidden Ones. A Neutral Zone is formed after the Forbidden Ones take one light year of territory.

2183-2186 War with Lykoi.

The Lykoi fight a war to the M9 star system and lose its fleets in the system. There is an unknown force there that no one can explain. No one knows who defeated them and the Alliance fleets. The M9 star system is very dangerous and is still a massive mystery to all. The Lykoi government was overthrown by the New Lord General and a new government was formed. Peace came to the Neutral Zone and the peace holds.

2190

New talks to make the New United Planets out of the Alliances of species. It will be a better galaxy. The forming of the United Planets will be sometime after 2200. We are looking at a newfound peace. Thousands of Alien species want to join.

Sometime after 2200.
Runaway.

A cargo freighter called the Kago flew near a planet. Captain: "Why did you scare him like that! You fools! He damaged the side of the ship! Where did he go?"

One of the crew looked out a window at the planet below. "The lifeboat is going into the planet, Sir."

An old lady ran to them: "You terrorized him! He is only seven. I could have had the other children help get him. He could have helped us in the new colony. Deim, why?! The poor boy. What planet is that? What planet is that?!"

The Captain looked at her: "Kailg, stop. Deim did not know the boy would jump into the lifeboat and launch it. We have to go down and get the lifeboat and the boy."

Diem looked at them: "That is M793! NO! Neator, tell them."

Neator looked at the planet: "There are monsters and ghosts down there. The boy is dead. There is no way we can get the lifeboat."

Kailg looked at them: "You are men! The boy needs you. Do not leave him down there. Captain, Please."

The Captain looked at her: "The boy fears his own shadow. That lifeboat is expensive. We do have to get it and put it back. The boy will be with the lifeboat. Do not worry Kailg, you will have the human boy back. He is your trouble after we bring him up. I would like to get him home to his own mother and father. He is not our problem. How did he know how to use the lifeboat? Get the work shuttle ready. Monsters, ghosts. You are children. Fear me! We are going down crew, let us get going." The crew boarded the shuttle. The captain looked at everyone. "Crew, we have weapons and those are animals down there. First mate, Terat, watch the ship. Tell the women to get the medical bay ready for the boy. We have to go down to this planet. Launch us when the hatches are closed." The twenty-long meter maintenance shuttle flew out of the freighter and down to the planet.

Deim looked back at the captain: "Sir, the lifeboat landed ten minutes ago. But…"

Captain: "But, what?! No ghost stories or boogeyman."

Deim: "It moved four hundred meters."

Neator looked at the screen: "I will put us there. What moved a thousand-pound lifeboat with ease?"

The captain looked at them: "Stop that child talk. It landed in the water and moved to the shore."

The shuttle broke through the clouds and then the captain stood up. "Wow, this is a graveyard of ships. I do not care. They look as if they have been here for years. They have to be a thousand meters or more from the other."

As the shuttle got closer, Beim pointed: "The lifeboat is there but everything in it is everywhere."

Neator looked: "Sir, there is no water near it."

Captain: "Get us there. It must have landed wrong. It rolled. Land near it."

Neator: "Sir, it was not moving for ten minutes."

Captain: "Quiet. Stop this talk of the boogeyman. It is getting tiring. Let us get the lifeboat and the kid and we leave. This planet is making me feel weird." The shuttle landed near the lifeboat. The crew opened the back ramp, and they climbed out. The captain looked around and felt weird.

Neator: "Sir, things are moving around us."

The Captain looked about: "Where? I do not see anything! Stop your crying it is small animals that are here. Crew, get that lifeboat loaded! Now! I want out of here in five minutes."

Neator: "The hand scanners are showing movement."

Captain: "There are animals moving around out there. Stop your panicking."

Diem pointed in at something in the distance: "What is that?"

Neator looked: "That is extinct in our world. That is a ten-meter-long dinosaur. Look at the claws and teeth on that thing. That will rip us apart. It is over there trying to move the large bolder. Look at the mythological monster behind it."

The captain looked around and saw many monster creatures moving about. He took steps back to the shuttle and he screamed out, "Get the Lifeboat! Let's get out of here! Forget everything else. Now!" He looked up and saw a nine-meter-long winged dragon fly over them. The crew worked quickly and loaded the shuttle with the escape pod. Some of them looked about and saw many creatures moving about. The crew started shooting their guns.

The captain screamed out, "What are you shooting at?!" He looked out of the back end of the shuttle and saw the crew running into the shuttle. He watched the forest come to life and monster-like creatures were coming out of the woods from everywhere.

The Captain screamed out, "Get in the shuttle! Close the ramp!"

The Captain ran to the shuttle bridge as they locked the ramp. The crew heard the creatures ripping and chewing on the hull of the shuttle. The captain jumped into the pilots' seat and through the throttle back. They shot into the air and missed a flying dragon-like dinosaur. They flew into space. Beim ran forward and said, "I heard the boy."

The captain looked at him: "You can go back and get him! Shut your mouth! That planet came to life and was going to eat us! No word of this! I saw a dragon! I am not going back! We looked and did not find the boy! That is what happened! Everyone, get to your stations."

The shuttle landed on the cargo ship and the crew studied the shuttle in the hanger. Kailg ran into the hanger. She looked at the ship and pointed at a bite mark three meters long. There were bite marks and claw marks all over the shuttle. Biem pulled a two-foot-long claw from the shuttle and Neator pulled a foot-long bone spike from the shuttle.

Kailg: "What happened down there? Where is the boy?"

The Captain looked at her: "Come with me to the library." They walked into the library and the Captain took out all the books on prehistoric animals and mythological creatures.

Captain: "That is all of them. Okay? That is what is down there from every living planet. Kailg, we looked for the boy but did not find him."

Kailg: "Wait, you were not down there that long."

Captain: "You see the shuttle?! The planet was going to eat us. I sent four of my men and they almost got eaten. No more questions."

Kailg: "But the boy."

Captain: "You want him? Get a shuttle and get him. Right now, there is no way down to him until we repair the shuttle. We cannot use the cargo shuttle and do not ask. Get your own shuttle."

Veartor walked in: "The shuttle needs to be overhauled. It will take days."

The captain walked onto the bridge: "Take us to M9. Get the cargo shuttle ready. I am going to my ready room."

Kailg followed him into the room: "Why are you changing dates and years on the report?"

Captain: "Kailg, I do not want to go back. If you saw what we saw you would do the same."

M793.

Tears rolled down his cheeks as he rolled up into a ball. The seven-year-old boy cried out as he watched the shuttle leave him under the bolder with the monster above.

Boy: "Do not leave me. Mom, where are you? Daddy, I need you. God help me! I need your help! I am sorry for being so weak. I can be stronger. Do not leave me." The boy was terrified of the dark and cried more. He moved more into the cave under the boulder and the monstrous creature clawed at the boulder trying to get to the boy. He turned and found something glowing in the dark. He wiped the tears from his face and picked up the large crystal. A foot long, four inch wide glowing crystal. It changed colors in his hand and lit up the cave. The cave opened up to a large cavern with a pool of water. He saw fish and other small animals moving about. There was a small building in the cave. He held the crystal above his head and walked to it. He opened the hatch that led into the building and walked in.

It is sometime after the year 2210.
The story begins.

The wind blew hard and cold as the blinding heavy snow fell. The sun tried to shine through the heavy clouds, but the light never made it through. The blinding wind howled past the outpost. Three of them watched from inside the command center as a special operations team walked around outside. The three inside of the building looked out through the large window and at the view screen. It was minus 85 degrees, and it was snowing harder.

The five-man special operations team walked through a small forest at the bridge of a mountain and could barely see the energy shield that surrounded the base through the blizzarding snow. The team walked under a massive tree. The warrant officer of the team looked at the frost on the sides of the faceplate on his helmet. "I need my equipment to see through this. I cannot see five feet in front of me."

The sergeant looked about in the woods: "Sir, I am happy these tactical combat space suits are working. I wish they had told us to use snowshoes. This snow is deep. You think he is out here?"

The Chief looked at the shield wall: "I am happy those energy shields are on. How does he get in here with the shield on? I do not think he is out here."

The Lieutenant felt the snow below his knees. He turned and looked at the team. "Knowing him he found us before we can find him and yes, he is out here. He does that and we do not know how. We do not know how he gets into the base or through the shields."

The microphone in the team leader's ear came to life: "Lieutenant, this is the Commodore. He found us again. Come back to base."

The team leader turned and pointed at the building: "You heard him, let's go!"

The Commodore pointed and raised his binoculars to his eyes: "Rear Admiral Trey in the massive tree over the team. Sir, the human boy is there. He is white Hispanic. He is one of yours. Rear Admiral Tray, Sir, you know I am a Gilardon species. We love you humans' skin and hair color. Sir, like you are brown skin and Captain Camille Davis is white with rose blonde hair."

The Admiral looked through his binoculars and saw something covered in snow. The boy sat there on a massive branch, and he looked at the base. Then the boy looked down at the team walking through the snow and then back toward the base. The boy was wrapped in some kind of blanket. Trey felt the boy looking at him. "So that is him. Can he see us? We cannot get him on scanners or infrared?"

Captain Camille Davis walked over: "Sir, it feels like he is looking at us. The boy looks a little sad. I cannot get him on any electronic device. Something to do with the planet." The Admiral saw the boy wearing animal skins and a wool cloak.

The Commodore lowered his binoculars: "Sir, he is a runaway. We found his parents, but they really do not care for him. They do not want him back and the boy really does not want to leave the planet, but he says he has to. Something to do with saving some girl he made a promise to. We asked him if he wanted to join the military and he said yes. We gave him the test and he scored high. We do not know how he can see through this storm."

Admiral Trey lowered his binoculars: "How did he survive here? Who helped him and how long was he here? Did the species help him? Why does he look a little sad?"

The Captain looked at the data tablet: "Commodore Sir, you were not here when they found him?"

Commodore: "No, I was not. I got here two years ago. I do not know how he can see through this, but the crew has said he can easily see through this. We know little of the inhabitants of this world or where they may be and how they survive this nightmare of a planet. The boy will not talk of them much or of his past here. He is protecting them or something. Sorry, Sir, I want off this rock. It is very scary on this planet. I heard there was some kind of battle some days ago. No one here knows about it, where it was, or even saw it, but we found out a lady called Moth died there with her servant, Sisur. They were very important to him. He does not say anything about them. All we know is that they are very important to him. He said he spent a lot of time with them and lived with them for a long time. Moth will let him run around freely. Sisur was his handler and watched over him. He said Moth first had him as a pet. He spoke about some other young lady with whitish purple hair. He promised himself and Moth he would free her. We never found the girl anywhere. What we know is what he told us, but we still do not know anything about him or the species on this planet. We know the species of this planet did not help him survive here. We do not know how he survived here. This here is a terrifying planet."

The Admiral looked at him: "The boy learned on his own or watched others. It is what I read here in this report. Do not worry. This program for training here failed, but we found him. That is one good thing, and we are getting him off this world."

Camille walked to the computer console: "Admiral, he was found by the archaeologist team, or he found them, and he led them to the ancient city. I am reading here what they wrote. Planet M793 is a large moon-sized planet. That goes around M9. It has a weird rotation. The planet's environment here is in the extremes, hot, cold, or gravity storms and other so called hellish storms. The planet disappears from time to time in a space cloud and then reappears before it comes out of the cloud. There is another report that states this planet stopped disappearing in the space cloud. What I read here is that he ran away from home at eight or nine years old. He was on the planet for over seven years. There is a report here from a freighter captain. There is more but it does not make much sense. Dates and years are off. It says seven years, then it says ten years. The freighter captain needs to get his computer fixed."

The Admiral turned and looked at her: "I want to know what all reports say."

Camille: "Yes, Sir. The report of the freighter captain about how the kid got to the planet. The captain states the child snuck onto the ship in the Earth spaceport of New York City. The crew found him robbing food and education data pads. The crew chased the boy and he jumped into the lifeboat, and he locked the hatch. They say he had to learn that from someone by watching the crew testing equipment. The child launched the lifeboat onto this planet. There is another report from one of the crew, but it was deleted. The deleted report had video and a study on the boy for a year. It is from an old lady who died from natural causes. The freighter captain deleted the report, and he died on a new colony. There is another report on the boy and a longer study on him, but that video and report has been deleted as well. A three-year study, but it does not say from who and why it was deleted. Sir, we can go to the colony and try to find the crew. We can ask them questions."

The Admiral studied the viewscreen: "No, that will take too much time and may be a waste of time. I do not think the boy wanted this planet. I think he wanted M9. So, why was the cargo ship here?"

Camille: "Sir, the cargo ship was dropping supplies off at the space station and an archaeologist site on Planet M9. They were driving by M793 when they found him. The crew said he did not know how to control the lifeboat and the craft crashed into the freighter. Then, the lifeboat crashed into Planet M793 and the crew went down to the planet and found the lifeboat but not the child. They recovered the lifeboat. They said they tried to look for the boy for several hours. They said the boy was dead, but we see here he is alive. The report says here they were terrified to be on the planet."

Trey looked at the view screen report: "I bet they did not try to find him. What is this on the report? It says the planet came to life."

Camille: "Sorry, Sir, I do not know. The report stops there."

The Commodore looked at the viewscreen: "This boy has survived here for seven years. Sir, his parents signed him over to the military."

The Admiral watched the boy in the trees as he saw the boy looking at him: "So, Captain, you want to study him. You will have your chance. I need to go to the Dracu system. I will take him to the star base after I come back."

The Commodore escorted the Admiral and the Captain to the hanger bay: "Sir, I will have him ready and cleaned up. We already have him trained to be a cadet."

Admiral: "Thank you, we will see you when we come back." The Admiral and Captain walked onto the waiting military supply ship. The side door closed, and the vessel flew out of the hanger into space. Admiral Trey sat in the lounge and felt the ship jump to warp.

Camille walked in: "Sir, you wanted to see me."

Admiral: "With your best medical and scientific expertise, can we make more humans able to survive heavy gravity like 3Gs?" Trey pointed at the chair across from him at the table.

The Captain sat down: "Admiral, may I speak freely?"

Admiral: "Yes, you can."

Captain: "Sir, with no disrespect, that planet is a gravitational and weather nightmare. The planet is just a nightmare. The gravity and weather fluctuates, and the special forces train under 2 or 3Gs. That boy somehow did not die there. Have you seen the animals there? Primal and prehistoric like all the prehistoric times were put together into one time with all the mythological creatures. I heard 10G storms happen on that planet. No Sir, we cannot make more like him. As a friend, how many people do you want to kill? It is one in a billion that may survive. Sir, we should leave the boy there. That is where he grew up. He will be difficult to control. The boy thinks primordial or barbaric. He is very dangerous or super dangerous. If that is where you are going with him."

Admiral: "There is something happening in this galaxy right now. I have no clue what it is. We need someone like him. Thank you, Captain. Need to know only." The Admiral got up and walked over to the windows and watched the stars fly by. "I do not like the planet we are going to."

The Captain looked at the admiral: "Sir, you mean the planet Searrun. I hear horror stories come from that world, but I was never there."

Admiral: "Well, it is a beautiful planet with large cities but the species loves slaves. It is a slave master race. The species is called the Ittors. Six eyes, four arms, and two legs. It will take us two days to get there. You should get the medical bay and the lab ready for the boy. I have paperwork to do. Oh, one last thing. We will be at an embassy compound, stay in the hanger with the ship. We will not be there long. Oh, one other thing, you are going to like his eyes."

Captain: "Sir, is there something you are not telling me?"

Admiral: "This is all confidential."

Captain: "Sir."

Admiral: "Need to know only."

M792.

Commodore: "I know I met the boy many times and I like this kid. He is always trying to be helpful and kind. So, Captain, the boy finally trusts us to take us to where he lives."

Captain: "Sir, not exactly. He takes us to the area. That is it."

The Commodore looked at the boy's spear. Captain: "Sir, you think he would have sharp sticks and sharpened rocks, not this complex metal weapons or clothing."

Commodore: "Captain, I was taught not to underestimate will of survival. This is a human design of a spear made by Japanese called Yari."

Captain: "Sir, that is his small one. The small blade is six inches, and the large one is twenty-four inches. His other spears are from Greek and Rome. He has weapons from medieval designs and others like the bearded axe and throwing weapons. The swords and knives are from America, Russia, Greece, Japan and Rome. The small bow is his design, and the arrow heads are from all the places I named. He has a shield and armor too. There is a mix of weapons from all these cultures and he knows how to set traps."

The Commodore cut his finger on the spear edge: "Ouch!"

Captain: "Careful! His weapons are extremely sharp."

Commodore looked at the blue blood coming from his finger: "Was he in a war here?"

Captain: "Sir, it is a long list. We asked and he spoke about fighting many wars with the plains, city, robots, dragons, monsters, kingdoms, tribes, gangs, hunters, pirates, slavers, valley, castles, and ancient ones. He called it the bringing of peace, order, and unity, and the ancient war. I do not know what he was talking about. We are still looking into it but now we will never know. We are all leaving in a month."

Commodore: "Well, put his things in the crate. It is amazing he has foldable weapons, and the spear and other weapons can be unscrewed."

Captain: "Sir, have you seen his wooden canteens or the tactical backpack? It is amazing to see his tools."

Two days later.

The military transport ship arrived at Planet Searrun. It was a clear day. The ship flew through traffic and the metropolis area. They entered the countryside. The ship flew over a farm, then a large water way with ships sailing through. It landed in a hanger bay on top of a small mountain in a luxurious embassy on Searrun.

Luxurious house

A young Ittors boy walked to his mother: "Mom, I cannot find her." The mother looked at her son: "You let her out of the cage again. She was massively expensive. That little beast cannot stay in her cage. My barn is getting a new cage because she is getting a little too big for the house. She must have her teeth shaved and she is to be declawed. The show handler wants her hair and everything done this weekend. Hopefully your father does not catch her in the field or he will have his way with her. I will tell the prince and he will kill him. My son, that is yours when you get to age. It is custom. That is if the prince will let you have her. If not, we will just buy you another."

In a dimly lit office in the house, a young girl crawled on her hands and knees. Her dress was caught under her knees and her long hair laid across her back. She tied a knot in her long hair and she hid each time she heard something moving. It was hard for her to see in the dimly lit room with a slave's helmet on. The room was dark. She crawled and found a desk. She felt around the desk with her hands and she found a large, crystallized bronze knife. She could see the outside sunlight peeking through the heavy curtains from the open dual doors. The curtains waved in the wind. The sun showed it was midday. She picked up the blade and crawled behind some curtains. The window was half open and she crawled out into the field quietly.

The slave helmet was heavy and slowed her down. It limited her view to only forward. She tried hard to take off the helmet and the knife did not help. She crawled through the muddy field and between the large plant growth. Something, or someone, grabbed her from the back of her helmet and grabbed her dress and tried to pull it off. Then, she was thrown through the air, and she landed hard in a mud puddle. The helmet detected fast movement and rushing air, so it closed the air vents. Then, the helmet opened its vents when she landed and stopped moving. She gasped for air and saw her slave master walking toward her with a smile on his face.

Slave master: "My son has picked the most beautiful one I have ever seen. You have curves and now I know why my wife wants to put you in the showcasing. You are my son's toy. It does not mean I cannot play too. No one will know or believe you." She heard some laughter behind him. It was a slave hunter. The slave hunters were very well known for their brutality and their unkindness.

Slave hunter: "Have fun Sir, I will be over here."

She watched her slave master take off his pants. She turned quickly and saw she was near a truck of some kind. She tried to crawl under it but was grabbed by her dress and pulled out from under the truck. The slave master flipped her over so he could see the front of her helmet and pulled her closer. He never saw the large knife in her right hand. The slave master moved his head close to her helmet. She moved quickly and forced the large knife up into his neck and the twelve inch crystal blade went up into his skull. She pulled the blade out of him and his blood sprayed her. She stabbed him in the neck a second time and as she pulled the blade out his whitish clear blood sprayed her again. His eyes rolled into his head and his lifeless body hit the ground next to her.

She reached for the side of the truck to help herself up but pulled down a satchel as she slipped in the mud. She put it on her back and crawled under the truck. She crawled through the field and muddy water as fast as she could. The mud covered her and made it hard for anyone to see her. She found a drainage ditch and crawled through the sewer drain. She stopped and turned as she heard screaming. The hunter looked about, "That beast killed him!" The Slave master's wife cried out, "That beast belongs to me! Find her! She is my property, and I will beat her tame! She is very expensive! Bring her back unharmed! My husband is a fool and a moron! I will pay well to get her back!"

The young lady jumped into the open sewer drain. As she jumped, she heard many people running toward the screaming. She fell into the rushing sewage water and she fought to keep her helmet up above the foul water. She hit a dividing pipe, and her body was thrown left. She gagged many times because of the smells and the foul matter in the gel-like water. She could not see a thing as the water level lowered and became a rushing stream. The water slowed to a slow stream and she laid there gagging and coughing. She got to her knees and saw a bright light at the end of the pipe. She could not stand because of the height of the pipe.

She saw the way out, so she crawled to the end of the pipe to the light and saw a large waterway. She looked around and saw a small ship landing on top of a small mountain. She put the knife into the satchel and looked down and saw deep water. She threw herself headfirst into the water. The helmet vents closed to prevent her from breathing under the water. She climbed onto the rocks under the pipe and looked around. She heard alarms and sirens sounding off and flying vehicles coming her way. She jumped into the water and swam with her head above the water. She dodged boats, ships, and hovercraft that were in the large waterway. All the vessels in the waterway were too big to see her swimming. She fought hard to keep her head above the water, and she made it to the other shore.

The young lady heard flying crafts on the other side of the waterway and looked back. She saw a flying craft around the beach on the other side of the waterway. She climbed onto the beach and up the rock face as fast as she could. She was halfway up and saw a ship fly out of the hangar bay. She watched the craft fly away up into the stars. She wondered if she could be free in the stars and if the boy remembered her. She thought of the places she met him and how she would get there. She knew he would keep her free there. She climbed higher and stopped. The flying craft was now under her. The young lady stood still, clenching the rocks tight. The flying craft left, and she climbed to the top where she could hear people talking.

Embassy Hanger

Admiral Trey walked off the ramp of the ship with Camille. They heard screaming in the distance. Trey: "Captain, that horrifying screaming is normal here." They saw one of the species of the planet walking toward them. Captain Davis looked at the species then turned and walked back onto the ship.

Dorock: "Hello, Rear Admiral, glad to see you again."

Admiral: "Dorock how may I help you?" The alarms and sirens were sounding. Dorock looked at the admiral and went to run when a Marine recruiter walked toward him.

Recruiter: "Dorock, I need your handprint and signature." He put his hand on the data pad and signed his slaves over to the military.

Dorock: "Admiral another time." Dorock ran out the embassy gates as they closed.

The Admiral looked at the recruiter: "Lieutenant. Report."

Recruiter: "Sir, that alarm says that a high ranking and very highly expensive slave escaped. One of the highest ruling families lost a lot of money."

Admiral: "How much do you think?"

Recruiter: "Sir, millions, or more I think. I do not know. I found out they got the military out looking and that is why our gates are closed." The Lieutenant escorted the Admiral to his ship.

The young lady climbed onto a landing pad and saw a ship. She slowly walked into the rear end of the hanger and walked around some boxes to hide. The ship ramp was down, and she saw no one around. She ran quietly to the ramp and walked on board the military ship. Then, someone tapped her on the shoulder. She jumped and spun around. A two legged two-armed creature jumped back as well. She did not know what it was. It had a uniform and its feet shined. She fell back onto the deck because only the slave masters had things on their feet.

Then it spoke, "Hi, I am Camille, stay calm. I will not hurt you." The Lieutenant saw her and ran to close the hanger doors. He ran back to the Admiral.

Lieutenant: "Sir, they cannot see in here and I know they are looking for her." The Admiral saw a very well-decorated helmet. The helmet had alien diamonds, gold, pearls, silver, and other very expensive alien materials.

The Captain studied the helmet: "Admiral, this helmet and her collar has very expensive materials on them. I have never seen one of them."

The Lieutenant looked at Admiral Trey: "Sir, if I was you, I would get her off this world and give her a chance at a life. Dorock gave us over 200 of them and you can smell he was drinking."

The Admiral smiled, "Good idea."

The Lieutenant walked back to clear the ramp. The young lady got up and ran into the ship. The Admiral ran after her as the Captain locked the ramp closed. The cargo ship rose into the air and flew out of the hanger. The transport ship flew into space.

The Lieutenant commander walked into the cargo hold: "Admiral, we are clear of the planet and warped out. We are being called. Sir, I know what to say."

Admiral Trey looked at the Lieutenant commander: "Do so. Call if you need help and max warp. She is up above the crates."

An Ensign stood at the hatch: "Sir, I can see her up above the crates. I scanned her as she climbed the cargo. She has a large knife or a short sword and data pads, three of them in her bag. She has blood all over her. It is not her blood."

Camille looked up at her as she looked down at Camille: "The back of her helmet is damaged and cracked on her visor. Her dress is ripped several places. She keeps pointing but I do not know at what."

The Admiral looked about for ideas: "The slave master helmet and collar are nasty things. Captain, you have education in the sciences, medicine, and psychology. You have this. I will close the door behind me. I will leave you with the Ensign. I am going to the bridge." The Ensign watched the Admiral walk through the hatch.

Admiral: "Ensign, stay there. We do not need her anywhere on the ship. Close the door behind me." Admiral Trey made his way to the bridge of the small ship.

The Lieutenant commander looked at him: "Admiral, Sir, I told the Ittors. We have no clue what the alarms are about. We rigged the scanners of the ship to show she was not on board. That fooled them for now."

Admiral: "Very good Lieutenant commander. You know, I was not on this ship for long. I have a question. How big is this ship?"

Lieutenant: "Sir, this ship is larger than a cargo shuttle. It is seventy-two meters and has two decks. One deck has the bridge, living quarters, and engineering. Second deck has medical, science, and a large cargo bay."

Admiral: "Thank you." Trey sat down at a computer console and looked at the cameras to see the cargo hold. The Admiral saw Captain Davis seated down on the floor talking and saw their visitor seated on top of the crates. The visitor was staying calm but she was nervous and looking around.

M793.

The Commadore looked at a Nurse: "I was looking through the files and putting them away. I came across yours. You were here the longest? Why? And were you here when they found the boy?"

Nurse: "Yes, Sir. I was here when they found him, and I was here for years."

Commodore: "You say in your report that you were terrorized by this planet. Why come back?"

Nurse: "Sir, for the boy. I was here when they built the base on the planet. I first came down with the archaeologist before the base was built. The first time I came down I was not coming back. The boy found us, even though some people say we found him. He warned us and told us to leave, to get back on the shuttles and leave. We did not listen. We just wanted to find and explore the ancient ruins. Then the planet came to life and started killing us. He saved us. He saved me and I keep trying to get him off of the planet, but he will not leave until he goes somewhere to free someone. Well, he is leaving because he can find this person to free them. Oh, he got us somewhere safe so we could get off the planet."

Commodore: "The planet came to life? What do you mean? Who is this someone?"

She looked down and looked at him with tears in her eyes: "No one knew this planet and they just looked at the planet from space. The planet's animals know how to hide extremely well and know how to ambush. The animals know how to fight extremely well. The boy mastered this. He will not say who this person is. He said he made a promise." She looked at the boy's crate and she walked over to it. "Sir, I know you were not here for that. A lot of people died. We told him we were coming back and would not leave him alone. We told him we wanted to know of the ruins. He saved us and told us where to land the next time to be safe. He told us where to put the base. I came back to get him off and the boy showed us the ancient ruins. There are cities here unexplored. It is too dangerous here." She picked up the boy's shield.

The Commadore walked over to her: "He is a mystery, and we want to know the answers."

Nurse: "Sir, have you seen him fight? It is like out of some great book of the past or a movie. Like he is Achilles himself. I read him the book. He is a mystery. He talked about some war here. No one can find evidence because everything gets eaten here. I was here for him and now he is leaving, and I am off of this world of nightmares. I can go home now. The boy's home will always be here on M793."

Commodore: "We are all off of this world. You are referring to Homer's book, The Iliad. They made movies of the Trojan War. I wish he would tell us of this person. You are right. He will come back here. It is his home."

On the planet Searrun

The prince looked down at the body of the slave master: "Where is she?!"

The wife of the dead man walked forward and kneeled at his feet: "Sir, we are looking for her now. We will find her."

He looked down at her: "Burn your husband's body out of disrespect!" The prince pointed at the hunter. "Call your boss! Tell him to call every boss! They will be paid very well! I want a meeting with them now. I want her back before the Emperor my father finds out."

M793.

The Chief walked up to the Commadore: "Sir, the boy is ready."

Commodore: "Chief, you were here when the base was placed here. Why did you stay here?"

Chief: "Sir, I do want to go home. I got here thinking the stories were lies. Boy was I wrong."

Commodore: "I was going through all the reports. You wanted off this world badly. You said it is terrifying to be here. Why did you stay?"

Chief: "Sir. The boy. Many people stayed here and kept coming back to see the boy leave. He has saved many of us."

Commodore: "How did he save you?"

Chief: "Sir, I should be smarter. I heard so many stories of this world and I thought I was tough. I went out for a hike. That was the worst thing I ever did. They said I was lucky the boy was there. Have you seen what he can do? You see, the security in the vents alone. We still do not know how he gets in here."

Commodore: "You said in a report that you asked him to take you to the bases on this world. How many are there?"

Chief: "Sir, he says there are hundreds of thousands. He got there before they put down a base and gave warning. They never listen. He came back in a day or two to find it empty. He just took what he wanted. The people were all dead. He also told me he would just find a base and it was empty. He knows the same happened there."

Commodore: "Did he show you some of the planet?"

Chief: "Yes, he did Sir. He took the science team out. They wanted to stay out there but they changed their minds quickly after they saw what was out there. You want him out there with you. This planet has destroyed ships here and hunting bases. There are some military bases but all of them are empty. There is no one there. The planet is beautiful but very dangerous. It is prehistoric. There are dinosaurs and dragons. Monsters."

Commodore: "Tell me of the ships you talked about."

Chief: "The ships that came down to mine or all the shuttles that still sit at these bases. Sir, I do not know what they come down here to mine. It was the last thing they ever did."

Commodore: "Well, Chief we are all going home."

Chief: "Sir, I know he will leave here but this is his home. There is one other thing the science team left out of the report. I also saw the medical team do the same on the boy's report. I learned why the mining ships are here. There is no way of getting any of it."

The Commadore looked at him: "Now tell me."

One hour later.

The Commodore looked at the science officer: "The boy took you out into the plains?"

Science officer: "Yes, Sir, he did. It is not that safe down there. It is in my report."

Commodore: "The Admiral wants to know. Tell me of this species on this world."

Science officer: "Sir, you mean species. There are more than one."

Commodore: "Tell me and speak freely."

Science officer: "Well, what the boy told me and showed me is that they are primitive and did war on the others but stopped. They are intelligent. They trade and work together. You want to know of the crystals?"

Commodore: "I want to learn about your findings. I am learning about why this world is so dangerous."

Science officer: "It is like someone had a lab and let all the monsters out at the same time. No one should be allowed anywhere near the M9 system. Planet M793 is like someone took all the prehistoric animals and mythological monsters from every world and put them here. The boy just happens to fall into the soup."

A day later.

The transport ship flew back to planet M793. The military ship landed in the hanger bay. The Commodore ordered all teams and hands to the hanger bay. The young man stood behind everyone and could not see what was going on. He looked up at the pipes in the back of the hanger. He wanted to get a better view. The ramp of the ship opened, and a young lady jumped out, but her satchel got snagged. It broke free from her and fell to the deck. She dodged and weaved around everyone on the hanger bay. She made it to the back of the hanger and climbed up some pipes. Camille was amazed by the boy's eyes. She stared at his golden green eyes and saw the light glimmering off the gold in his eyes.

The Captain thought, *the report says the boy has brown eyes. How did he get those golden green eyes?* Camille wanted to get closer to the boy but somehow, he disappeared. She looked around franticly, but she could not find him. The young lady made it to the top of the pipes. Admiral Trey screamed out, "Stop chasing her, but do not allow her out of the hanger!" The young lady looked down at everyone, then to her right and saw the young man sitting up there with her.

The boy: "Hi, my name is Joseph. Are you hungry or do you want something to drink? What is your name?"

She looked at Joseph: "Are you going to eat me?"

Joseph laughed: "No one will eat you or hurt you. I promise you. Like I did before." Joseph looked at her ripped dress and her half naked body. She was shivering because of the cold. "Are you cold?" She shook her head yes. Joseph slowly stood up. He took off his heavy coat and slowly put it around her. She was surprised someone cared. The young lady put her arms through the sleeves, then Joseph zipped it up. It was big on her, but it was big on Joseph too. She felt warmer and they both sat down. "No one here wants to hurt you. So, are you hungry, do you like fish? They gave meal bars. I like the fish bars they are good."

Joseph took a fish bar from his winter overalls and opened the wrapper, then he gave it to her. The young lady's helmet opened a little and she began to eat. Admiral Trey smiled, "Captain you are right. It did work. Now how do we get them down?"

Captain Davis smiled: "Sorry Sir, one thing at a time." She thought to herself, *how did he get up there?* A master chief walked over to Camille and gave her a satchel with a broken strap.

Master chief: "Captain, the Admiral told me to give this to you."

Camille: "Thank you, Master chief." Camile took the bag and looked into it. The Captain saw the large knife and saw the blood on it. "Ensign, can you put this in the ship's medical bay? Thank you." The ensign took the bag and walked onto the ship.

Joseph clapped his hands: "Anyone have a canteen or water bottle?" A staff sergeant pulled a water bottle out of a box and threw the water bottle up to him. He opened the water bottle and handed it to the young lady. She could not drink from it. "Let me help."

She looked at him: "Okay."

Joseph looked at some tools left behind by a work crew. He picked up a hand scanner and scanned her helmet. Then he looked down and saw someone on a computer console. The person put in how to open her helmet. The information went to the scanner. Joseph remembered his training and opened her helmet. The helmet opened and he saw her face. He looked into her eyes. "Wow, you are as beautiful as I remember."

She looked down and smiled back at him: "It is forbidden for my helmet to be opened like this. I do remember you a little. I am untouched."

He smiled: "I won't tell if you won't tell."

She drank from the water bottle and smiled: "My name is Orka. I remember you."

They heard from some of the crew: "What does she look like?" Orka closed her helmet slowly.

Joseph looked down: "You are free now as I promised I was going to do. Let us get down and I promise you I will protect you." She looked at him and shook her head yes. He turned around and she climbed on his back.

Joseph climbed down with ease and Orka climbed off his back. A nurse walked over and scanned Orka. Admiral Trey walked over to them as the nurse walked over to Captain Davis. Orka looked at the Admiral and said, "I want to join the military. I want to be like her." She pointed at the Captain.

Camille smiled: "We can help with that."

Admiral Trey looked at the captain: "I wonder where she got that from. Thank you everyone. Now let us get on the ship so we can drop them off to the military base. Commodore, thank you for everything."

Commodore: "No problem, Sir. Let's get you on your way."

The special operations teams and the station crew went back to their tasks. The hanger crew put a crate on the ship and closed the ramp. They walked onto the ship from a side entrance and the ship's doors closed. They watched Orka carefully and walked to the medical bay. The transport ship rose up in the air and flew out of the hanger.

In the medical bay Orka was looking out the window at the snow. "What is that?" she asked.

Camille walked up to her and stood behind her: "That is snow."

Orka: "And what is that?"

Camille: "We are in space." They felt the ship go to warp. "What is that?"

The Captain smiled: "There is a lot for you to learn."

Orka: "Learn? My people are not allowed to learn."

Captain: "Well, that changes now. Learn everything you can and want to."

Orka: "I will not get in trouble?"

Captain: "No, you will not. You are with us." Joseph heard the door to the bay luck.

The Admiral stood at the door: "Cadet, there are tasks you need to do in the medical office. I need you to read the cadet manual first."

Joseph walked into the office and saw the door lock behind him. He sat down and saw Orka through the window office. She can easily see him. He got to studying. Admiral Trey opened the door and pointed. Joseph got up and walked into the medical bay. Orka was ready to fight.

Joseph: "Let them help you." Orka looked at him and lowered her hands and Joseph walked back to the office.

Camille walked over to her: "Okay, I need to get you cleaned up and get you scanned. Orka is your name?" She shook her head yes. "I need you to take everything off and get into this small room. It is called a shower. It is like it is raining on you. Then I need you to lay down on this bed here." The Captain walked into the office and closed the curtain to the window, then he turned off the viewing cameras in the office. Camille looked at Joseph studying and walked out of the office. The Captain grabbed some clothing and walked into the medical bay. Camille put the clothing on a bed as Orka showered.

The Captain walked to the shower and felt the freezing cold water. "Orka, there is warm water."

She looked at Camille: "Can I ask for it?"

Camille: "Yes, you can. This is freedom."

Orka: "Yes, please."

The Captain pushed the button and the water got warmer. "I will be back." Orka felt like she was in heaven as the water washed over her.

Admiral Trey sat on one of the far beds. "Captain, I do want to know."

Captain: "Well Sir, she was not raped or inappropriately touched. She killed whoever was going to hurt her. Sir, they will be looking for her."

Admiral: "Captain, something is telling me that someone needs your help. Behind you."

Camille turned and walked over to Orka: "Wait, go back in and hit the button. That will help you dry." Orka hit a button and felt warm air rush over her. She was dry and walked over to the bed. She climbed into the bed and Captain Davis put a blanket over her.

The Lieutenant commander walked into the medical bay and put a tool bag down. "Orka, we need to remove the helmet and collar. This will not hurt." She looked at them and shook her head yes. As he began to take her collar off, Camille walked over and held Orka's hand. The Lieutenant commander removed the collar and then the helmet. He then put the collar and the helmet on the table. The Lieutenant commander walked out of the medical bay and the door locked behind him. Orka's dress was placed on the table and the Admiral studied it. He noticed it was a very expensive dress. Then he picked up the scanner and the data pad.

Camille took blood from Orka and put it in a machine to start scanning it. The Captain looked at Orka. "I like your whitish purple hair and you have no nose. Your iris is purple, and you are voluptuous. Now this bed is a machine, and it will put you in 0 gravity. Just lay there. It will keep you in the middle of it and trust me it will not hurt you. It will scan you. As we scan you, I need you to take this test. We are just seeing how smart you are. You have three hours on the test, okay?" Camille gave Orka a data pad and Orka shook her head yes. The Captain took the blanket away and closed the hatch over her body. Then the hatch closed over her head.

Camille walked to the office: "Joseph, I need you to get in the scanner." As he got up and walked around the desk, she looked at his face. "Joseph, you get into a lot of fights on that planet?"

He looked at the captain: "Only when I hunt or in war. Some guy came to the planet and wanted the weapons and ships. I said there was nothing there. He said he was God. I asked him why does God need weapons and ships? He got mad and started a fight. I made him bleed. I said to him God does not bleed. His friends came and got him. He calls himself the Grand Master."

Camille looked at him: "Who won?"

Joseph: "He did. He killed friends, family, and pets. He knocked me down a shaft and killed some of my friends. He killed Moth and Sisur." Joseph took off all of his clothing and climbed into a bed. Admiral Trey pointed at Joseph. She closed the hatch over him. The Captain gave him a data pad. "There are some tests for you. Have fun." She closed him in and started the scans.

Admiral Trey looked at Captain Davis: "There are scars on his body but there are none on his face? He looks as if he has been in many wars."

Captain Davis: "He had to get them on the planet."

The Captain tinted the scanner windows. Camille turned on the view screen to see Joseph and Orka. The overhead speakers came to life. "Admiral to the bridge." Admiral Trey looked at Camille and she was hard at work. He turned and walked out of the medical bay. He walked onto the bridge and looked at the view screens. "Hello Ambassador Tara, I hear you are looking for me."

The Ambassador of the Ittors' people was on the screen and she had her fore arms crossed. "Hello Admiral Trey, we have a situation. Your ship left our world quickly and I will ask for you to return."

Admiral: "Ambassador, you know the laws."

Ambassador: "Yes, I do. I am just asking."

Admiral: "We cannot do that right now. We are late with some cadets and important cargo. You know various species we have to pick up going to bootcamp. We landed on many planets and star bases. We landed on that ice world, and we got some of those bear species. May I ask, why do you want me back to your world?"

The Ambassador looked down then at the view screen: "Admiral, you do not have to return. I know this planet and it drops to minus eighty degrees. If you did have a stowaway, you would have found them there."

Admiral: "Ambassador, who are you looking for?"

Ambassador: "Someone's property. Thank you, Admiral." The view screen faded back to space.

Admiral Trey looked at the Lieutenant commander: "I need a normal helmet for her, and we might be followed."

Lieutenant: "Sir, I have scanned behind us. There is no one there. They may send a ship to where we have dropped cadets before."

Admiral: "Change course and we drop them at the star base 31. Where we drop off cadets. We cannot do a thing except drop them off and hope the transport ship is there to get them." Admiral Trey walked back into the medical bay and found the lights dimmed. The Admiral looked at his watch. The medical scanners were off and he could see both cadets sleeping. He walked into the medical office where Camille was reading a data pad. He tapped the desk and pointed at the science lab. She looked up at him.

The Captain got up and walked to the lab with the Admiral. The Admiral walked over to the holographic table and turned it on. "There is a news report that Orka killed or murdered her master. The fifth in charge of their government. A very wealthy man."

Camille hit a button on the table and the image showed. "They bought Orka at a young age. You are going to like this. They moved her by armored vehicle, the Army, and the Navy. We incinerated her clothing and the satchel. The knife is a small sword and some kind of artifact. I had the crew bring me Joseph's crate. I put the sword, collar, and helmet in his crate. The crate will go to my office and stay there."

Admiral: "Captain, the data pads?"

Camille: "Sir, her master's data pads have a lot of information. I found some alarming things. The history of her people. They were not even in the bronze age when they were invaded and forced into slavery. They were just coming out of the stone age. Sorry, Sir, Orka's species does not have a name yet. Her people were slaves for over one hundred years. Orka's people were not only slaves but they're DNA was altered to be more pleasing to the slave masters. Other DNA was put into their bodies. Their tales were removed and their skin was changed. Even their skeletal system was changed. Orka's people still hold a lot of her people's original DNA. They are a few thousand years old."

Camille hit a button and the image changed. It showed Orka and a prehistoric cousin. There was an image of DNA. Admiral Trey studied the images. "Sir, what do you see?"

Admiral: "Captain, I need a female up there with her."

Camille: "Sir, that is two young ladies at the same age. You can see they had hair, but they are different." Admiral Trey studied the DNA. "Admiral, you see it and they are mixed with humans. That is why she looks a little human. Yes, they are hefty, and they breathe under the water. They are known to swim deep, like miles under water. They had two thumbs on one hand, no nose, pointed ears, dual skin with fat in between but they could smell. They have the five senses."

The table changed holographic images. "This is Orka's home world. It is a heavily defended planet. The people are mammals, and the planet is a habitable sea world. It has no solid land mass, like continents. It is an island planet with oceans around them."

Admiral: "Captain where is this planet?"

Camille: "Sir, when you were on the bridge, I looked up star charts and it is not there or anywhere. I looked through the three data pads. One of the data pads has a lot of top secret stuff. There was history and star charts. I asked the data pad for help, and it said not on the net."

Admiral Trey changed the table to star charts. "The Ittors are part of the United Planets, but what is there dealing in the Beta quadrant and her planet. Where is it? We are both in intelligence and these gifts fall in our hands."

Camille: "Yes, Sir, I do not know what they are doing in the Beta quadrant."

Admiral: "Captain, we are the United Planets. We only explored five percent out of a hundred percent of our galaxy. We have to get better at this."

Camille: "Sir, I have done some experiments on Orka and Joseph and need to do more. Orka scored high for her people, and she is different from her species. She has a very high chance of becoming a doctor. I asked Orka what she likes to learn, and she said yes to science and medicine. I also talked to them both and they agree to stay silent about each other."

Admiral: "Okay, Captain, I am going to get some rest. This ship will be at star base 31 thirty-six hours from now." Admiral Trey turned and walked out of the medical bay to his small living quarters. Camille turned off the equipment and thought to herself, *Admiral, what are you hiding about these two? I know you have a plan.*

On the planet Searrun.

A large man walked into a palace office. There were area rugs everywhere on the marble floors. The office walls where well painted with royal colors. A very large very expensive desk sat on an area rug with a very large executive chair behind it. Dorock kneeled with his head bowed in front of the desk. The new head Ambassador walked in from a side room. She clapped her hands and the private guards walked out. They locked the doors behind them. "It is good to see you again. Dorock how did you become the boss of bosses? Dorock you're a fool. I know of all your underhanded endeavors. All the shady business deals. You are part of an organization and a criminal syndicate. Too bad I need you, but first how many slaves did you give to the United Planets?" The Ambassador walked to the window and looked out at the night city lights.

Dorock did not move and replied, "I am sorry. I do not know. I think one hundred."

Ambassador: "I should have your entrails ripped from your body! I should kill you and how fun it will be! You, Dorock, gave them two hundred slaves. I bet you wonder why I have you here in the middle of the night."

Dorock: "Sorry Ambassador, I would like to know." Dorock knew why he was not dead. Ambassador Tara needed him to do a lot of criminal activities.

Ambassador: "I know you heard by now. The single most priceless slave has escaped or was stolen. They are giving the most handsome of a reward. That little beast did me a favor and I should let the animal go but capturing her will give me more power and money." Tara looked at the night sky then walked back to her desk and sat down. "They are sending your two hundred to a planet we, the Ittors, are not allowed on, but what we do not know we cannot prevent. We need to get her before they get there. I need you to go and call your hunter. Send the hunter to Star Base 31 where the ship will dock. Have your hunter find her and get her unharmed. Net her and meet up with a science ship. The hunter will board the science ship and the ship will bring them here." She tapped the desk and pointed up. Dorock stood up. "Dorock I want you to go to the Beta quadrant. I want you and your colleagues to start some trouble there. I will give you twenty percent of all weapons sales."

Ambassador Tara waved him away. Dorock pulled his data phone from his belt and started to make calls as he walked out of her office.

The doors closed behind him and a secret door opened. The Ambassador looked at the elite soldier. "I want you on that science ship. When the hunter gets there kill him, bring me the girl, and after that I need you to go to the Beta quadrant to start a war that will get Dorock and his colleagues killed. You have any questions?"

Soldier: "Ambassador, and the data pads?"

Ambassador: "Forget them and I want the beast to be my pet. I need a massive war. I want to be Empress. That old fool does not know what I have planned."

The military transport ship flew through warp space.

Trey cleaned himself up and walked into the medical bay. He saw the experiments underway. Orka and Joseph were showing off their skills to each other. The medical bay had two electrical shields erected around a space four meters high and seven meters round. One was full of water. Orka was doing tasks as she watched Joseph lifting weights and he watched her swimming around. Trey walked over to Camille writing on her data tablet. "Hello, Admiral Trey, a warning Sir. Do not enter any of the shields. I have her in a shield, and it is pressurized water. Joseph is in a shield with gravitational forces. Did you see Orka's eyes? She can turn them black. Her eyes help her see in the water and in the darkness in deep water. She is over a mile down and the data pad we gave her got crushed."

Admiral: "Captain, I have a plan. I need you to put everything of Orka's in Joseph's crate. I need you on Earth before I get there. Captain, you need to find these two Ambassadors. Then have a meeting with them and high

153

command" He handed her a data pad. Trey turned to walk out and said, "I have to make some calls." The door closed behind him. Camille walked over to the water tank. Orka hit the button. "Ma'am, after I am done here can you read to me the book you are reading, Hero? I need a hero." Camille smiled and then hit the button. "Cadet, you have a lot of training to do and a lot of manuals to read. Maybe later you can read Hero." Captain Davis walked to the holographic room and prepared it for more experiments.

A lieutenant walked into the medical bay.

Lieutenant: "Hello, captain, I have the new helmet and collar. It is made to look like the others. Ma'am, it also has improvements. The young lady will be able to take it off when she wants, and she can see around her better. She will be able to breathe in the water. The helmet has a new number on it, and it is in the gray color they come in."

Captain: "Thank you, Lieutenant. I will have her train with it before we get to the station. Put it in the office on the desk." The Lieutenant put the helmet and collar on the desk then walked out.

Star Base 31, 30 hours later

A hunter walked through the first group of cadets that got off the ship onto the star base. He looked at the alien's bluest white marble floors and the ancient pillars that held the walkway and stores above. He looked at the third-floor train, and out the massive windows above and beside each terminal. Everyone could see ships of all kinds coming and going out of the star base. He looked at the alien wood and long steel benches and the potted alien plants beside them and looked at the long rectangle potted alien shrubs that split the floor from the sidewalk and the roadway. The wheel and hover vehicles traffic were getting lighter. As the transport ships stopped coming in. At the later time.

Hunter: "Dorock there are thousands of cadet slaves here and thousands of other cadets here. None of them are yours. I heard your slaves went to Star Base 4829. She is not here. I did what you told me. I paid the transport crew off to leave early. The science ship is at the outskirts of the system."

Dorock keyed the mic. "I know that. There are more by the star base by the Asta star system. Forget that. They want her. She is not at that star base. We have people there. She has to be there somewhere. Pay off everyone there! They are paying one gold platinum bar for expenses alone. The big bar, not the small one. Pay off the authorities to stay out of the area."

Hunter: "Dorock, I paid everyone off like you said. I just saw a two-man military fighter. It is just sitting outside in space."

Dorock: "Hunter, I am not paying you to sightsee! Keep your eyes open! She is worth a lot of money. Remember that! Use the nets. Remember not to harm her."

Hunter: "Sir, this is a crazy question. You think of keeping this one and selling her for more?"

Dorock yelled over the mic. "What are you crazy?! My colleagues will report us, and they will not pay a thing! The bosses are terrified of this hunt! They do not want anything to do with this! You are mad! There is nowhere we will be able to hide. These people we are working for now can find us with warships and troops of millions! Remember, I fear no one but them! Remember that!"

Hunter: "Dorock, the transport left. There are no more cadets here. There are no more vehicles moving about. Sorry, I do not know who is paying for this."

Dorock: "Remember, these people see and know everything. Find her!"

Six hours later.

The hunter stretched out and yawned on the wooded bench. He heard the overhead computer. "Ship docking at bay 136." He looked at the bay dock number and saw he was at exit 136. He looked out the massive window and saw the military transport flying around and flew into the dock. He keyed his mic. "Dorock, the second ship is here, but it is flying around the station. It is docking now. I will call you back, over." The hunter put his phone on his belt. He walked to the huge bay doors and sat thirty two feet across from the doors.

There was no one there on the promenade. So, he had an easy view to the doors. The hunter walked another twelve meters away. It was taking too long for the doors to open. He walked to the window. The ship was still docked. Then, he saw the dock hands. A dock hand waved at him and did hand signals at him. Then, the dock hand ran away. The hand signals said they are not allowing anyone near or on the dock to see. The hunter saw the fighter leave the hanger and instantly jump to maximum warp. Then, the ship left the dock and jumped to warp. He hoped she was hiding in the dock for the next transport. All the shops were closed and there was no one to be seen.

The hunter walked further away, and he can barely see the doors. The transport was gone and that meant the next one would be there at 4 AM. The time was 8 PM. He moved to get a better view. When one of the doors opened, two young cadets walked out, and they both wore military coveralls. One was human male, light peach color skin, black hair to his shoulders and broad shoulders. He was a medium built male. He stood five feet five inches. He was a sixteen year old human boy. The hunter saw her. Coveralls and covered from head to toe. Shoes, gloves, turtleneck, and a hair cut above her shoulders. Her helmet visor was up. She had a human-like face but no nose and beautiful lips. Her hair was whitish purple. She had grayish skin with light whitish ghost gray markings just behind and above her eyes. She stood five foot five inches. He knew she would be taller than any human girl her age. The porpoise girl of her age fourteen stands tall or taller than a human boy. It was her. She closed her visor.

She wore a slave military helmet and it was the wrong color. She was not wearing the right slave military clothing and she had no skin showing. He thought to himself, *It will be easy to kill the human.* Joseph walked out first and looked around. "There is no one here. You can come out." Orka walked out and looked around. The door closed behind them. They walked to an eating area to some chairs and round tables. Joseph looked at Orka. "Can I call you Micky?" A robot voice came from her helmet. "What is Micky?" He pointed at the letters and numbers on her helmet. "Your helmet M9I3C7K5Y. I took the letters from your helmet."

She looked down. "Yes, you can, but do not tell anyone."

Joseph: "Okay, Micky. The transport left early. I wonder why they did that, and the overhead signs are not working to tell us were to get to our transport." Joseph looked around and then at Orka. "I am going to run around and look for any information. Are you hungry or thirsty?" Orka smiled and shook her head yes. Joseph: "Micky, why do you look down at your feet?"

Orka: "Yes, I am thirsty and hungry. I never had shoes or these soft things inside. They are called socks and these things on my hands are called gloves."

Joseph smiled. "Yes, they are. Well, you stay here. They gave me credits. I will be back with food and drinks. I am going to look around to find out where we have to be for the next transport." He ran off. Orka sat down on the ground and looked around. She smiled and looked up at the walkway above her. It had to be over six meters up. She looked at her hand and wiggled her fingers. Then she looked at her feet and wiggled her toes. Orka could not hear Joseph running anymore. He had to be far away. The promenade was dead quiet. There was no one around her.

Orka got up and walked over to a chair and table. She looked around and felt someone watching her, but there was no one there and she sat down. Orka crossed her arms on the table and put her head down on her arms. She heard something behind her. Orka turned quickly but there was nothing there. She put her head back down and closed her eyes. Orka was small for the tall chair and her legs dangled. She wiggled her toes and waved her legs beneath her. The helmet lens closed to show she was asleep. Something grabbed Orka from the back of her helmet and threw her into a statue sixteen feet away. Orka hit the statue hard. She gasped as the air was knocked out of her. She saw stars and blue lights. Someone tall and muscular was walking toward her. The person had cloth body armor on. Hunter: "Oh, this is going to be an easy one."

Other side of the station.

Joseph looked back in the direction of Orka and knew he was over seventeen thousand meters from her. He saw a small restaurant and a convenience store open. He felt something in the air. Something was warning him. Something was wrong. An old lizard lady walked to him from the restaurant. "Hello cadet you are looking for where you get the transport? You get it here and the cadets normally get things from the two stores." She looked at him. "What is wrong?"

Joseph: "Sorry, Ma'am. One of the cadets needs me." Joseph ran at top speed back to Orka. The old lady watched him run and whispered, "Wow, he can run. Save her!"

Sometime before. In the docking bay.
The Past

Admiral Trey sat down in the medical bay. He remembered what Captain Camille Davis told him. They walked to the ramp of the ship. The Ensign put a medical box in Joseph's crate. The pilot and the ensign loaded the crate on the fighter. The captain looked at the Admiral. "Sir, Planet M793 made Joseph superhuman. He is a mystery. There will be no way to know what he can do without him showing us what he can do. He could have very good combat skills. Joseph had to fight everything on that planet to survive. That planet's environment is a nightmare. The planet's life is amazing and dangerous. He spent seven years or more on that planet with different gravitational forces on his body. His DNA had to change to survive. Joseph's whole body is reinforced. His skeletal system, muscular system, his internals, and his senses are highly tuned. His skin is hard to pierce. His eyes allow him to see in any environment. The strange thing is, he has crystals in his blood. Right now, he is three times stronger, faster, and jumps higher than any human his age, but when he gets older, he will be ten times or more. He can breathe under the water, and I have no idea how that happened. Oh, Joseph is sixteen or seventeen and Orka is fourteen, but they like each other. I recommend not to separate them. They can help each other, and they both need family. I was studying Joseph and how to clone him, but that is impossible. Something is stopping us from getting his full DNA. There are crystals in his DNA. We taught Joseph some combat skills and he is very cunning and agile in combat. Joseph is perfect for your special forces program. Admiral what is one of the special forces' sayings? It's not the smartest, it's not the strongest, it's not the fastest, it is the will. He is the person you need. He may not be the one you want, but he is the one you need. I have everything in the frozen medical box. I took samples from them both. I will have the meeting ready for you as you ask."

Admiral: "Thank you." Captain Camille Davis walked to the fighter. She climbed into the military aircraft and the canopy closed. The fighter flew out of the hanger, and it went to warp.

Admiral: "Ensign where are the cadets?"

Ensign: "Sir, they're in the hallway for departure. They will leave there the time you requested." The ramp closed on the transport ship. As Admiral Trey walked to the bridge, he remembered a conversation between him and the boy, Joseph. *"Sir, I do remember you. It is good to see you again. I see you made Rear Admiral. I will not tell anyone we met before. I will not tell anyone what we talked about." "I know Joseph. I am happy you are off. I know you are good at hiding things and keeping secrets." "Will you help me stop them?" "I told you I would. Sorry for your loss."* The Admiral walked onto the bridge and said, "Lieutenant Commander, get us out of here." The ship flew out and they went to warp.

Star base 31.
The Present

Orka looked up at the hunter. The hunter grabbed her by her wrist and picked her up. "Your name is Orka. You are going to make me rich. You are fourteen and over five feet tall." He held her high in the air by her wrist. The hunter stood over seven feet tall. Orka could not touch the ground with her feet. The hunter smiled and used his other hand to remove her glove. He saw the purples, blues, and white gray in her hand. The hunter looked at her claws and then looked into her purple eyes. "You, beast was never declawed, and you are expensive. I can see why."

Orka kicked him in the stomach as hard as she could. The hunter curled forward and then he threw Orka ten meters into a wall. "Do you remember me?! I was there when you murdered your master!" He grabbed his netting gun. "No one would care if I threw you around a little. Time to bring you home you pet!" The hunter could see she was dizzy. He walked up to her and heard Orka say, "God, Iosa, I need my hero. Bring me a hero." The hunter laughed. "What did these humans try to teach you? You need a hero. That is a myth."

He laughed as Orka pulled herself up off the ground and she saw double. She put her arms up to fight and to protect herself. The hunter laughed more. "You do not know how to fight." He reached down to grab her, but he grabbed a muscular shoulder. Joseph was now standing in the way between Orka and the hunter. "Human boy! I do not care to kill you and there are no orders to let you live!" He threw Joseph into the chairs and tables. Joseph flew and hit the wall twenty meters away. The hunter watched the human fly and crash through everything. He laughed. "That takes care of your hero. That human is dead. They will find his body later. I will be gone by that time." The hunter looked down and Orka was gone. He turned his head to see her running behind a statue. The hunter got hit hard from behind. He flipped through the air by the impact of a table. He hit the ground hard and got halfway up.

The hunter looked where the table came from, and Joseph was standing there. "How?" Then a chair hit the hunter from the other side and saw Orka standing, ready for the fight. They let the hunter stand. "You human, what are you?! Forget it! You will be dead, and she will be in a cage!" Joseph jumped at the hunter and punched him in the face. Orka pulled off the other glove. Orka protruded her two-inch-long claws. She jumped at the hunter's back and stabbed him. The hunter screamed out in pain. He hit Joseph into some tables and chairs. He swung his arm back and knocked Orka into a pillar. The hunter grabbed his net gun and shot Orka. She got entangled in the net. Then, he saw Joseph stand up and then the hunter shot Joseph, but the net was not strong enough. The boy easily ripped out of the steel cable net and growled at him. "You human are a beast. A foul beast." The hunter reached for his gun but it was gone. He lost it in the fight.

The boy leaped at him. The hunter knocked him out of the air. He grabbed Joseph with his four arms by his arms and legs. "Human! I will rip you apart!" He pulled at Joseph's arms and legs, but the boy pulled himself into a ball and looked into the hunter's eyes. "How human?!" The boy attacked the hunter with a headbutt then jumped back. The hunter grabbed his face and saw blood on his hand. "How, no human has that strength." He kicked the boy away. Joseph flew back then landed on his feet and he lunged back at him. He hit the boy across his chest with the netting gun and the gun was destroyed. Joseph toppled over hitting the ground. The hunter kicked him with all his force. Joseph flew through sales carts, chairs, tables, and heavy garbage containers. "How are you not dead?!"

The hunter turned and ran. He grabbed Orka in the net and ran as fast as he could. The hunter touched his back, and it was bleeding. He touched his face and it hurt and bled. Joseph kicked him in the back. The hunter dropped Orka, and he tumbled forward. Orka slid across the ground and she freed herself from the net. The hunter got to his knees. He grabbed a marble bench and broke the bench against Joseph's back. Joseph flew down the hallway. The hunter tried to stand up when he was struck hard across his head with a helmet. He fell forward by the impact. The hunter looked up to see Orka without her helmet. He was in shock to see her helmet off. She attacked with fury. Orka hit his head with the helmet, left to right and up and down. The hunter kicked her away. "Get away from me beast." Orka went flying and her helmet slid across the floor. Orka crashed into some bushes before she hit the ground.

The helmet stopped at someone's foot. Joseph jumped at the hunter. The hunter swung and missed Joseph. Joseph grabbed his arm and broke it. The hunter screamed out, "I still have three more to kill you beast!" He pounded down at the boy with his three other fists. Joseph swept the hunter's legs out from under him.

Joseph: "You talk too much!"

The hunter kicked at the boy. Joseph grabbed the hunter's legs and threw the hunter through the statue. The statue broke apart by the impact. The hunter hit the ground hard. Orka began to get up to fight with fury in her heart. She wanted her freedom. She wanted to be free of those monsters. She wanted nothing to do with them. The hunter got up and spit blood out of his mouth. He reached for his data phone and it was gone. The hunter saw his plasma pistol on the ground. He grabbed his gun and aimed it at Joseph.

Joseph dove behind a pillar. When Orka and Joseph heard the pulse pistol fire from behind them, the hunter was shot four times in the chest and twice in the head. The hunter collapsed lifeless. They looked in the direction of the shooter. The old lizard lady was putting her pistol away in the holster behind her apron. She picked up the data phone and turned it off. Then she put it in her pocket. "I am with Admiral Trey. Come with me now before the alarms go off." Joseph ran and picked up Orka's gloves. Orka picked up her helmet. They walked with the old lady to a side door. The old lady closed the door and walked over to a computer console. She took a card from the computer and the alarms sounded. "You kids need to learn how to fight faster and smarter. Oh, your helmet is the wrong gray. Light gray is for the females. Dark gray is for the males. Grayish blue is not on the list."

She looked at both of them and hugged Orka. The old lady walked with her arm around her. "You look hurt." Orka shook her head yes and put her helmet on. They walked through the back corridors and back rooms to the restaurant. The room had four couches, chairs, and a large table. They heard security forces and emergency services running to where the alarms sounded. The old lady closed the back door to the restaurant. She walked them to an office with two couches. "I own both the restaurant and the store. I will bring medical equipment, food, and drinks"

She walked out, and a minute later another lady walked in. "I am a medic." She worked on their bruises. They heard the chief of security. "Hello, how are you? Did you hear or see anything?" "I am an old lady it is hard from me to hear, and my eyesight is no longer good. I need my glasses. I will stay here to help the cadets. Where did this happen?"

Medic: "On the other side of the star base."

The old lady laughed. "The other side. No one can hear that on this side."

Medic: "Thank you, Ma'am. Sorry for bothering you. Have a good night." Then she walked to a hallway between stores and then they heard. The old lady talking to someone. "He should have never taken the job or the money. Take that to him." She gave the person an envelope with something thick inside it and the data phone the old lady got off the floor where they fought. The other person ran away. A minute later, the old lady walked back into the office. She carried two trays full of food and the other had juice, drinks, and water. She put it on the desk in the middle of the room.

Old Lady: "Are they okay?"

The medic put their things away. "They are okay. I gave them some shots. Bruising will be gone in eight hours. I also gave them something for their pain. The last shots were for their muscles and vitamins." The medic walked out.

Old Lady: "Food and drink. After you both eat get some rest." She walked over to the light switch and dimmed the lights. "Both of you have seven hours till the transport gets here. Also, the bathroom is over there, get cleaned up."

She walked out then heard the police. "Hello Ma'am."

Old Lady: "I already talked to security. Officers, I did not hear a thing. I was here and that terminal is on the other side of the station. My old body makes it hard to hear, see, and move around."

Officer: "Thank you, Ma'am."

The police walked away. Joseph sat down and opened one of the cartons as Orka sat down. He slid the carton over to Orka as she took off her helmet. A big smile came across her face. Raw fish were now her favorite sushi of all sorts. The old lady looked into the office after one hour and both of them were sleeping. She walked over to a phone and called Earth. "Captain Davis. They are okay now. The Admiral told me to call you and give a report."

Sometime later.

Joseph felt someone tap his foot. He opened his eyes. The old lady looked down at him. "Your face looks better. The transport will be here in an hour and a half. Get the lady up. There are other cadets out there and police. You both ate all that food and drink. Wow, you both were hungry. Well, I took it away and I put breakfast down with drinks. I have information for you. The head drill sergeant will be waiting on you. Sergeant Calup is going to give you hell, but he is the best of the best. Good luck, you are going to need it." She walked out and turned on the lights.

On the planet Searrun.

Dorock was kneeling in the Ambassador's office. Tara walked in with a data pad. "What happened Dorock? Your hunter never made it to the ship, never left the star base, and he is dead. His ship was impounded. Do you know this?"

Dorock: "Ma'am, my inside man told me. She had help, a team of people were there to help the cadets."

Tara: "So, Dorock, where do you think she is? What is her name, Orka?"

Dorock: "Ma'am, we are searching the Earth's water."

Tara: "She is not in the Earth's waters! The Ittors are not allowed there. Get your people out of there. Now! Before the humans park a fleet at our home world and they will not leave for a year. The humans will become annoying to our plan. They are taking her to a base planet where we will not be able to Go! We had war with those short people and we have had peace for over a hundred years, but we get close to any of their star systems and they will start shooting at us. The Emperor will have my head! That is why you are here."

Dorock: "Ma'am, she could be on that base. She could be there for a year to six months. There will be no way to get her until she is in a unit or on a ship."

Tara: "Dorock, the Beta plan."

Dorock: "As you ordered. They say that they will make a small war that will last a few months."

Tara: "Good!" She waved her hand. Dorock left the office. She walked to the window and looked at the night sky.

Luxury farmhouse.

Dorock walked into a large luxurious house. "Sir, you called."

A young man sat at his father's desk. "My mother and I want Orka back. We will pay you to get some of the beast's blood. Where is she?"

Dorock looked at the boy: "I do not know, but I can find out."

Young man: "My family has paid you well before and we will do the same again." Dorock bowed his head and walked out. The young man waited for one of his slave servants to tell him Dorock was gone. "Mother, why do you need her blood? I want my property Orka back."

She looked at her son: "We were already doing experiments on her blood for a new beauty product that everyone could use on their skin. We make these beasts to serve us. You know we sell them to other alien races. They are here to serve our needs. That is what she is for."

Star Base 31.

They thanked the old lady and got in line. The guard at the gate looked at their military coveralls and passes. He waved them through and they walked on the transport. Then, they walked on with all the other cadets. Joseph and Orka walked to the back of the transport where there was no one. They climbed into their seats. The stewardess walked to them. "That is a first to see." She looked at them both. "I have never seen them sit with anyone else." The stewardess pointed at Orka. They were trained by the old lady to know what to say and when to say it.

Joseph: "They told me to escort her to bootcamp. They could not get her with her group."

The stewardess looked at them both: "Does she talk, because what I know they do not."

Joseph looked at Orka: "Their species is extremely shy."

Stewardess: "They are robots or cyborgs?"

He looked at the stewardess: "I do not know, but they do eat and drink."

She looked at them both and saw Orka squeezing his arm: "So, what does she want?"

Joseph: "Ma'am, do you have breakfast, she wants some."

The stewardess smiled: "Yes, we serve breakfast. We will be leaving at 5 AM. We normally do not get it at this time. There are sergeants that normally get on with them. I am happy to see they have a chance now. At 520 AM we will serve breakfast and we will make it to the base on Kallos at 7am, but Kallos time will be 5am. You two are going to want to run. You are going to be late.

You both are first year?" They both shook their heads yes. "And good luck." She walked away to attend to other passengers. The transport left on time.

On Earth at a United Planets building.

A meeting was under way in the capital of the Unified Earth. Captain Davis walked through the large doors with a data pad in her right hand. She stood next to a pew where a young alien lady sat who looked up at Captain Davis and tapped her data tablet with the Captain's data pad. The young lady read her tablet. She then tapped the tablet to the pad. Camille turned and walked out. She walked down three marble corridors and walked into the same meeting, but it was a different door with the pad in her left hand. Camille stood next to another pew. The short alien lady looked at her and tapped her tablet to the Captain's data pad. She read it and tapped it to the Captain's data pad. Camille walked out and walked to the human Ambassador's office where the secretary tapped the data pad. Captain Davis walked to a waiting hover car. She read the pad, and saw what the alien allies agreed. The car drove her to the air force to a waiting shuttle.

On the transport.

Orka opened her eyes slowly and could barely see in the dim light. She was about to change her eyes so she could see better in the dark. Someone sat across the aisle from Joseph. Joseph left a seat empty between them to better protect Orka and to act as if she was alone. The person was a lady and she looked straight at Orka. She looked at Joseph's eyes closed. Then, Orka heard a lady's voice come from the alien species who sat at the seat. "Yes, humans can sleep, and boy can they."

Joseph laughed: "I have been watching you and boy are you loud, hunter. Like a stampede of mammoths running through a dense forest."

The hunter looked at him: "Be careful human!"

Joseph: "What, hunter, you have no weapons. The stewardesses, cadets, and more than hundreds of military personnel will come to the new cadets' aid."

Hunter: "Human! I will pay you very well if you give her to me. You can make a new life and never have to serve in the military. A new life as a rich man and buy yourself an island on any planet."

Joseph: "NO! I see you do not remember me."

Hunter: "We never met. Did we meet?"

Orka watched Joseph open his eyes: "Yes, we did some time ago. I will do to you as you did to me. I heard of a name Dorock. He was there. You work for him?"

Hunter: "Yes, I do human. What did I do to you?"

Joseph: "Hunter, I am new at this very dangerous game and I want nothing to do with, but I am learning fast."

The stewardess walked up to the hunter. She took out some credits to give to the stewardess, to walk away.

Stewardess: "Ma'am, put that money away and go back to your seat. These two cadets are back here alone and leave them alone. Do not look at me like that. If you will not go back to your seat I will call for the officers. I do not think you want a hundred guns shoved into your face."

The hunter got up and walked back to her seat. The stewardess turned and looked at Joseph and Orka. "I am with Admiral Trey." She walked away.

Joseph looked at Orka and her helmet lens was closed. He knew her eyes were closed. He closed his eyes.

On planet Searrun.

In the emperor's palace. "Father, I need to talk to you." Prince Korien walked to his father.

Emperor looked at his son: "Yes, son."

Prince: "Where are you going father?"

Emperor: "For my exercises."

Prince Korien looked at his father's private guard: "I need to talk in private."

Emperor: "No, son, we can talk in front of my personal guard. Now son talk to me. What is it?"

Prince: "Okay, father. The pet. I can use him in the shows. He should have a collar and helmet. The beast can be dangerous." Emperor Xona breathed in deeply then exhaled and waved his hand in frustration. Prince Korien took a step back and bowed his head. He knew his father was upset.

Emperor: "No! He is a boy, and he is no pet. He is not dangerous. His people will be freed, and they did not have time to learn what to call themselves. His people should have been left alone to grow. You are not going to put that poor boy in a show. His family was ripped from him. Well, I found his family and I will put them back together. You touch him and I will more than exile you this time. I will put you in the hell fire myself. Did you find her? I do not see her here!"

Prince: "Sorry father, I am still looking."

Emperor: "Find her or I will exile you again. I am tired of this. I told you never go to that world, but you went there with her. Find her. I will give her to the boy of that planet. She is his. Now be gone. Leave now, I am going for my exercises. Find me later. Now leave!" The Prince walked away. Something moved under the Emperor's cloak as he made sure his son was gone.

No one saw the four legs under the Emperor's cloak. He pulled his cloak back and looked at the little boy. "Hi there. That is a good hiding spot Kor." Kor barely came up to the Emperor's hip. "Let's go and play ball. Then, we can go and get some ice cream. You want some ice cream?" Kor shook his head yes. "Okay let's go. Let's go and have fun." The guard looked at Kor, then the Emperor.

Guard: "Sir, I will miss him and all the fun we have."

A tear came to the Emperor's eyes: "We will take him to that world ourselves. I want to make sure he gets there safely. It is the only way to keep him safe. I will miss him too."

Guard: "Sir, I will be there with you. I will miss him as well."

Siogai home world Kalgan.

A father looked at his daughter on the view screen. He looked at her half-red half-black color hair and black lipstick on her lips. He wished she kept her normal hair color that was whitish green. He knows she wanted to be gothic. He never wanted her to stop expressing herself. She was young and still needed to learn.

Father: "Alice! Why?!"

Alice: "Dad, I want to go into medicine, and I always want to do more, like save people. The military will help me."

Father: "Alice, the United Planets military is still new. They do not know what they are doing. Come home and I will help you here."

Alice: "Dad too late, I am here, and it will start shortly. I am leaving the hotel."

Father: "Alice. You are young and you need to think about this."

Alice: "Dad, I want to help the New United Planets. Is that not what you are doing? The best way is this way."

Father: "Alice! Do not do this. I know you ran away before and did stupid things before, but if anything happens now, I cannot come to help you."

Alice: "Dad, I am okay. I learned from you. The recruiter is here."

Father: "You are underage. They cannot take you in."

Alice: "Dad, I am a runaway and a criminal. They can do this. You helped pass the law, remember?"

Father: "Alice! Please."

Alice: "Dad, enjoy being the Head Ambassador."

Father: "Alice Oakwing. I love you. I will see you soon."

Alice: "Bye, Dad, I love you too. They need me." The screen went dead.

The father punched the view screen and he looked at one of his staff. "Find out what branch of the military. I know she will never join the Marines. Find her so I can talk some sense into her."

On the transport.

The stewardess tapped Joseph on the shoulder to get him up. When the lights came on, the transport came out of warp and flew to the planet. Orka and Joseph both looked out the window and saw the sun beginning to come over the horizon, but it was still dark. The streetlights showed the trees' leaves were changing color and there was a fog between the trees. The ship landed and then the doors opened. There was a chill in the air. A drill sergeant ran on board the transport. He found Orka and Joseph standing at attention and began screaming at them. The instructor pointed at the rear door. "You two are lucky! Admiral Trey called! Get off the transport, run, run, run! Let's Go! Let's go cadets!" They ran out the rear door and found out it was only the two of them. The sergeant got them to a waiting small bus. The bus driver scanned them and their ID that was given to them by the Sergeant. The bus driver drove to the gate and off the space port.

The bus drove up to the base's front gate. The military police came onto the bus and scanned them. The bus drove through many gates and security was very tight. The driver drove to the front of a huge bus. The sergeant got off first. Joseph came out and was shoved to the right where a drill sergeant grabbed him by the back of his neck. They shoved him to a four-by-four white square on the ground with two yellow spots. They did the same to Orka. A drill sergeant screamed out. "Welcome to the Marine Corps! We are the Marines! The Elite Fighting Force! A Marine can take out thousands of any troops. The Marines are forged in the hell fire and cooled right in heaven. God inspects us himself and gives the okay if we are made right. That is why God loves us. He made the Marines himself to keep fresh souls coming to heaven. The Marines kill everything we see. We sure do not start it but by sure will finish it. We will turn you into men and women of the corps! We will make you Marines! You will feel hungry. You will feel cold. You will be wet. You will feel tired. You will feel hurt. You will feel pain. You will be in hell. That is God forging you by the Marine Corps massive hammer! I am the head drill instructor here. You, boys and girls, are under me! The lucky ones have me for three months. The others, the unlucky ones, have me for six months or a year! Oh, will this be fun! Welcome to hell! I will make sure you live in hell the whole time you are here! You will be miserable every second of the day. I will make sure of it. I am Drill Sergeant Calup! You belong to the Marines and that means you belong to me! You two cadets owe me for being late one hour! That means you owe me twenty-four hours of hell on the two who were late. I will get the time from you later. You will be Marines. One other thing, you will learn about Marines and our history. Like Lieutenant General Chesty Puller and Sargeant Major Daniel Daly and thousands of others. A lot of learning. Welcome to hell boys and girls. Instructors, get them moving!" The screaming started at the cadets and the young adults were separated.

The girls went left, and the boys went right. The instructors hit hard, shoved, and pushed the cadets. The cadets went into two different buildings. They were taken to a room with desks with large boxes built into them. Every cadet had to stand in front of a box desk. They lined the boys up next to each other and they did the same to the girls. The drill sergeant screamed out, "Put everything in your pockets in the box that is in front of you! Your pockets will be empty." Everyone did as they were ordered. The instructors ran around the room and screamed at the cadets. They ran up to Joseph and hit and screamed at him. They put their hands in his pockets and did the same to all the cadets. The sergeants took the cadets into another room with phones on the wall.

The cadets were told they had two minutes to make their last call. Joseph stood back, then a sergeant grabbed him and shoved him into the next room. When everyone was done with their calls they entered the next room. The cadets stood shoulder to shoulder. They were told to get naked and get in line to start seeing the medics. The cadets stood one meter apart from each other. They were examined, then injected with all kinds of drugs. The boys got their head shaved, and the girls got short haircuts to the bottom of their ears. They walked them into the showers, and the next room the boys put on green briefs and the girls put on green briefs and green sports bras.

The sergeant walked them to the next room where they received classes on how to wear their clothes. The cadets came out looking the same in dark green. The cadet training class began. The instructors marched them out of the buildings. The cadets were taken to the cafeteria and were fed. The sergeants marched the cadets into the next building for class. They received classes on how to pack their clothes in a duffle bag. The cadets were marched to a huge hanger and each cadet was given a space on the floor to put their equipment. The instructors wanted to make sure the cadets got all the equipment together. The cadets were given warnings to lock their foot locker and their closet or their things would be thrown everywhere in the barracks.

Orka saw Joseph getting his gear and he saw her doing the same. Joseph looked to his left and saw a male of Orka's species. He was looking at her and studying her. He tried to walk to Orka, and the instructor jumped at him. The cadet jumped and stood at attention as the instructor pointed his knife hand at the cadet and screamed in his face. "What do you think you are doing cadet?! What do you think you are doing?! Get back to your job! You have a job to do! We gave you a job to do! You want out?! We will take you to the ocean! But you will not disrespect orders and you will not disrespect me! You will not disrespect the Marine Corp! Get to your job cadet! Get back! Run Cadet Run! Run!" The cadet ran back to his equipment and got back to his task. He looked at Joseph and then got back to work. They got their private foot lockers and were taught how to put their things in them.

The cadets were done getting their equipment and they all stood at attention. Sergeant Calup walked out, "This is where we start making Marines. We will turn you girls to ladies and boys to men." Sergeant Calup looked at his watch. "This whole beginning program takes two days for us to get you ready for training. Some of you have different tasks in the Marines, but you all go through training for the Marines. You are going to be Marines! You will be Marines!" He looked at the drill sergeants. "Get them fed and put them to bed."

Female Barracks

The cadets marched to their barracks. A female drill instructor screamed out in the female barracks. "Orka, your bunk buddy is Alice. You two will help each other. Orka, do you know how to read?"

Orka: "Sergeant, a little, Sergeant."

Sergeant: "A little is not good at all. You cadets will help this species learn to read. You will help each other, or you all will fail. I will make sure you all get extra servings of hell. Get to your assigned bunks and get your things into place as we showed you." Alice and Orka helped each other with their new equipment.

Alice: "Hi, your species has a name. I never knew your species. Hi, I am Alice."

Orka: "Hi, I am Orka. I do not know, what is species Alice?"

Alice: "Well, species is a race. I am from the Siogai species. That is my race. You are the only one of your species here. I heard the other cadets before us had ten of your species with them."

Orka: "I do not know my species name, Alice."

Alice: "That is okay. You do not have to end every sentence with my name. You are free. Well, free in the military."

Orka: "I was taught to end every sentence with a master's name."

Alice: "Oh, there are no masters here. I will help you learn to read. So, what do you want to do in the marines?"

Orka: "Doctor, scientist."

Alice: "Oh, I can help you there. I want to be a doctor. You need to learn to read. I thought your species was cyborgs. Do not ask what cyborgs are. You will learn that."

Orka: "Thank you, Alice."

Alice: "No, thanks are needed. Hope you like my crazy side."

Orka: "I do not know this crazy side, but I hope we can be friends."

Alice: "Orka, that we can be. I will teach you how to read like the other ladies here. You're in good hands. So, Orka what is your last name? I am Alice Oakwing. Does your species have last names?"

Orka looked at her: "What is last name?"

Alice: "There is a lot for you to learn. You are not going to be cannon fodder. Oh, Cannon Fodder is people that are highly expendable."

Orka: "What is that word?"

Alice: "There is a lot of learning to do. Ladies, I need your help here. Okay, Orka how old are you?"

Orka: "What you mean by that?"

Alice: "I am fourteen, you look as old as me."

Orka: "Age, I know this word. How many seasons you lived."

Alice: "Yes."

Orka: "I am fourteen."

Alice: "That is a start. Now we may have to teach you math too. Do you know how to write?"

Orka: "Write, Math?"

Alice: "Ladies, need help here. Oh, one other thing. Who is that human boy that had the long hair you keep looking at?"

Orka looked at Alice: "He is mine! He is like me, from a prehistoric time. That is what the Captain told me."

Alice took a step back and raised her hands: "Whoa. Stop, I was just asking. He is human. Where did you learn that word from? Prehistoric."

Orka: "From Captain Davis."

Alice: "Well, you learn fast. We are not in prehistoric times anymore. Can you change your eyes back from black and put the long nails back in your fingers."

Orka: "Sorry. I thought you were challenging me."

Alice: "Nothing to be sorry about. I am not challenging you. You like him. So, you know him?"

Orka: "Yes, I do. We met before. He is my warrior and hunter. He is my hero. I want him to be my mate."

Alice: "Okay. Let's be friends. Let us talk to the girls about guys. Let's get you modernized. Like men's code of conduct, love, family, and a women's code of conduct. It is the same."

The drill instructor looked at the cadets: "Everyone to me! We have a small meeting, then go to bed. Come to me!"

Male Barracks

The drill sergeant called out to Thomas. Thomas stood up from the floor. "Yes, Drill Sergeant. Yes."

Drill Sergeant: "You failed twice but still want in. I have a special mission for you."

Thomas: "Yes, Drill Sergeant. Yes."

Drill Sergeant: "You are a counselor, therapist, and have your psychology degree. You are with Joseph. He will help you pass boot camp, and you will help him as well as all the cadets here. You all pass or you all fail. Work together cadets."

Thomas grabbed the heavy footlocker with both hands and he carried it to his bunk. He watched Joseph pick it up with ease with one hand and walked to the bunk. "Hi, my name is Thomas. I am human. You look human are you human? Nice eyes."

Joseph looked at him: "Oh, this footlocker is heavy. I am Joseph. Yes, I am human." Joseph grabbed the footlocker with both hands.

Thomas looked at him: "I have a question. These footlockers are heavy. How are you able to pick it up like that?"

Joseph: "They told me not to tell anyone where I came from or what planet I came from. I was born on Earth."

Thomas put down his footlocker and watched Joseph place down his. "They asked me to help the last time I failed. Well, I said yes and wanted to pass. This boot camp thing is hard work."

Joseph: "Yes, I heard. We can do it. I need help adjusting to this life. Camille told me. Well, she is human."

Thomas: "Who is she?"

Joseph: "A lady who took me from my home world and brought me here. I joined the Marines."

Thomas looked around: "I thought your home world was Earth? What type of world? Can I ask that?"

Joseph: "Yes, you can. I left Earth when I was young. The other world became my home world. They said the planet is primeval or prehistoric. I do not know what that means."

Thomas took a step back and the drill sergeant stopped him: "Joseph, they told you. They may have forgotten to tell you of the planet thing. So do not say no more."

Joseph: "Yes, Drill Sergeant. Yes."

Thomas looked at the instructor: "Sorry, Drill Sergeant. I just wanted to know how to help better."

Drill Sergeant: "That is okay. Stop asking questions. We need you to help him to be human and civilized. No more questions about where he came from or anything about that, carry on." The instructor turned and walked away.

Thomas looked around: "Okay, I can do this. Civilized Human. Who is that girl I see you looking at? The Porpoise species?" Joseph took a step at him and Thomas raised his hands and took steps back. "Is it something I said? Wait! Is she your mate? No, wait."

Joseph: "You are not challenging me?"

Thomas: "No, it is what we call talk. It is what civilized humans do."

Joseph: "Oh, sorry."

Thomas took a deep breath: "Okay, I stopped myself from getting killed. Wow. So, who is she?"

Joseph: "She was to be given to me, but I wanted her to be free. We both want to be together and left alone. Camille said it. Learn everything, make a life, give each other freedom and free choice."

Thomas: "It is okay. You both like each other. I can see that."

Joseph: "We want to be mates."

Thomas: "Okay, this is going to be a bit hard. Civilized human."

Joseph: "Yes."

Thomas looked Joseph over: "Well, let us work together and pass this boot camp. Make you civilized. Oh, do not hurt or kill anyone. They will train you. Learn everything." Thomas thought to himself, *Joseph is the boy they got from M793. I heard my father speak about it. Everyone wants it to be kept a secret. Who is that girl?*

Thomas: "Joseph, you need to talk to me about every feeling you have after training. Oh, not mates now. She is your girl if she wants."

Joseph: "Orka said she wants to be my mate. Camille said no making babies until we learn to be civilized."

Thomas: "So, she is not civilized either. Okay, they are training her. There is work to be done. Let's make you civilized. Is she from your world?"

Joseph: "No, she is not, but she wants to be there with me. I promised to free her and give her free choice."

Thomas: "That is good. Why did you promise her freedom?"

Joseph: "She is a slave, and she is property. I believe no one is anyone's slave or property. They tried that with me. It did not work."

Thomas: "Who tried?"

Joseph: "The species of my planet. They learned the hard way. I cannot speak of it. Maybe later we talk."

Thomas: "Good, yes, we can talk later about this. Now let us get you and Orka civilized. What are you looking at out the window?"

Joseph pointed: "She is there. In that barracks. Talking to that girl."

Thomas looked out the window: "Wow, that is hard to see. Looks like they are helping Orka. Let us get ready for bed. You take the top bunk, and I will take the bottom."

The Drill Sergeant called everyone to him: "Cadets, to me. We have a meeting. Cadets to me."

A star base over Pluto.

The Ambassadors and President of the United Planets walked out of the meeting, but one person stood still. He waited for everyone to be gone. Ambassador Ishton Oakwing walked to the windows.

Ambassador: "Admiral Trey, I have some questions. This has nothing to do with the meeting." Trey walked over to him and sat down across from him. "Rear Admiral Trey, your bosses super soldier program did not work. The boy from planet M793 cannot be cloned. He is now at boot camp, and I will ask, the girl is there too?"

The Admiral looked at him: "Ambassador, they are there. He also told me he met you."

Ambassador Ishton smiled: "Yes, we did. He is a very brave and smart boy. He is a new species of human or new species altogether and you have plans to make ten billion off of him. He is going to be a Daddy and she will be a Mommy."

Admiral Trey looked at the table then out the window past the ambassador: "So, you know."

Ambassador: "Yes, I do. I have eyes you know."

Admiral: "They will not know. We put the samples in the banks and all we need are carriers. The children that will be born will only have twenty five percent of his strength." Ishton turned and sat down as he watched Captain Davis sit down with them.

Captain Davis: "Admiral, will anyone ever learn not to do this. The boy and girl will be a family of a hundred billion children. That is not okay with me. Just stop trying to make super soldiers! That has failed every time. You remember history and the Forbidden Ones. Our species and other species sent super soldiers to a planet and we thought they would kill each other. We were wrong and they now have a light year of planets. The Forbidden Ones now want to be left alone."

Admiral Trey looked at Ambassador Ishton: "We have stopped."

Ambassador: "No, you have not."

The Ambassador looked at them both: "You humans are very interesting. I remember reading the history of our species meeting. We were meeting humans and only knew of four other aliens. Your government of the time was trying hard to control everything the humans did at the time. Before the war, before World War Three. The old leaders started it and never thought it would get out of control. They were wrong and they paid with their lives and the lives of billions. Forty years of war. The humans had space travel and your technology at that time could have put humans on Pluto. After your third world war, not one of you humans ever followed the rules they set out. We landed on Earth with one of your humans, and the new friendship started. Humans made it to warp overnight. The humans thought they made first contact, but we told you we were already talking to your governments. The new governments were a lot better. We all made great peace and trade. The four alien species came together with us. We came to Earth and helped you humans fix Earth. We all came together and explored space. After we got to a thousand aliens, we made the United Planets."

Admiral Trey: "The United Planets is ten years old now."

Ambassador Ishton looked at them: "Yes, ten years. With antiquated military equipment or thrown away military equipment and now I am learning the Ittors species have a split in their government. I do not like them for having slaves. We have to find a way to free them, and we have new threats we are just learning about. We need to know what side of their government to stand for and find out what is going on in the Beta sector. Now, Joseph tells us of this Grand Master who thinks he is a God, and he allies with the Ittors. This is what you humans say. Our cold war of spying. Let it begin."

Admiral Trey stood up: "I know the military. We can work with what we have. We need to start getting the information we need so we can get the equipment we need. We can come out on top with this."

Ambassador: "I hope so."

Admiral: "Ishton, we showed you before. We can do it again. We just need time."

Ambassador: "Well, that is something I hope we have."

Boot camp.

Joseph opened his eyes when he heard a light switch turn on. He looked and the lights in the barracks and they were off, but the outer hall lights were on. He heard a group of people gathering in the hallway. Some people walked in with something big. The lights turned on in both buildings and the drill instructors threw their metal trash cans down the middle of the barracks. The trash cans collided into each other making a godly horrifying noise. The drill sergeants stormed into the barracks screaming at the cadets to get up and get ready. They woke everyone up and the screaming started again. The instructors got the recruits up and had them make their beds. The cadets were showered and dressed in 10 minutes. The recruits stormed out of the barracks at 0300 or 3AM. It was freezing out that morning and no cadets felt it. The recruits began their morning exercises. By 0600 or 6AM the recruits ran to the mess hall and ate their chow. By 0630 the drill sergeant ran them to their first class of the day. The class was over at 0900 then more exercises and obstacle courses.

The cadets felt their bodies by 1200, and they ate like hungry monsters. The whole day they exercised, ran, went to class, and went through obstacle courses. The recruits were extremely exhausted the first day of boot camp. They finally got back to the barracks and the cadets felt satisfied to feel the icy cold water on their skin and all the dirt and mud off their bodies. The instructors had the cadets in bed by 2100 or 9PM. Drill Sergeant Calup pushed and motivated the cadets. He hit, pushed, shoved, and screamed at the cadets. He took interest in Joseph and was extremely abusive to him. He screamed in his face: "What are you fighting for?! You have no Family! No one wants you! You ran away to hide, why?! I will make a man out of you! You need something to fight for! Why are you here in my Corps?! Are you wasting my time?! Why are you holding back?! Are you here only to get good marines killed?!"

The second day the helmets and collars came off of Orka's species. Everyone was given military helmets to train in. At the end of the second week, the recruits were used to the extreme weather and extreme mud and dirt fields. They went through extreme obstacle courses, extreme exercises, ran further, and they did hand to hand combat classes every second of the day. They all learned the meaning of living in hell. They all learned the meaning of cold, wet, and hungry. They all learned the meaning of the true word pain. They all felt like they were in hell every second of the day. The cold days there was mud, dirt, water, and ice were thrown on them. On hot days they were trained in mud and dirt, and ice-cold water was hosed down on them. They ran into the ocean and ran out. They learned Marine history, tactics, and strategy.

They started new classes and were given body armor. It was heavier than the normal armor and very uncomfortable. They had to learn to sleep in it. The third week, the cadets took a gas mask class and they entered a room to get gassed. The cadets were given heavier weighted guns, and they had to sleep with their guns and equipment. The drill instructor trained the recruits hard. Sergeant Calup stepped on Joseph and beat him all the time. The drill sergeants took the recruits to combat training and class. The cadets were brought to a building to perform combat with robots.

Sergeant Calup pulled Joseph from the team and screamed in his face: "You stand there! You can hear your new battle brothers and sisters lose. You want them to lose! Not a word out of you! Hear them scream for help! You will not help them will you cave man?! You will let your new family, the Marines, down! Cave Man! You Human coward! Cadets, you need to defeat the robots to get out. Work together. You will win. He will not come and help. You'll see." The cadets stormed into the training room and Sergeant Calup went into the control room.

Camille stood up and pointed at him: "This is abuse! This is wrong First Sergeant and I want you to stop."

Admiral Trey walked over to her and raised his hand: "Captain, let it happen. Sergeant, proceed."

Sergeant Calup looked at them both: "Sir, Ma'am. He needs something to fight for. Something happened to him. Talks in the barracks was with his new friends asking for help. They told him they were his new family and to fight for them. They will fight for him. They also said to forget his old family. They told him the dead wanted him to live and to fight for the living. The cadets were motivating him. Now he can do two things, either walk away or go in and fight for them. I will say if Joseph hears his friends fighting and needing help, he will fight." Sergeant Calup hit a button, "Joseph, you can hear me."

Joseph looked up at the speaker. Calup looked at the computer screen at Joseph. "I want you to hear them lose." The sergeant hit a button and the doors opened. "Cadets, fight!" He hit another button. "Joseph, you hear them? The robots are stronger than normal. They need your help and I know only you can help them. I put only all your new friends in there. I put the closest thirty together. I know you can help them." Joseph heard them screaming. He heard Alice, Orka, and others fighting. Joseph looked around and ran to the front door.

Sergeant Calup smiled, and Admiral Trey looked at him: "You did not know he would fight for them. The second he heard them cry out you knew he had to do something."

Sergeant: "Sorry Sir, yes, I bet on Joseph. Oh, he is impressive."

Captain Davis looked at Sergeant Calup: "Open the door for him."

Calup pointed at the window that overlooked the training hanger: "What door? He ripped through the door. Joseph is ripping apart the first robots I put in the first room for him. I made those robots special for him, but I need to get stronger robots for him. Sir, you need to call the government and get funding for better robots. We need better robots to fight Joseph." Trey and Camille jumped to their feet to watch Joseph destroy the combat robots as the robots teamed up and attacked him all around. Alice watched Orka get attacked by a robot and fall over as David jumped to her aid.

David: "These robots are stronger!"

A robot attacked David and Alice saw Zor trying to help Karg. Alice jumped to the aid of Orka who was now fighting on the floor and saw a big robot coming after her. Orka screamed out, "Help me!"

Thomas jumped to help Orka to fight off the robot and helped her stand. A larger robot stormed into the room. Asta jumped on the back of a combat robot only to get knock off into a wall. Alice watched the large robot attack her.

Orka fell over the second time with Thomas. Tanga was thrown into Karg and Isash. Orka screamed, "Joseph you promised!" Luke tried to help Zor but there was too many robots now. Alice was thrown forward and something ripped through the wall behind her. She looked up and the large robot was now gone and destroyed. Orka screamed, "He is here!" The cadets watched Joseph rip apart five robots. Orka got up and ripped apart a robot with Alice. Joseph looked at everyone, "Lets fight together!"

Sergeant Calup smiled, and Camille looked at him: "You did not know, like the Admiral said. You hoped to God he would fight and turn the battle."

Sergeant Calup: "Yes, Ma'am. Joseph never had someone push him or believe in him or not tell him he was a pet or a slave. He was on a planet for seven years. It will get him ready for that military life."

Camille looked at them: "What if there were others on the planet he did fight for?"

Sergeant Calup: "Ma'am, I do not know but I know now he has a big reason to fight."

The recruits were allowed to destroy the combat robots, but it was no easy task. They fought with each other with foam sticks and the cadets had body armor on. They received harsh training. The cadets received survival classes in space, planetary, and other survival training. The last week of training, the cadets were used to the extremely hard exercises, obstacle courses, classes, and other training. The recruits were never given a break until the last day.

Joseph walked into the robot combat range, but there was no one there. He saw First Sergeant Calup at the control room. A general walked in and said, "Hi, cadet I am Marine Brigadier General Tatius. I am in charge of this military base. Let loose son." The doors closed behind Joseph, and he was angry for all the abuse. The robots came out fast and were destroyed just as fast. The training safeties were turned off and each robot got harder to beat. All the recruits went through the last day of training. Joseph walked out of the main building when he heard a familiar voice.

Orka: "How did you do?"

Joseph looked and saw Orka sitting on a bench. Joseph smiled: "I passed everything Micky. How about you?"

She smiled and looked up at the sky: "I passed as well. I remember the first day we were here. First Sergeant Calup was right. Welcome to hell. He was right about three months of it too. He got us ready for the future. Now things get easier. We just have to train."

Joseph looked at his watch: "Want to go to lunch?"

Orka stood up and looked at him: "Are you asking me to lunch?"

Joseph smiled: "Yes, and you are a fast learner."

Orka closed the book about medical aid she was reading: "And you are a fast learner too."

Joseph: "Can I carry your book?"

Orka: "Yes, you can." Joseph carried Orka's book as they walked to the mess hall.

At the space port of Kallos.

They took the children off the military transport ship. Kor looked around as all the other children looked at the ground terrified. They loaded the children onto trucks.

One of the workers looked at Kor and said, "This one does not have a helmet and does not stink. He is not filthy."

A lady walked over. "The leader of those slave masters brought him and cried about leaving him. I found out today he gave a lot of money to the academy. Do you believe that? The Ittors Emperor cried for that kid. Put him with the children. They are all going to the new academy."

The man put Kor next to other children. "Hay, the boy next to the kid with no helmet. He has no letters on his helmet, and he has all nines on his helmet. We can call him Nine."

She looked at him. "Do not worry about that. The doctors will give them names. Like they know what that is. We get them to the academy."

They closed the back door. Nine looked at Kor and spoke in a whisper because he was terrified, "Why they put me with you? Where is your helmet and collar? They will beat us for you losing your helmet and collar. What is academy?"

A girl shoved Kor in the back, and she whispered, "Stop looking around they will beat us harder and do not talk. They may not feed us."

Kor looked down and the boy next to him elbowed Kor. "Stop smiling and do what they want, or they will beat us and not feed us for days. I hope they do not eat us." Kor felt terrified and looked down at the ground. The man drove the truck onto the military base and drove past the guards.

He looked at the lady. "This is a much faster way. We will be at their barracks and the medical center in no time." The truck stopped in front of the medical center. They took the children out of the truck and the lady looked at Kor. "Why is he not looking around anymore and why is he looking down?"

A doctor looked at her. "Do not worry. He will look around in days or weeks. Where is his helmet and collar?"

The man walked over. "He did not come in with one."

The doctor looked into the medical center and screamed out. "I need nurses here. We need to get all these children cleaned up and get their helmets and collars off. They do not know how to read, write, or do math, and these kids are not smart. They do not know where they are."

The nurse put Kor in an examination room and the doctor walked in. Kor looked down as the doctor walked in. "So, what will we name you?"

Kor looked at the doctor. "My name is Kor and I know where I am."

The Doctor looked at him. "Hi, Kor, so where are you?"

Kor: "I am on planet Kallos. I am in a medical center where people go if they are sick or hurt. You are a doctor, and she is a nurse." He looked down and the doctor looked at the nurse.

Doctor: "Kor, how do you know you are in a medical center?"

Kor kept looking down. "I read it off the wall."

The doctor was impressed, and he studied Kor. Doctor: "Okay, nurse. We got a smart one here. He is also clean. Someone taught him. Kor, I want you not to look down. What do you want to be in your future? Do you understand?"

Kor looked at them both. "I do understand. I want to fly like an eagle. I want to be a pilot of a fast plane." The nurse looked at the doctor as he looked at her.

Doctor: "Okay, nurse, you know the routine. Get him checked out. Kor, where did you learn to read?" Kor looked at the nurse taking off his shoes. The nurse looked up.

Nurse: "Doctor! He has shoes on. This one is different. They all come in with no shoes."

The doctor asked Kor again, "Kor, answer the question."

Kor looked a little down. "My friends, who dropped me off on this planet. They told me they did not want to leave me, but it will be safer for me here and I can find my family here." Kor took out a piece of paper from his pocket and gave it to the doctor. The doctor read the names, ages, and where they were.

The doctor looked at him. "Okay, Kor, where did you learn to read? Who are your friends?" The doctor knew very well the Ittors had strict laws against teaching the slaves.

Kor: "Emperor Xona, his general staff, his special, elite, private guards and troops." The doctor took steps back.

The nurse looked at him. "Doctor, the chart and report says, Emperor Xona brought him here himself."

The doctor continued, "You got some friends. I am going to help, but it looks like you will be going to school here."

Kor watched the doctor walk out of the room and overheard someone saying, "I need the head nurse and the counselor. I want the older one found. The older one is married. The other one is too young. Oh, one last thing, make sure the General knows."

Kor looked across the hall into another examination room. A young girl his age waved at him. She was sitting on a table. He waved back. She was not of his species, and she had a horse's tail. Kor climbed down and ran to the door. He looked both ways before running across the hall. "Hi, I am Kor."

She smiled. "Hi, I am Barhar Jupitor."

Kor: "Do you want to be friends?"

Barhar: "Yes, I would like to be friends."

Kor: "Okay, I have no friends here."

Barhar: "Me too." The nurse looked into the room. "Kor, you can talk with her. I will be back. We have to get everything ready for you two, and Kor, we have someone coming to talk to you, okay?" Kor looked up at her. "Okay."

On the Base.

Orka put her helmet on and got in line. She stood in front of Joseph. They sat down together. Someone flipped Joseph's chair and threw him to the ground. He rolled across the cafeteria and then stood up ready for a fight when he saw the same male species of Orka's ready to fight him. Joseph recognized him from the beginning of boot camp. He was about to charge at the person who was challenging him, but he stopped himself. He tried to walk over to Orka, and the instructors stopped him. Orka jumped in the way. Everyone was watching, even First Sergeant Calup. The Sergeants in the room did not do anything but watch.

Orka screamed out, "Ion! What do you think you are doing?!"

Joseph was puzzled and Orka looked at Joseph ready to jump into the fight. Orka: "Wait! Do not hurt him."

Ion looked at her. "He is human! He cannot hurt me! You should not be here, and you should not be with the monkey human."

Orka looked at Ion in his eyes. "Ion, I escaped a day after Dorock took you away."

Ion: "You should not be here, Orka!" Ion went to grab her, but Joseph moved and grabbed Ion's arm. Ion jumped back and Orka jumped in the way again. "Ion, I am here now, and no one will ever bring me back! Those humans saved me and one of the humans is Joseph. He saved me."

Ion took a step back. "When I saw you on the first day in boot camp I tried to talk to you, but they did not let me see you until now." Joseph did not know what to do and he took a step back.

Orka looked at Joseph. "Do not go, Ion is my brother. Ion, what do you think or where should I be?"

Ion looked at Orka. "Not here and not with him! That ape human!"

She looked at her brother. "Here is where I want to be, and you must except it. Sit with us."

Ion looked at them. "No, I sit with no ape monkey human. I will go with the others like me. Where you should be. Your name is Joseph! I will challenge you to the sandpit. You will learn how strong my people are. I will easily defeat you." He turned and walked away. Joseph sat down with Orka. Then they saw First Sergeant Calup watching everyone.

Orka looked at Joseph. "You think First Sergeant Calup knows?"

Joseph looked at her. "Oh, he knows. He saw the whole thing. He walked in as we were looking for a table and we need to talk about your brother."

Orka: "Sorry, I saw him and did not know until the shooting range."

Joseph: "That is okay, Micky."

The main building on the base.

General Tatius called his medical staff to a meeting room. Tatius gave the head doctor a clear plastic bag with a medical vial in it. The Doctor looked in the vial and saw a flexible computer chip. It was one inch square with three-inch wires coming from it. The General turned on the huge screen on the wall. It showed three bodies on the screen. Tatius looked at everyone. "I want that medical bag passed around and everyone look at the screen. The two on the right are still alive. I talked to Admiral Trey and Captain Davis. Medical staff, this was taken from them. Sorry, I do not want to call them slaves. They are free here. We need a name for their species. Let us get back to what I was talking about, the chip. They did heavy scans on one who died on the transport here. She was sick and she died of mistreatment by her masters. The computer chip is some kind of control chip. The two that are alive do not have it at all. One of them escaped her masters and the other was born outside the Ittors control. This species that come from the slave camps have chips. I want this species deeply scanned. Command wants the chips out. Removing the chip will not kill them, so start removing them."

A nurse raised his hand. Tatius looked at the nurse and he stood. "Sir, did you get the report?"

Tatius looked at him. "Yes, I did, about the family. I would like to have a meeting about that. I would like to get them together. We have an Emperor, one of his sons, and some Ambassadors working with us on that."

Surplus building.

Orka and Joseph were walking away from the building with their dress uniforms. Joseph felt someone knock on his helmet that was on his head. They both turned around and saw First Sergeant Calup standing there with his hand out. "Helmet." Joseph took off his helmet and placed it in the sergeant's hand.

Calup put a black, dark green and gray line on it. "Your group always gets the line last. Shadows. It is good to see you are becoming a marine." Calup handed the helmet back to Joseph and the sergeant walked away. Joseph put the helmet back on his head.

Orka looked at his helmet. "Joseph, what is the black, dark green, and gray line mean and what does he mean shadows?"

He looked at her. "I do not know. The green, blue, white, and red line is on your helmet. You are science and medical. They have every color in the book except black and gray until now. They walked back to the barracks. Joseph looked around at some people's tags on their uniforms. Some of them had the same lines as his on their tags. He wondered what Calup meant by shadows.

Next Day.

The next day, at the end of graduation, Joseph saw them gather all of Orka's people and march them out of the parade grounds. He watched Orka march to the barracks. They dismissed the recruits, and they gave the cadets leave for three hours to be with family, but they had to return. Joseph walked back to the barracks alone. A cadet ran up to him. "Hi, Joseph."

He looked at her. "Hi, you are one of Orka's friends."

Cadet: "Yes, I am. My name is Nicole. Do you know they took Orka's people to medical bay for some test, but I saw Orka walking out. She was carrying clothing in some small bag."

Joseph replied, "That is for her medical work."

Another cadet walked up to them. Nicole: "Hi, Thomas. I heard you are going to the academy?"

Joseph: "Yes, he is. We will call him, Doc."

Nicole: "Thomas, I saw you with your family. Anything special?"

Thomas: "No, just going to be with the family. Look at Joseph. He looks like a lost puppy without Orka."

Nicole: "You see them the last three days, the two of them? They are attached at the hip."

Joseph: "Okay, enough."

Thomas looked at them both. "I have to go. I have a family lunch." They both ran from Joseph. Night came and Joseph had just finished dinner with Orka, and he escorted her back to the ladies' barracks. He walked into the men's barracks and saw some of the cadets. He got himself ready for the morning.

Some of the recruits were having a sleep over with loved ones or family. He closed his eyes.

Sometime in the middle of the night.

Someone walked into the barracks. "Joseph, get up and get dressed you have two minutes." Joseph opened his eyes and saw First Sergeant Calup. He jumped out of bed and got dressed quickly.

Calup looked at Joseph. "Follow me."

They walked to the main building to a meeting room. Sergeant Calup pointed. "Go in." Joseph walked into a room full of Generals and Admirals.

An Army General pointed at a chair. "Sit recruit."

Joseph sat down. An Air Force General pointed at the helmet on the table. "The black and gray line on the helmet means special intelligence. You wanted Special Operations, too. Dark green. We will test you. We already know you can keep a serious secret. We want to see how high up you go in the training. You have three years of training, good luck."

Marine General: "Joseph, you are not to talk to anyone about this meeting. You come to this building and go into the special operations room and ask for specific classes. We want you to take them all. We will see how you do on them. Then you move on."

The Admiral looked at him. "Take all the training Joseph, and good luck. Get sleep, you will have to be at the training grounds at 0200." Joseph was escorted back to the barracks.

First Sergeant Callup looked at him. "I will come and get you. Oh, you will learn how to work in the shadows. Get sleep."

Joseph: "Yes, First Seargent, yes."

Following day

Orka got up the next day. She walked outside and heard in the distance a massive battle and explosions. She looked at her watch and it was 0400 (4AM). Orka did not see Joseph. She ran to Ion. "I need your help."

Ion looked at her: "What happened to the monkey human ape?"

Orka: "Stop that! I cannot go into the male barracks. I need you to go in and see if Joseph is there."

Ion: "Oh, the human went missing? The foul smelling beast left with some girl. The humans have no loyalty."

Orka: "Ion, I will rip you apart right now! I will make sure you never have children if you do not go in and see if Joseph is in there."

He looked at her. "What is wrong with you? Humans are not good people."

Orka: "Ion! You have proved to me my people are not to be trusted by your actions."

Ion: "Fine I will go in and look. Stay here." Ion walked into the barracks and walked around the barracks. He walked up the stairs to the second floor and a cadet looked at him. Cadet: "Yea man, what you want?"

Ion: "I am looking for Joseph."

Cadet: "Well, what I know is he left at two. They sent him somewhere. He will be back, and his stuff is here. There is a note and sign here. A Lieutenant from staff HQ put it there. You know, headquarters. He will be back."

Ion looked at the sign and note. "Thanks." He walked out and looked at his sister standing outside.

Orka: "What is it, Ion?"

Ion: "HQ has him doing something. There is a note there, but it says move if need staff only." They heard extreme fighting in the distance.

Orka looked at him. "Okay, we have to get to morning exercise. I will find him later or he will fine me."

Ion looked at her. "What is up with this human? Why you choose him? We have people of your kind."

Orka hit her brother. "Mupet! Look at him. He will beat you and all our people in any fight. You have not seen what I have seen."

Ion: "The human has strange eyes. Not like the others."

Orka: "Ion, forget it for now."

Orka went on her day but wondered about him and thought about Joseph all day. All day the base heard the severe battle in the distance. For seventy-six hours straight, or a little over three days, everyone could hear the battle going on in the distance. On the fourth day, Orka had an early shift in the medical bay. She walked out of the barracks, and it was quiet. The battle training was over, but Joseph was not at morning exercise at 0400. His things were moved for him to the new barracks. Orka walked into the medical bay thinking of Joseph and what he may be doing. She saw First Sergeant Calup in a medical bed after not seeing him for three days.

Calup: "Doctor, put me back together before the new recruits come in."

The Doctor ran in. "Sergeant! What the hell?! You look like what came out of me this morning. You look like someone put you through the building then through the planet."

The Sergeant laughed. "Oh, it hurts. I should not have challenged him. It hurts."

General Tatius stormed in. "What the hell?! We got all those new battle robots and mech robots to fight him! We got those new robot tanks and robot air vehicles too! You stopped the fight! Why?! What the hell?! I need you for the new recruits! What did you do to yourself?! You challenged him, didn't you?! I told you not to challenge him. You are brain dead. You know how hard this guy hits. I know you are a rock species. You, dumb rock. You have rocks in your head. The Sergeant is going to have one of his bad days. Doctor, I need you to put him back together. After that, First Sergeant, I want you in my office. You will have that day after I am finished with you. What happened with Cadet Joseph Ramiro?"

The doctor looked at the general. "Sir, he carried Calup in and put him on the bed and he sat down over there. I let him go back to the barracks. He does have injuries, but not as bad as the Sergeant." Orka walked slowly to the head nurse. The nurse looked up at her and smiled and whispered, "Your boyfriend is back. Quiet."

The Doctor looked at Orka. "General, he will need a few days here. You're lucky he did not hit harder, and I know he can. General, I can have him ready for the new recruits. Cadet, I am giving you a special pass. I need you to go check on Joseph Ramiro. The nurse knows where you need to go. This is good training for you to learn how to use your scanner and medical equipment. Take the manual and read it. I will have the nurse check on you from time to time. Call if you have questions."

Calup smiled and looked at the General. "Sir, he could have fought for the whole week. I am sorry, Sir, for messing it up."

The General looked at him. "Oh, you will feel sorry, Sargeant. You wanted to be extra abusive to him. You get what you deserve. Man, you look like something I left in the bathroom this morning."

The doctor looked at the General and laughed. "Sir, I got to get to work on him."

General: "Go ahead."

The head nurse smiled at Orka and gave her a pass. "Your boyfriend is back. Go see him. He is in the new barracks." Orka walked out of the medical bay, then ran at top speed to the new barracks. The military police looked at the medical pass and scanned it. He let her in.

The MP pointed. "He is upstairs, third floor. A cadet brought him in. You will find him up there. Oh, I sent in to command. He needs new equipment." Orka walked up the stairs. She saw Ion cleaning up dirt, metal, sand, and mud. Ion looked up at Orka, and he pointed at the showers.

Ion: "A cadet brought him in. They asked me to help because I was doing guard duty." She slowly walked into the shower room. Orka walked until she saw him with hot steaming water running over his body. Joseph had cuts and bruises all over his body.

He opened his eyes slowly and saw Orka smiling at him. She was looking at him up and down. Joseph held onto the safety bar around the showers. Joseph: "Okay, now I feel violated. Hi, Mickey." They both laughed. Orka took his huge towel, and he turned off the water. She put the towel around him. They embraced, but she had to take a step back because Joseph collapsed on her. Ion ran to her aid. Joseph put his feet back under him. Orka looked at his bruised and cut face. They got him dressed and walked Joseph back to his bunk. Orka put Joseph to bed as Ion went out to get food and drinks. He ran back and looked at Orka.

Ion: "What is he?"

She looked at him. "You will learn." They put Joseph in his bed. The doctor walked in and handed Orka a hand scanner with a data pad and an attached data phone. The data pad was in a carry bag. She put the strap over her shoulder.

The doctor then had her scan, Joseph. Joseph was well asleep because of exhaustion. Doctor: "Orka, I want you to watch over him. He should be up in about ten to twelve hours. If anything changes, call the medical bay and we will come over. You, Orka, will stay here and watch him. This is your patient, and I will send you a nurse occasionally to relieve you for breaks and to check your scanner. The nurse will help you learn the scanner."

Orka: "Sir, doctor, I have a question."

The doctor closed a heavy curtain to Joseph's six bunk quarters. Doctor: "No cadet, you may not. He is hurt, not wounded, and he just needs sleep. I am teaching you something all medical cadets learn on their first patient."

The doctor walked up to Ion and looked at his head. Doctor: "You need to go to medical bay eight. You should be back in a week. More than enough time for your infantry training." He walked out with Ion, and he looked at Ion.

Doctor: "You will be back in two days from your surgery, but we want you to meet someone. You will go first to General Tatius' office."

In the cafeteria.

Kor looked at Nine. "You, okay?"

Nine looked around. "These people are weird. They want to help us or want to serve us, but why? Our masters say we must serve, and we were made to serve. Why do they want to serve us and help us? A lot of them are dressed in green and look the same. They make us look the same too."

Kor: "Nine, you had to see the nurse, why?"

Nine: "My center hurt and I threw up. That is what they called what happened to me. It was hard to eat and I really wanted to eat. The nurse called my center stomach, I do not know what that word is, and she asked if it hurt. I told her yes and begged her not to kill me. She looked at me and told me no one would hurt me here. The nurse gave me something to drink, and it tasted bad, but it helped my stomach. I can now eat better, and I do not throw up."

Kor smiled and looked out the window at the night sky. He thought to himself, *I am happy Xona helped me.* Kor: "What did they say we get tonight after dinner?"

A girl tapped Kor's arm. He looked at Five. Kor "Yeah."

Five: "They call it jelly pudding. It looks funny. It looks alive. It moves on that plate over there. It smells good, it's like a fruit. I hope it does not bite us. Its skin is wet."

Kor turned and looked at the large jelly pudding sitting on the serving table. Kor: "Where are its eyes and its mouth? You can see through it. You think they took off the skin or they ate the skin and the head?"

Nine looked at them. "No, I think it feels its way around. Look, they are cutting it, and it does not scream. It is dead. What kind of animal do you think it is? Wait, it can be a, oh, we learned it in class. I remember, it's a fruit, but wait where are the seeds? Quiet, they are coming and giving it out."

A teacher laughed behind them. Teacher: "Please talk, it is too quiet in here. They call it Jello pudding and it is a dessert. It is sweet. It is not an animal or a fruit. They cook it. You will love it." The children looked at him as he put the Jello in front of them.

Teacher: "Eat, eat and enjoy." They waited for Kor or one of the others to try it. By the end of the night the children loved the Jello. They walked the children to the barracks and Kor walked to a teacher.

Teacher: "Yes Kor."

Kor: "The counselor told me I would meet Teacher Novear, Miss Novear, or Mrs. Novear." The teacher smiled as they entered the barracks.

Teacher: "You are still learning the difference. It is Mrs. Novear. She is married. She is your species. Your class has her tomorrow. Oh, you have to go to the office. You meet her tonight. I will be taking you to the office."

Later that night.

Kor laid in his bed and listened to the rain hit the window outside. He looked around his cubicle. He looked at the top bunk and at his closet. He got up, leaned forward, and looked down the line of cubicles. He looked into the hallway and saw the light on. He looked up at the camera. He climbed out of bed and saw the teacher working on their laptop. Kor snuck by the teacher quietly. He made it out into the hallway and heard someone downstairs. Kor slowly walked down the stairs and saw Barhar laying on the bench with a blanket and pillow.

Kor walked up to her. Kor: "Are you okay?"

She looked at him. "I am scared. This is how the war started on my home world." She sat up and Kor sat next to her.

Kor: "I will protect you. I will stay here with you. So, what happen on your home world and what species are you?"

Barhar: "I am a horse species, and they call my species Equus. What do they call your species?" Barhar put her head on his shoulder.

Kor looked at her. "I do not know what my species is named. They never gave us a name. So, what happened on your world?"

Barhar looked at Kor: "That is sad, your species does not have a name. Maybe they will give your species a name now. Oh, there is a civil war going on in my world. My mom and dad took my brothers and sisters to the space port and to my uncles on the nearby moon. My aunt and uncle could not take care of us. My brothers and sisters went to the academy, and they sent me here." Barhar put her head on Kor's shoulder.

Kor put his head on her head. "I will stay with you."

Barhar whispered, "They said I was rebellious. What is rebellious?"

Kor: "I do not know, but we can find out tomorrow." Barhar through the blanket over both of them. The children both fell asleep on the bench where a teacher would find them the following morning.

In the barracks.

Thomas walked in with his duffle bag. He walked up to Orka who was sitting in a chair by a cubicle with the heavy curtain closed. Then, he looked up at a number and a letter on the ceiling. He walked into the cubicle next to the closed curtain. He looked at the three bunk beds and three personal closets per cubicle. He put his footlocker on the floor and put his bag down next to the rolled-up mattress. Thomas: "This is better. The other barracks had beds in a line, closets on the walls, and footlockers at the end of the bed. Here they got a place in the closet for your footlocker. Look at this. There is a pullout desk in the closet. This closet has more room in it." He walked and looked behind the curtains.

Thomas smiled and looked at her. "What did you do to him?" He laughed quietly.

Orka looked up at him strangely. "I did nothing to him. I would like to, but I want to do it like the tradition of my people."

Thomas: "Okay, what happened to him?"

Orka: "I do not know. He was missing for four days, and someone was at the training ground, the urban one. There was a massive battle there."

Thomas: "I do not want to know. It is best not to know or ask."

A cadet from Orka's medical group came walking in. She put an emergency medical box down. Cadet: "I heard you both talking, and the doctor told me to give this to you. Oh, I have two brothers. One in the special forces and the other one is a Military Police. I now know gray and dark green is two kinds of special forces. There is a color that means intelligence. My brother told me. Do not ask about black. They are some kind of special elite intelligence special forces. There is an all-branches military special forces, a very nasty group. One of the new military police was doing a patrol one night and saw

Generals and Admirals walking around the outside of the main building. The head military police officer told him there was no one there and the new officer walked the other way to do his patrol. He said they were meeting with cadets with the black line. The recruits went missing for a day and a half."

A military police officer interrupted them. "What is the saying? Loose lips sink ships! To save lives do not talk or say anything to anyone! Talk to your superiors about it! What you see and hear! So, learn to shut up to save lives and families! This conversation is over! All of you be on your way or get back to work!" The MP stood there watching over them. The cadet walked off the floor and back to the medical bay. Thomas walked to his bunk to fix his things. Orka began to read her medical science manual. The MP slowly walked away.

After some time had passed.

The military police officer slowly walked off the floor. Thomas walked to Orka. "I do not want to know."

He looked around. "All I know is they are peacekeepers by their secret wars."

He looked around. "I am going to be an uncle again by my sister and her husband. They wanted to try this Carrier birth, which is where they put the egg and the sperm in a female. The lady is the carrier. I want to be a doctor. I do not want to know anything about the dark green, black, or gray line, or any of those lines."

Orka looked up at him. "I do not want to know, but I will be here for him."

Thomas: "Okay, when Joseph wakes up my boyfriend and I want to take you both on a date. Tomy has to leave a day before infantry one training."

Orka smiled and looked at Joseph sleeping. "Okay, it will be nice. I have a question."

Thomas: "Yes." Orka: "Thomas, why are you back early? The first infantry training is not for three weeks."

He smiled. "I signed on for this month's weekend off only and signed up to train in the medical bay and hospital for training for upcoming doctor. I have to do infantry training and classes." Thomas walked out to the mess hall for lunch. Alice ran in and looked at Orka.

Alice: "Hi, so, he is back. You are watching over Joseph?"

Orka looked at her. "Yes, I am. I do not like these medical scanners. I wish I knew how to make them work better."

Alice: "They got these tech classes we can take during off time. I want to take the class. Take it with me. We have to go to the main building, then to the security office."

Orka: "Oh, yes, I will take the class with you. Then we could fix these scanners and get them to work better." Alice opened the curtain and looked at Joseph sleeping. She smiled and looked at Orka.

Alice: "He looks so cute sleeping there. You think he will, you know?"

Orka's claws came out. "No! Stay away from him."

Alice: "Okay, okay. I am just joking with you. I am teasing you."

Orka: "Alice, Go away!"

Alice: "Maybe I will be the next to watch him." She changed her eyes as Alice raised her hands.

Alice: "Okay."

Orka: "Alice, you play too much."

Alice: "Okay, calm down." She changed her eyes back and retracted her claws. Alice went to walk away.

Alice: "Orka, I will come back and kiss him in his sleep. When you are not here." Orka smacked Alice's backside and Alice jumped.

Alice: "Hay, that hurt."

Orka smiled. "You like to joke."

Alice: "Okay, I am going." As Alice was about to leave, Orka extracted one of her claws and poked her in the back side. Alice jumped up and ran away a little.

She looked back. Alice: "Ouch, you! What was that?"

Orka turned in her chair. "You have a crazy side. I have a crazy side. I like to play to and tease."

Alice: "Okay, you started it."

Orka: "No, you started it."

Alice: "We are still friends."

Orka: "We're still friends."

Alice: "Okay, I got you."

Orka looked at her. "Let the friend war start."

Alice: "Oh, okay." Orka: "I love you, Alice. Now get going."

Alice: "It is, go away. I will be nice. Love you too Orka. I will kiss your mate."
Alice turned and ran off the floor as Orka jumped up and chased her off.

On the planet Searrun.

Prince Korien sat outside looking up at the stars. He looked at his aide. "So, he overthrew his species' government. Good. The boy and the girl?"

Aid: "Sir, on Kallos. On the base."

Korien: "My father should never be leader. Like my grandfather said. I want the boy to give him away as a gift and I want to give the girl away as a gift. I still want the same handler, but with stricter rules. Call Dorock, tell him I will pay more for them both. Make sure Tara knows and watch her. She is a sly thing she is."

Aid: "Sir, should I call the mercenary you like?"

The Prince looked at the sky and drank his wine. "Yes, call him, but I have a job for his group first."

Aid: "Sir, should I have him call you?"

Korien put the goblet on the table. "Have the Professor call me. I want him to subvert a government as well."

On the planet Kallos in the barracks.

Joseph opened his eyes and saw a medical cadet working on her scanner and learning the medical scanner. The heavy curtain was pulled open. The cadet was somewhat in the dark. Joseph looked at the glowing digital clock on the wall. He had slept over fourteen hours. It was 03:00 (3AM). Joseph looked around the barracks and saw very little cadets there. He looked at the medical cadet and she was too busy learning her medical scanner. Joseph heard some alarm clocks going off. Then, the lights came on, he sat up, and put his feet on the cold floor. The medical cadet jumped to her feet and dropped the medical tablet.

She turned on the light next to her as the hall lights came on. Many of the heavy curtains were pulled open and the cadets that were there got themselves ready for the day. Medical cadet: "Hi, Joseph."

He looked at the medical cadet. "Yes, you have to scan me." She looked at his muscular body. She smiled and scanned Joseph slowly.

Medical cadet: "Okay, I will make sure the doctor gets these scans." The medical cadet walked out. Thomas looked at Joseph and laughed.

Thomas: "You think she can scan you even slower than that?"

Joseph laughed. "Get ready for morning exercises."

Joseph opened his closet and found some of Orka's books. She left her medical scanner. He got himself ready and ran outside into the cold. Joseph was walking when someone tapped him on the shoulder. He turned and saw Orka. She looked at the bruises on his face and neck. She looked him over.

Orka: "Hi, Joseph, you look better."

Joseph: "Orka, it hurts still, but I will live."

She gave him a hug. "Okay, let's get to morning exercises." They walked to the parade grounds. Orka joined the female cadets' section and Joseph joined the male section. First Sergeant Calup saw Joseph getting in line.

Calup walked up to Joseph and put his hand on Joseph's chest. "I honor you and I am proud of you. You will make an honorable Marine." Sergeant Calup walked away and gave the signal to start the morning exercises.

After the morning exercises, the cadets ran to the mess hall. Orka sat down with Joseph and other friends. Thomas sat next to Orka. "Orka did you ask him?" Joseph had a puzzled look on his face.

Alice sat down. "Where is Ion?"

Orka looked at Alice. "He is in the medical bay."

Another friend sat down. "I just saw him in medical and they told him he had something that weakened his immune system, but he is going to be fine."

Another one of her friends sat down. "I saw him too. They worked on the back of his head. He's fine."

Alice looked at Orka. "Ion is doing fine. It is strange that all your people are in medical but you."

Orka: "No, I never received any of the surgeries they gave to my species. They had to have messed up somewhere."

One of the ladies that sat at their table said, "It is nice, you Orka, are getting your people to join everyone."

Joseph interrupted everyone. "Stop! Orka, you were going to ask me something."

Thomas looked at Joseph. "That is rude!"

Joseph looked at him. "Excuse me?!"

Thomas laughed and put his hands over his face. "I forgot."

Joseph: "Look, she was asking a question. I just want to know what she was asking. I have to go and see the General. I need to know if Orka is going to be in medical so I can meet up with her later."

Orka looked down and blushed. "Sorry Joseph. Thomas wants to know if we want to go to dinner with him and Tomy."

Joseph looked at her and smiled. "Yes, if you would like."

She smiled. "Yes, but I have to be in medical."

Joseph: "I will see you later then."

Orka: "Yes." He turned and walked away.

Thomas: "So, it is a date. You two make the perfect couple."

Orka: "What is a couple and date?"

Thomas: "Tomy and I will help explain that on the date."

In the hospital building.

Thomas was working on the top floor. He saw Alice walking up to him. Alice: "I have a question. Why are they letting this relationship happen with Joseph and Orka when the rest of us have to do it quietly. Where in the manual does it say it is forbidden?"

Thomas: "The truth."

He looked around. "Joseph told me of some planet he is from. Not the one he was born on, Earth."

She looked at him. "You mean planet M793? He has to be lying about that. That planet is a killer. No one can survive there for long. Everything there tries to kill you. There is no colony there and it is a graveyard of ships trying to get the gold there."

Thomas looked around. "Yes, planet M793 is a killer world, but somehow Joseph lived there for seven years. It is true. You saw what he can do. I am human and I cannot do that. In training our squad took on robots. They told us to let loose. Well, you went in before me, right? Remember the enemy is in the middle building."

She looked at him. "That is why he is sent in last now."

Thomas: "Yes, Alice. I watched him destroy ten of the training combat robots. He also has different fighting styles. Joseph switches out as fast as he wants. That is why computers or robots cannot keep up. He jumps for cover when he is shot at. When we got our stuff on the first or second day, I did not mean to bump into him, but he felt like steel."

Alice looked around. "Then why the relationship?"

Thomas: "Think Alice. Slave girl and runaway. They have no family. They will kill anyone who will try to hurt them. They do not know what freedom means. They are learning how to read, write, and math. Orka is different than her species. They found there are over twenty-five cultures in her species like her. Everyone else has thousands. Orka's people believe in mates for life. Joseph comes from an old family or believes in it. Orka has her eye on Joseph, and he has his eye on her."

Alice: "I do not get it."

Thomas: "Okay Alice. Remember nuclear weapon class where a nuke can destroy a city or anything in a hundred miles? Well, they are like the nukes and the safety devices."

Alice: "They are unsafe."

Thomas looked at her. "No, they are safe. They just want a life of peace and freedom. They will let the relationship happen. They both are very deadly, but they want a peaceful life."

Alice looked at the people walking by in the large hallway. "Well, I think they should stay together."

He smiled. "That is why I am trying to help."

Alice laughed. "What can I do?"

Thomas looked at the people walking by. "Just be you."

Alice started walking away and laughed. "Just act crazy and ask you about something I know the answers about. Have you ramble about."

Thomas chased Alice off the floor. "Come here! Stop running! When I get you, I will throw you out one of these windows!"

At the young academy.

Novear looked at one of the teachers. "You cannot give my species' children straight chocolate. You will get them drunk. You have to mix it with something like ice cream, pudding, cake, something edible, or drinks. We can eat straight chocolate as teens or adults." She walked into the medical center.

The nurse smiled at her. "Hi, I guess you heard."

Novear smiled. "Yes."

The nurse looked at the children in the beds. "Their teacher did not know. He had them dress up in costume for an Earth holiday. He did not know and gave them chocolate. He said they started laughing uncontrollably, they could not walk straight, and they acted drunk. He thought the children were acting funny but knew there was something wrong. He had them lay on the floor and called for medical. We got there and knew what was wrong. The other alien species' children wanted to help their new friends, but the teacher just had them sit next to them. We told all the children their friends would be back."

Novear looked at Kor laying in a bed. "How long will they be here?"

The nurse looked at the medical chart. "Doctor wants them here for three more hours."

Novear laughed and walked to Kor. "How do you feel?"

Kor looked at her. "I feel funny and weird. I cannot talk right. The doctor gave us this water. I felt like I was spinning and floating. I tried to walk but my feet wanted to walk some other way. I cannot stand up. I laid down and felt the planet was moving out of control."

Novear looked at the other children. Nine raised his hand and she pointed at him. "Ohh, I do not want to move my head. Why is everything still moving as I lay still? Are we going to be back in class? I like that computer thing. No, I mean work."

Star raised her hand and waited to be pointed at. "Are we going to have fun time with our friends and watch more weird cartoons?"

Five did the same and waited. "Are we to still have the Halloween party?"

Novear smiled. "Yes, to all your questions. After you see the doctor, you will go back to school. We just have to change something. I know it tastes really good, but no more chocolate bars. The teachers will watch this."

One of the children raised his hand. "I do not feel good. Aamm."

The nurse ran to him. "Children drink your water! The buckets are next to you!"

Date

Tomy drove to a nice restaurant. He jumped out of the hover car. Joseph climbed out of the car and walked around the vehicle. He opened the door for Orka. Tomy looked at them both. "Oh my God. I am so happy you let me dress both of you up. That tie, the dress shirt, the slacks, and the cowboy boots make you, Joseph. You look good. What do you say, Orka?"

Orka: "Yes Tomy. He does."

Thomas smiled. "Orka looks good in that red dress with that belt and the small thick heeled black and white sneaker boots with laces in front. Her hair is made up. She looks good right, Joseph?"

Joseph: "She looks beautiful." They both blushed a little.

Tomy looked at both of them. "Okay, we have rules right, because of the theater. We look military right, but no killing or hunting anyone down. Anyone who hits on any one of you, you cannot hurt them or kill them. Orka, I know you got upset with that lady for hitting on Joseph. She now has scars on her chest. Thank God the military is going to help her remove the scars. Joseph, no ripping arms off or heads off, and no ripping the building down or destroying it. The military has to fix that building. That poor guy. Joseph, that guy should not have put his arm around Orka. Orka, you almost stabbed him in the chest. You both cannot do that. Joseph, you cannot fight, kill, or throw people hundreds of feet into walls. I know he went through glass, and he will not be that hurt. The military took him to the hospital. Thank God."

Thomas smiled. "Well, I am glad the theater manager let us in after the General promised to have military police there and pay for damages. We have to see the General in the morning."

Tomy looked at them. "I hope you all are not in trouble."

Thomas smiled and looked at Orka and Joseph. "No, we are not. The General said they need training to be able to be with the civilians." They walked into the restaurant and they were seated at a table that sat four people.

Thomas tapped Tomy on the shoulder. "The bar has military police there. I did tell them we had dinner reservations here."

Tomy looked at the menu. "Let them be. I am happy they are there. Orka look, there is a lot of fish on the menu for you."

Orka looked at Tomy. "What is squid?"

Someone pulled a chair to a table next to them and sat next to Orka. It was the lady hunter. "Hello, Dear, you are breaking the laws and what are you wearing? You are breaking another law. You have to wear at all times military clothing and your hair and no earrings. You look atrocious."

Orka's eyes changed color to black and her nails extended. Orka looked at the hunter. "I have a question. Is she on the menu? I heard she taste like crabs."

Thomas looked at the hunter. "This is a private dinner. Who do you think you are?"

The hunter smiled. "It is not allowed to speak, and it speaks. The beast broke another law and I work for the high Ambassador"

She was rudely interrupted by Joseph. "No, you do not. You work for a crime boss named Dorock."

The hunter looked at Joseph. "I now remember you boy. Human boy, you are beginning to piss me off. Human, I am twice the strength of any human."

Tomy was laughing. "Honey, you are not that smart. Oh, look, crabs are on the menu."

The military police walked over and looked down at the hunter. "Are you a hunter? You are not allowed on this planet."

The hunter looked at the Officers. "I am a visitor. The beast has broken the laws, and she needs to be escorted by a high-ranking officer. There are none here. I see no officers. You are Sergeant rank. Take the beast back to base."

A low voice came from behind them. "What about us?" Two Colonels were coming out of a booth.

One of the colonels looked at Orka. "You look ravishing young lady."

The other Colonel pointed at the hunter. "Sergeant, get that trash out of here. A lot of military personnel come here. So, she is on the base."

The military police went to grab the hunter. The hunter raised her arms. "I am leaving. Do not touch me." The hunter stood up and she was escorted out.

Orka looked down. "I am sorry. I am going back to the base."

Joseph grabbed her hand and did not know what to say. Tomy and Thomas kicked Joseph under the table. Joseph: "Stay and enjoy the night."

Tomy looked as if he wanted to cry. Thomas looked at him. "What is it?"

Tomy: "I wanted Orka and Joseph to rip the hunter apart." Thomas laughed. After dinner, Orka and Joseph were dropped off at the gate of the base and they walked slowly to the barracks.

In a private hanger.

The hunter sat back in her chair in her ship. She looked at the screen. "Dorock, I found them both."

Dorock looked at her through the view screen. "What planet and what base?"

She picked up her drink. "Star system Asta, planet Kallos, on the military base Ralvur. He is some General who beat us in a war. That is before my time."

Dorock: "Security! I need to know."

She drank and put down her drink. "The boy and girl. The boy is under heavy security, but we have to wait for a class trip. The girl, we can get her easily. There are woods around us. She has training or classes in it. We can take her there. They will never know we have her. We will be off the planet before they know she is missing."

Dorock wrote it down. "What do you need?"

She looked down at her computer. "I need hunters."

He smiled. "I will send them. What is it?"

Huntress: "The human. I remember him from somewhere."

Dorock: "What about him?"

Huntress: "He is the same one from the star base and the transport. He is different than the other humans. He is fearless."

Dorock laughed. "What, the human boy? Kill him and get it over with. Do you know how much credits you will get? Finish the job."

The hunter looked at him. "How did the humans beat us?"

Dorock looked at her. "The humans are very skilled and know war better than anyone. Forget the history. Smack the human boy, kill the human, and get him out of the way."

She smiled "I will send a hunter to kill him."

On the base.

It was morning, and Thomas looked at General Tatius. Tatius: "This is my fault. I talked with Admiral Trey. Cadet you will not be allowed to take them out without permission in advance. We need to give them civilian training. Without that training they will be dangerous to civilians. I know you have infantry and advanced infantry training. Then the academy. Tell me what you will be in the Marines?" Tatius looked at a picture of them last night together.

Thomas: "Yes, Sir. I am becoming a doctor. Sir."

Tatius: "Well, they need a life too. You will have time to take them back out without an escort. Sorry, but this time they will be escorted. You are dismissed." Thomas walked out and saw Joseph waiting on him.

Joseph: "Everything is, okay?"

Thomas: "Yes, Joseph, no one is in trouble. Come on we have training."

General Tatius waited for the Colonel to walk into his office. "Colonel, I want to increase security on the base. I want more patrols in the forest."

Colonel: "Sir, there is a lot of land out in the woods and that desert."

Tatius: "Colonel, we have pilots and drones. Get cadet squads doing patrol drills out there. Use those wheel drones too. Use everything and make more training operations."

Colonel: "Sir, anything I need to know?"

Tatius: "Yes, there is a crime lord out there called Dorock. He has no regard for the peace treaty. I am expecting a hundred hunters or more."

Colonel: "Sir, I will get on it at once."

A shuttle came out of warp outside the planet Kallos moons.

The Shuttle of Admiral Trey was flying to the base. The door opened to the computer bay. Trey: "Captain Davis, are you ready?"

Camille: "Sir, almost ready."

Trey: "Good, we have to keep our eyes open."

Trey turned on the view screen. "General Tatius, where is Orka?"

Tatius: "Sir, she is in the medical bay working." Trey: "General, put her in the brig."

Tatius had a puzzled look on his face. "What?!"

Trey: "General Tatius you heard me right and make sure she only gets out for training. I will explain. I am almost at the base."

Base

Joseph walked to lunch with a skip in his step and a smile on his face. He got to the mess hall and did not see Orka. He looked around and did not see his friends or Orka's friends from medical. He walked around then walked out the other end of the mess hall to the medical bay. When Joseph got there, he saw a row of armed troops, tanks, gunships in the air, and armored personnel carriers waiting for him. He looked past them and saw Orka in handcuffs. She was escorted out of the medical bay to a waiting military police car. Joseph did not understand what was happening. He was about to jump into battle when he heard Thomas scream. "Stop! Do not turn this into a warzone!"

Then General Tatius walked up to him. "Son, let this play out. She needs you on a mission to win this and I need you. I have a spy watching the base for a crime lord. I have a spy and three hunters."

The General handed Joseph a piece of paper and a map. "That is where you will find the spy, the three hunters, and any information. Take this young man. It will help hide you from cameras, scanners, and radar devices." Joseph took the small device and looked at the paper and the map. Then, he ran to find the spy. When Joseph was gone, Tatius breathed a sigh of relief.

Tatius: "Okay everyone, I want this place ready."

Thomas looked at the General. "Sir."

Tatius: "Son, we will get a lot of hunters. Help the doctors to get medical bay ready."

DEATH COUNT

At an apartment complex some distance from the base.

An alien species heard someone knocking on the door. He walked over and looked out the peephole and saw no one there and walked away from the door. Then, the knocking started again. He walked to the door, opened it, and looked down the hallway both ways and saw no one. He closed the door behind him. He heard knocking again. He saw someone trying to look into the apartment through the peephole. He looked at the door and the knocking got louder. He got his gun and slowly walked to the door. The door exploded inward. He jumped out of the way. The door flew through the apartment and crashed through the patio window. The door fell ten stories down. He walked to the opening of the door, and he looked both ways down the hall but there was no one there.

He walked backwards into the apartment. He walked backwards and hit the wall, but he thought to himself, *what wall is behind me?* He was spun around and Joseph threw him out the window. As the spy fell, Joseph jumped out the window on top of him, crushing and killing the spy as Joseph landed. He scaled up the wall to climb back into the window. It was dark now in the apartment. Joseph looked about the apartment and found an empty sports bag. He picked up the gun. A curious neighbor slowly walked into the apartment. The neighbor ran out when Joseph pointed the gun at him. The neighbor saw the police in the hall and told them he had a gun and he saw him on the ceiling. The police slowly went into the apartment and found no one. They looked out the window and looked down. They saw other police with the body on the ground. The police pointed up. "He went up to the roof!" The police stormed onto the roof and found no one. The police looked through the apartment and found the cameras and computers were gone.

At the seaport.

At the furthest hanger, a hunter was watching the beach as the other walked around their small ship. One of the hunters saw someone running on the beach. He walked back into the hanger to the ship to get binoculars. The head hunter was sitting in the ship and she looked at him. "Yes." Hunter "Ma'am, someone is coming down the beach. I just want a better look." He walked out of the ship. She heard over the police radio that the police were looking for someone who evaded them. They said there was a murder and a robbery.

She picked up her data phone and sat down. "Dorock."

Dorock: "This is Dorock."

Huntress: "You told me if I need back up you would send me troops."

Dorock: "Yes, I am sending hunters too. How many troops?"

Huntress: "I need two hundred troops. I can get her. I have a plan." She heard over the police radio the spy's address and the apartment number.

Dorock came back over the radio. "I can get you the troops, but I am sending three hundred."

She watched the hunter's lifeless body slam into the floor behind the ramp of the ship. She screamed, jumped up to her feet, and pulled her gun. The huntress looked at the hunter's mangled lifeless body. Huntress: "I have never been this scared. Something threw him over the ship. The length of the ship is twenty-eight meters, almost a hundred feet."

She looked at the blood on the front windshield. "Where is the other hunter?" She walked down the ramp slowly to see the other hunter was decapitated and his body was mangled. The binoculars were forced into his head.

Then, she ran back up the ramp and closed it. "What can do that to a body? What is out there?!"

Searrun

The last thing Dorock heard from the huntress was. Huntress: "What the hell?! How did you get in here?"

Her gun hit the ground. "You are the hu." The phone went dead and then the phone roared to life with horrifying screaming and crying of torturous pain. Then, he heard gargling screaming.

She begged for death. "I remember you now! I remember what I did to you! Please, I will tell you anything. Please let me go!"

She screamed, "You are hurting me! Please stop! What do you want?! Please, I will do anything you want!"

They heard her scream louder, "Please stop hurting me and kill me!"

A horrifying scream followed. Dorock cringed as he heard her bones break and her limbs being ripped from her body. He now knew what the gargling noise was. Her mouth was full of her blood as she screamed for mercy. Dorock heard her being ripped apart and it sounded like she was being devoured. Then, he heard her body being ripped open as she begged for death. Then, something crushed her main organs and her breathing stopped. Dorock and Tara heard her last breath. The data phone went dead. Dorock was shaking so bad with fear he could not talk, and he could not stand. He fell to his knees. The high Ambassador Tara screamed as she heard the ordeal. She was shaking in fear, and she could not stand. "What was that?! What did that?! I heard her body being crushed and ripped open!"

Dorock got back to his feet and got on the data phone. "Who are you? Talk to me! Do you know who I am and what I can do to you?!"

The Ambassador looked at him. "She was ripped apart and crushed. What does that?!"

Dorock looked at the data phone. "Come on! I know you hear me!" The phone came to life. Tara and Dorock heard silence, then they heard the rear ramp of the ship open. Whatever it was, it was moving without a sound. They heard police sirens in the distance coming over the phone. Then, it spoke the word they dread. "DEATH!" The data phone went dead then turned off.

Ambassador Tara breathed hard. "Death?! Death?! What is Death?! That is what it said! That was horrifying! You can hear her body being crushed, mangled, and ripped open! She was mutilated! You can hear it! That thing just did that! How did that thing have the strength to rip open her shell then the bones to her rib cage?!! What the hell did they make?!"

She got up and walked to him. "You get one thousand troops. I want to know what that thing is! I want hunters and elite hunters on this."

She sat down. "Get out of my office!"

Tara put her hands over her ears. "What savage thing is that?! I cannot get those sounds out of my head! Get out!" He ran from her office. Dorock ran out into the rain, and he looked up at the night sky. He fell in the street and cried out in horror. He wiped his face with his hands. He told himself, *get it together Dorock*. He got himself up and climbed into the car and thought, *I want out, but I am too far in. I have to find it to destroy it or get it to work for me. Oh, no, destroy it is better. It will kill me and take over. No, no destroy it! What savage beast does that?*

On the planet Kallos.

Joseph remembered the flight training he received from special forces officers on planet M793. He flew and landed the ship of the huntress. He landed the ship in a hanger bay on the base. The intelligence officers took charge of the ship. Joseph ran from the airfield to the barracks to get cleaned up. Thomas saw Joseph covered in alien blood and went to walk to the barracks from the medical bay. The doctor grabbed him. Doctor: "Oh no you will not. Cadet, if you are his friend, be his friend and be there for him. Right now, be in medical. Ignore whatever he did."

Thomas turned and looked at the doctor. "I just want to help, but you are right. I do not want to know. It is safer that way." Doctor: "Yes, it is." On the overhead speaker they heard, "The alarm is over stand down, stand down. Alarm over, alarm one over." The head doctor walked to the barracks, then came back after some time.

The next day.

Joseph walked into General Tatius' office. He recognized Captain Davis, and she was pointing at him to come to her. "Yes Ma'am."

Camille: "Joseph, take a seat in this room. You are part of this." He walked into the meeting room and saw a Siogai female seated at the large table before he fully walked in and sat down.

Joseph: "Hello Ambassador Ishton." The Ambassador was seated right next to the large view screen.

He smiled. "Joseph, you amazed me still and thank you for saving my life on planet M793. I must say thank you for that beautiful bow that helped me finish the hunt. Do not tell anyone I was there on that hunt. Remember, I am not here."

Joseph looked down. "Like you were not on that planet."

Ambassador Ishton smiled. "Exactly." Joseph can hear arguing in the General's office but could not make out what was being said. He knew how to focus his ears, but he did not.

Office

General Tatius: "Admiral, I know I am out of line, but have you seen the police report or the military police report?! Have you seen these pictures of these bodies? Did you see what he did to the huntress? We intercepted and listened into the calls. You do not want to hear it. I have my military police in medical. They got sick for what they saw! It looks like an animal ripped them apart viciously. The civilians are terrified and asking for this thing to be hunted down. They want answers. The base is on this silent alert status. It is safer to move them to some other place. This planet will become a warzone in time with them. I know they want to be here in the military. I know they want normal lives. Look what he can do! What did you get off that planet? Have you seen the reports from his combat fight in the city we built? Now I know why they put on his report to never take him from that world. What are you not telling me about this boy? We put people away for doing things like this."

Trey looked at Tatius. "They stay here, and he stays here. This is the safest place and if this place becomes a warzone. I want to win this! Just get them ready."

Meeting room, minutes later

The Admiral walked into the meeting room and put his hand up to stop Joseph from standing up. The General and Admiral sat down. The Captain hit a button and the screen came to life. The High Ambassador Tara of the Ittors species came on screen. Admiral Trey spoke before the High Ambassador Tara could say anything. Trey: "What did your species put on this planet? We are at Defense Five. We have troops running around with guns. There is something here that killed three of your species. The beast killed four. It has the ability to upset electronic devices. There were witnesses. It went into the apartment and killed the first victim by breaking his neck and crushing him. Do you want to see the videos?! I saw them and I am sick."

Ambassador Tara raised her hands, closed her eyes, and she looked queasy. "No! I do not know anything of this. What about the other two and their ship?"

Trey: "Well, the General has a video of your three getting devoured. The three of them are hunters and the ship is impounded. It is covered in blood, in and out. Do you want to see those videos? I will be happy to show you them."

Tara: "No! Please. I do not want to see that. We are here for the murderer of one on my world and the other one on Star Base 31."

Trey: "What about the murder of the three on this world?"

Tara: "Admiral, your authorities there will take care of that." Admiral Trey looked across from him to the Siogai species lady.

She stood up. "Hello, my name is Luthien. I am a United Planets government lawyer and work for High Ambassador Ishton. I would like to know how you know she is here? We all know your hunters and how ruthless they are. We do not need to know how Orka escaped. High Ambassador Tara, you say Orka is a murderer of two people. What is the evidence? You say there was a robbery, but you will not tell us what was taken. You have no video. You say the two cadets killed an Ittor at Star Base 31, but our evidence shows they got off the ship with no weapons and got on the transport with no weapons. We are not allowed to see the bodies and the other body was a hunter and your people took him. The hunter had his gun on him and a lot of money on him. They say the cameras were turned off on Star Base 31. Yes, there were claw marks on him, but we do not know if they are Orka's claws. You did not allow us to study the body. The hunters hunt down all of her species. You left us nothing to look at or study for ourselves. The cadets have no bruises or marks of any fight. We cannot just take your word on this."

Ambassador Tara looked at Luthien. "Well, well. A little lawyer. This is going to the courts. She belongs to us."

General Tatius held up a data pad and hit a button. "Dorock signed her over and that is his handprint. Orka's name is on this list."

Tara clapped her hands and looked down, then back up at the view screen. "Orka is to be in a combat unit and to stay there. She is not to be trained in anything. That is the agreement, and it is the law."

Trey looked at his data pad then at the screen. "Yes, and she will. Is that all?"

"That is all." High Ambassador Tara turned off the viewscreen.

Ambassador Ishton got up from the side of the view screen and sat down at the large table. "Emperor Xona changed the agreement. We can train them. Those videos have been altered."

Trey looked at the Ambassador. "Sir, the electro interference alone is good enough. We have to talk about the beast and keep to the story."

Luthien looked at everyone. "You look at her hands? All four of them, they were shaking. She was terrified of the report of the beast. Joseph, was she on the data phone?" She looked at Joseph and studied him.

Joseph: "I promise I did not eat them."

Everyone looked at him with some kind of fear in them as they thought, *what did we bring off that world of M793?* Ishton looked at Joseph. "Just answer."

Joseph: "Dorock was on the phone and the Ambassador was whispering to him. She was demanding to know what was the thing that killed the hunters. I heard her and Dorock listening to me crushing the huntress. After I crushed her hand, she told me she would tell me anything. I said nothing and then I crushed her knee in my hand. I tortured her because Orka told me about the horrors of what her people are going through. I also remembered what she did to me on my world. Sir, I am sorry for my actions. I know it was wrong. Just because something is done to you does not mean you have the right to do the same to others or to the person who did it to you."

General Tatius dismissed Joseph. Captain Davis closed the door behind him. Camille sat down at the table and Ambassador Ishton looked at the Admiral. "Is there something you are not telling me?"

Trey looked at him. "I told him to mutilate them. I studied him for a very long time. The history of Joseph and Orka. This cannot leave this room. This is top secret."

Mess Hall

Joseph walked to the mess hall, and he saw new cadets there. He remembered how they taught to eat civilized. He got his food and drink. Joseph found his friends and sat with them. Thomas looked at him. "You know she is safe there."

David moved Joseph's drink and sat down. "Orka is okay. I was there training as military police. She is safe there. You know more are coming."

Joseph looked at his food. "Yes, I know. I cannot wait."

Zor put his hand on his shoulder. "You know, my species are peaceful but some of us choose to sacrifice ourselves to keep that peace. Stay with peace as you ask me to teach you. Orka will be free in time."

Karg tapped the table. "Brother, I can see what you are going through. Remember, the wind shall blow, and the sun shall rise on you and her again. Your time will come to take on the great enemy. Be strong as the Earth and ready yourself. The time is near."

Asta looked at Karg. "Man, we want Joseph in good spirits, but what are you guys talking about? We do not want him in war paint. Man, we all see Orka as we work around the base. They let her out for training. Dude, remember, she wants you to do the right thing."

Tanga threw a wadded-up napkin across the table. "Eat your food. Orka was in tech class with Alice. She is okay. I was talking to her. Orka is fine. They will let her out."

Isash tapped his drink on the table. "Brother, keep the peace. They will move her to the academy. They said in the main building. She will still be with us."

Luke looked at them all. "Joseph, we know what you can do, but man, do not turn this into a warzone. Things will get better. Do your classes. She thinks of you as you think of her. They have the base on this silent alert. They are making sure they can stop these hunters and mercenaries. Orka will be out."

Mar tapped Joseph on his shoulder. "Peace and love defeat the evil. The great spirit God will be there with you. Meditate and pray to the one God. He made you. You are his finest warrior. You are here to fight for the great peace. You keep the love and peace in your heart. You will win."

Thomas looked at them all. "You guys are great. Joseph, get some rest and train. You got the NAV (navigation) class tonight, do that. You passed day one. Orka is doing the same."

Alice and Orka's friends walked over to Joseph. They all hugged him. Alice looked at Joseph. "Orka asked us to hug you for her."

On the planet Searrun.

Dorock pointed his finger at a hunter. "Zaire do not talk."

Zaire: "Why Sir?"

Dorock frowned at him. "You talk crazy. Get your one hundred hunters and go to Kallos."

Zaire: "Oh, boy. You want your best at this. I am your best."

Dorock: "Shut that hole. You will go and get the girl and bring her here untouched and the boy will be next."

Zaire: "Sir, no one will touch her. I know what they will do to me if I do."

Dorock: "Zaire, what I say! Max warp there. Kill this human boy that might be helping her. There will be an army coming up behind you. There is some beast the High Ambassador wants too. Now get out."

Zaire got up. "I will be back shortly."

Dorock waited and then he picked up the phone. "High Ambassador Tara I will come to see you. I have sent out one of my best elite hunters and his men of a hundred. You will have the beast on your wall, and the girl and boy."

The following day on the planet Kallos.

Joseph saw Orka at the morning exercises, but he could not get close to her. He prepared himself for night NAV class and walked to the head military police office. Joseph stood at attention. The head officer opened his door to the office. "Enter cadet."

Joseph walked in and the door closed behind him. "Cadet, give me the jammer, your watch, and your dog tags." Joseph did as he was ordered. The office put a dark green, black, and dark gray tag on the chain.

He handed a small box, tactical belt, and Joseph's dog tags to him. "This is yours. This wristwatch has a jammer, compass, and a small screen with maps. The belt has a jammer on it, and a small computer screen. Take the tech class to upgrade everything. It will be a storm tonight, have fun passing the class."

In a private hanger.

Zaire walked off his ship. He looked at the dried blood all over the place. It looked as if someone painted the wall and ground with it. A young lady walked to him. "Sir, Joseph will go on a night run. The run is a long one. The girl is in a jail cell, and they will move her to the academy. You can get her in between."

Zaire looked at her. "Keep your watch on the base. You are the new lead."

He waved his hand. "I want ten of you to kill the human. It will be easy. He is a human boy on a night run."

The General's office.

Camille walked to General Tatius. "I have a question, Sir. How did this spy get the photos and these taped conversations?"

Tatius looked at the pictures of Orka and Joseph in the mess hall. Then Captain Davis gave him a blueprint of the base. "There is a spy on the base, but who? We have to ask the informer."

Camille looked at the spy's computer. "There has to be more than one. A lot of these pictures are taken at the same time."

Tatius opened a map and looked at the spy's tablet. "They mapped out the whole forest. There must be more than one to map out a twenty mile square in this short of time. Is there a flying drone in the bag?"

Camille looked in the sports bag. "No, there is no drone."

Tatius looked through the tablets. "Well, there has to be another place with more equipment. I will have Joseph sent out after his infantry training."

She looked through the computer. "The informer will give us more help."

The barracks.

Joseph walked to his bunk and found a box on his bed. The box had three bush knives. He took his Ka bar marine knife and put the other knives away. He walked away from the barracks and looked at the night's cloudy sky. Joseph walked to the instructor of the class and the military police at the gate to the woods. The wind began to blow harder. Lieutenant: "Joseph, you are the only one here. The rest of the class will do their NAV class tomorrow. There is a storm coming, have fun. Here is your map and a compass. Good luck. See you in six hours. Well, with the storm it will be eight. Start now."

Joseph: "Sir, Yes, Sir." Joseph started to walk out of the gate. The path went dark as he walked around the bend. The lightning struck and it lit up the night sky. The rain began to fall hard as the wind blew harder. Joseph found one of the NAV class's billboards. He stopped and looked at his map and saw a NAV point on the map two miles away from him. He saw coordinates he had to follow. He wrote it down on his map with a wax pencil and looked at his compass as it began to rain hard.

The General's office.

Camille saw a picture of the entrance to the students NAV hike. Then, she found one taken at night at the gate. The General had retired for the night. Camille grabbed the phone. MP: "This is military police station four."

Camille: "This is Captain Camille Davis, Intelligence officer. Is there a NAV class tonight?"

MP: "Ma'am, let me see. Yes, ma'am. A harsh weather NAV class. One student and he is Cadet Joseph Ramiro. He went through the gate three hours ago."

Camille: "Who is the highest rank there?"

MP: "That is me ma'am. Second Lieutenant."

Camille: "Okay Second Lieutenant. We have an emergency, and we need to get that cadet back to the barracks."

MP: "Ma'am, we just got a tornado warning. There is nothing we can do at this time. We have five trees down and two crashed vehicles. One crushed by a tree by us and the storm is making things worse. We are right now cleaning things up. This storm is bad. That cadet is on his own. Sorry, but I will call the head office for help and that is all I can do for now."

Camille: "Does he have a radio?"

MP: "No, ma'am. The cadets do not get radios at this stage, but if he has radio training, he will have one."

Camille: "Call the head military police. Tell him to call me. I will try him on the radio. I will be in the comms room in the main building." She ran to the comms room and used her pass to get in. The phone rang and she picked it up.

Camille: "Captain Davis, here."

Captain: "Ma'am, this is the Marine Captain. I am second in charge. I looked here and if Joseph has his tactical belt, you can call him on special forces line Alfa 793. I do not know what is happening, but it is an emergency. I will have the military police get him. We are going to try from the main roads and the rear roads. The beach road you will need a boat at this time."

Colonel: "This is the Colonel. I will send out some teams. Can you tell me what is the emergency?" Captain: "Ittors Slave Hunters in the forest. I see a report here. They are hunting the cadet." Colonel: "Okay. I am sending the teams out." Camille keyed the numbers into the radio.

In the forest.

Joseph saw something move. He kneeled down in the ankle high water by a tree. It was hard to see in the heavy fog, heavy wind, and heavy rain. The heavy wind and lightning made it worse with trees falling over, and tree limbs breaking off or flying about. He looked at some hunters moving about. Joseph's earpiece came to life. "Sss m sss k sss l ss are ss u sss k ss I ss ll ss them sss all." He tried to fix the radio. "Mission sss Cadet. Ssss now. There ssss hunter sss" He worked to clear the noise, then he saw movement out of the corner of his eye. It was moving in the shadows.

In the private hanger.

Zaire drank and laughed. He called Dorock. "Sir, they see the human boy. They will have him."

Dorock: "I want to hear."

Zaire sat in the ship and he plugged the phone into the computer. "You can hear them now."

They heard a scream come from the other side of the radio. "What is that?! Look at those golden eyes over there. There is something out here with us! Where did the boy go?!"

Dorock slammed his fist down. "Get them out of there!"

Zaire looked at the phone. "Why? You do not want to give me the glory and the radios or phones are not working at this time. This is some kind of electrical storm."

A hunter screamed out on the other side of the radio. "What killed him?! How did he go through that tree?! Whose greenish golden eyes are over there?! Who is that?! Over There!"

Then they heard a crushing noise. "What crushed his head?!" They could hear screaming in the background and a crushing noise. One hunter screamed, "It ripped him in half!" Another hunter screamed out, "All hunters on me! We make a defensive circle! We need more men here!" A hunter screamed out, "How did it rip his head off?! I was looking at him! Where did it go?!" There was more screaming, "It dragged him into the darkness! You saw its eyes! They shine in the light like Gold! Let's get out of here! Run!" There was screaming, "How did that tree explode?! Run!"

High Ambassador Tara screamed, "Turn it off or I will kill you both now!"

Zaire hit the button and turned off the hunters' phones. "Ma'am the phone is off! What was that out there? Where are my men?"

Dorock: "Forget them. They are dead. Get everyone on the ship and sleep in space tonight. You were told about this beast! It is coming to you."

Zaire heard one of his men scream out in the hanger, "What happened to the hunter by the door of this hanger?!" They heard rushing wind enter into the hanger. The roof shook violently. Zaire closed the ramp and opened the side door. They heard one of the hunters scream as something dragged him into the night.

Zaire: "Open the hanger door we are leaving! Everyone on the ship. We are leaving!"

Zaire heard heavy rain hit the roof of the ship and something jumped on top of the ship. The lights went out in the hanger, then screaming and wild gun fire started in the dark hanger. He heard, "It is over there!" "Shoot it!" "No, it is over there. This thing is fast!" "Shoot at it! Fire, Fire!" The ship rocked wildly, and he could hear metal ripping. The hunters began screaming and blood sprayed into the open door. Zaire watched as one of his men was grabbed by something and thrown into the darkness by a shadow. The shadow was gone. In a panic, Zaire hit the button and the door closed. He quickly turned off the lights and ran and hid in the bathroom with his gun ready.

Zaire looked down at the phone and saw Dorock hung up the phone. He tried to call Dorock, but no one answered. He could hear wild gun fire and his men were dying. Their bodies were being slammed up against the hall. Heard people pleading and begging for death. Zaire heard limbs ripping from bodies, bones breaking and being crushed, then he heard someone gargling. Zaire turned on the data pad. There were red lights across the board for the ship. Something ripped the engines out of the ship and the reactor. The systems showed the wing was first ripped in two, then ripped off the ship. He tried the cameras, but they did not work. The rear ramp was ripped off the ship and the ship rocked violently. Zaire heard something rip the side door off, then it went quiet.

At the gate to the base.

It rained like pouring water. Joseph got to the gate as the military police drove through. One of the officers saw Joseph fall and get back up. The officer ran to him. "Are you the cadet they are looking for? What is your name?"

Joseph: "Sir, Cadet Ramiro, Sir."

The military police waved his hand. "He found us. The cadet is here."

Another officer ran over. "It must be bad out there look at his wet tattered clothing. Get him too medical."

MP: "Sir, look here he finished the course. Cadet, you passed your class."

Second lieutenant: "Well, it took you longer because of the harsh storm. Now get him too medical."

Barracks temporary living quarters.

Camille heard knocking on her door. She opened the door and saw Admiral Trey. Trey: "I checked the floor, we are good. Captain, what happened last night?"

Camille: "I told Joseph his mission was over and to get back to base and to be careful because there may be hunters out there. Luckily, he got back. I do not know if he heard me."

Trey: "Joseph's radio got severely damaged in the storm. Get cleaned up, I need you to talk to Joseph. He killed one hundred plus hunters last night. I need you in the office. The Ambassadors are talking. Oh, Joseph passed his class last night."

Camille put her hand over her mouth and looked at the ground. "Captain, this is no one's fault. He also had an old radio. No one checked it before he left."

In the meeting room of the main building.

Camille walked in and saw Ambassador Ishton slam his hand down on a button and the view screen went off. "She really thinks I am to believe a hundred plus hunters came here to get three bodies." He turned and looked at Captain Davis. "Is he safe?!"

Camille: "Yes Sir."

Ishton: "Is he safe?!"

Camille: "Sir, he is one hundred percent safe. Yes, he is safe."

Luthien raised a folder to Camille. "Take a look. The kid needs training to be human. He thinks he is an animal."

She put the folder in front of Camille. "Joseph was on a planet alone for how long? What type of planet was it? Where he had to be an animal!"

General Tatius hit a button. "Captain Davis. That shed destroyed on screen is the hanger. The tornado hit there last night. After the electrical explosion, the police ran in. Someone was ripped from the ship's bathroom. The hunter fired wildly into the night and then shot himself. Joseph had left already, and the bathroom was hanging from the damaged ship. The hunter was so terrified in the bathroom he thought he was going to die, so he shot himself. The other hunters, some of them panicked and they shot their friends, they shot at each other. One of the hunters opened the hanger door and he tripped and fell but the wind got to the door and started the fight. That is what the police put on the report and that is what we see as well. Your boy killed more people, and it is normal for him to kill."

Captain Davis looked at everyone as Admiral Trey walked in. Trey: "Joseph helped destroyed the building and the ship. They think he killed fifty people. No one can see in the hanger. He did kill ten in the woods. Joseph needs etiquette class like we give Orka's people. I have to put him in class for tech, radio, and orders. Oh, Joseph stopped talking. I have a way to get him to talk again. Captain Davis, you will be stationed here until they learn to live with civilians. I need you to find those spies and stop the hunters. Get yourself a place here. You will be here for some time. There is a little boy I want you to talk to."

In the mess hall.

Joseph barely talked to his friends. Ion walked to him. "Joseph, you have a good heart. Be strong. We still have enemies among us. You are her hero." Joseph got up to throw away his tray of trash when someone tackled him. They both rolled across the floor. Joseph ended on his back looking up at Orka. She held tightly onto him. They embraced and their friends cheered. Their friends helped with the cleanup of the mess hall. Admiral Trey, Captain Davis, and General Tatius stood at the entrance of the mess hall smiling. The morning exercises were different this time. There was a fast ceremony. The cadets became Marines and received their first rank of private. They were assigned to fifteen-man squads. The new privates started their new classes and their field training. The infantry training started. The squad was mixed with male and female. There was combat medics in training. The drill sergeants' screaming returned to the new privates. The new marines lived outside and trained extremely hard. They learned in class and only had two days in the barracks.

Over the planet Kallos.

Dorock looked at the view screen. "Effie, take your five elite hunters. Go get the girl. I want this done quietly."

Effie: "I am at planet Kallos now. No one will know we are here. We are going to scout out everything. You will have your girl."

The screen went dead. High Ambassador Tara crossed her arms. "This better work."

Dorock: "Ma'am it will. She will go and grab one person. Let them do their scouting."

Fourteen weeks in.

General Tatius walked into the meeting room. "How may I help you?" He looked at a much older man past his sixties with a cane. He was an Ittors species but he was different and wore armor. "General, my name is Gesa. I was sent here by my government to watch the transition of our troops, or species, we sent you. You know a lot of the politics garble. General, they do this once a year."

Tatius sat down next to him. "You know, you are early. I sent a message to Command for an Admiral and a Captain to be present. Where is the other person that normally does this?"

Gesa: "General, they changed this up. Do you want the number to call?"

Tatius: "No, that is not necessary. We checked your credentials. You do check out."

Gesa: "Okay, General, you know me and my men have to be escorted. I will enjoy the star base until Command staff gets here. Call me and I will come back. I am waiting for retirement, and I hate leaving my world now."

Tatius: "I will try to get the Admiral here so we can get this over with. I have a question."

Gesa: "Yes."

Tatius: "Why do you walk with a cane? I never saw one of your species with one."

Gesa: "My Emperor has one."

Tatius: "That was because of a battle wound. He told me himself."

Gesa: "Well, I went hunting and a savage through a spear into my leg. My cane is made by the wood of that spear."

Tatius: "I have a stone knife that has that wood on it."

Gesa: "How nice." Tatius: "Yes, you can go."

Gesa: "Bye."

The old man got up and walked out. The General thought, *that wood from his cane is from M793. How did he get the wood? No one is allowed to hunt there or be there.* General Tatius waited to hear the military police. The officer called and told Tatius that Gesa left the base. He walked to his office and turned on the view screen. "Admiral Trey, he left."

Trey: "Okay, hold Gesa up as long as you can. I need to get some friends together. Captain Davis will be here at the end of the week."

Tatius: "Sir, I must say. This is the first time an inspector came in a three-hundred-meter-long ship and did not go to the Embassy or stay there. You know the Ittors. They want us to meet them there. Gesa calls it a personal yacht. We tried scanning it, but he has reflectors on it."

Old Glory! In the grassy field.

A fifteen-man squad was laying in the grass after their infantry basic training. Everyone was laughing as Ion teased Thomas. Orka looked at the sky. "I like this freedom. I understand why so many are willing to fight and die for it. It is beautiful. There was a great man who said in 2041, America can never be defeated. The founding fathers made this for us all and was thinking of us all. They gave us the greatest powers and wanted us to protect them. The power of education, the power to read, write, and do math. The United States of America will always be a Constitutional Republic. It is not a country, it is not a government, it is not a flag. It is the people. It is in all the people. The people were the ones who made the flag. It is in our hearts and minds. United States is freedom and shall and will always be free because of the people. Freedom is in everyone's hearts and minds. He said what the red, white, and blue mean on the flag of his country. Stars mean the states. Stripes mean the thirteen colonies. Blue means sea to shining sea. White means peace and prosperity. Red means the blood of the men and women who sacrificed themselves and their families sacrificed for their peoples' freedoms. That is the highest of all honors."

Joseph smiled with his eyes closed. "That is beautiful. Orka, you asked me to train you better to fight."

Ion grabbed his arm. "Yes, I want to learn."

Thomas turned and grabbed Ion's leg. "Yes, me too."

Alice tried dragging Joseph by his leg. "Come on, let us train. That should be fun."

Thomas looked at him. "Joseph, yes let's train."

Joseph looked at everyone. "I said Orka, not you others. Okay I will train the rest of you misfits."

The following morning.

Joseph was helping clean the barracks. He put his things in his closet properly. "Joseph."

He looked and saw Captain Davis. He stood at attention. "Ma'am, yes ma'am."

She pointed at the tags on his battle dress shirt. "I see you got your tags. Oh, General Tatius wants to see you in his office. Dismissed." Joseph closed his closet and walked to the main building.

Office

Orka and Joseph stood in front of General Tatius. "Sorry to inform you. You're outing you had planned. It is canceled. Joseph, you are allowed to leave the base to go to the stores around the base only. Then return. The military police have to be on station. The beach and waterways on base only. That is all, dismissed."

Barracks

Orka was in the barracks moving around some books. A Lance Corporal saw Orka's closet open. There was a picture on the inside door. "Is he your boyfriend?"

Orka jumped and closed the closet door. "No!"

Alice opened her mouth loudly. "Yes, he is! That is your boyfriend! You love, love him!" Alice and the ladies of the barracks laughed. Orka threw a toilet paper roll at Alice's head. The roll hit her and it bounced off her head. The ladies all laughed.

Orka looked at Alice. "Leave me alone."

Lance Corporal looked at Orka. "How old are you?"

She smiled. "Fifteen now."

Alice jumped in again. "Fifteen tomorrow and Joseph will be seventeen." Lance Corporal looked at Alice acting girl crazy and teasing Orka.

Alice: "You love him. Just admit it."

The lance Corporal looked at Orka. "I will say this. Maybe you both are not ready for that love step, but I see you both care for each other. That is beautiful." Alice jumped to attention, and everyone jumped too.

Captain Davis walked in. "Ladies relax. I am here tonight for lady talk."

Late night in the mess hall.

Camille walked into the cafeteria. The lady behind the counter stood up and looked at her as an old man cleaned and mopped the floors. All the tables were moved and numbered. The middle-age woman walked closer. "How may I help you?"

Captain Davis turned on her jammer on her belt. "Hi, can I see IDs and is this mess hall open all night? Is it twenty-four hours?"

The lady had her ID on a chain where it was visible. She showed the Captain. "Yes, this cafeteria is open twenty-four hours."

Camille scanned the ID and looked at the data pad. Camille: "You've worked here for ten years?"

Lady: "Oh, yes, I do. I like this night work."

Camille: "See anything strange?"

The lady took a step back. "Is this an investigation? Am I being Investigated? I am sorry for taking the food. It was going to go bad."

Camille put her hand up. "You are okay. It is okay to take some food. I am looking into something happening on the base. I cannot say anything."

The lady looked down. "Sorry. There was something. I told the new boss. He said forget it."

Camille looked around the cafeteria. "Tell me."

Lady: "Well, Freyja, the old man, was not working that night and a new guy worked for him. Only that night. A maintenance crew came to work on the tables. It was strange because they just removed the legs and put new ones on. The other strange thing was they were not military. I never saw the new guy again or that crew. The new boss numbered the tables and told Freyja to put the tables where the numbers say. Oh, they put something in the ground. There were other things. They put them in the trees and the bushes. They put small lamps for the walkway and around other buildings. The old lady on that day said they worked with the gardeners. Her granddaughter goes to the academy."

The Captain pointed. "Is that Freyja?"

Lady: "Yes, that is."

Camille: "Okay, do not tell anyone we talked and tell the old lady I want to see her in the General's office. The old lady's name?"

Lady: "Oh, yes. I will not. Her name is Nora."

Captain Davis walked to the old man. "Your name is Freyja?"

Freyja looked at her. "It is about time. I put that report in months ago. The new boss took the report and told me he would put in the report. I wrote a new report up and walked it to the main building. I gave it to a Captain. He told me he would make sure the General would get it."

Camille looked at him. "You remember what Captain?"

He looked at her. "He is military police and he said he was intelligence. He had a MP on his arm."

Camille: "What's on the reports?"

Freyja: "The table leg I fixed and the things in the ground also. The ground lamp I broke."

Camille: "Where is the broken lamp?"

Freyja: "Go to that table that is standing up and look at it. The lamp is still in my locker." She looked at the table. "Can you bring me the broken lamp?"

Freyja: "Yes, it will take me some time. I will be right back." Freyja walked away as Camille walked to the table. She scanned the table. The Captain found antennas and electrical listening devices in the legs of the table. She scanned the floor and found scanners in the floor.

Freyja walked back with the bag. "You can have this."

Camille: "Do not tell anyone that we talked."

Freyja: "I am not saying a thing."

Camille walked to the lady behind the counter and held up her data pad. Camille: "Was he here?"

The lady looked at the picture. "That is the new guy that was here."

Captain smiled. "Thank you, and remember I was not here." She walked out of the building and saw Joseph sitting on a small wall.

Camille walked to him. "Hi, you do not have to get up. Joseph, what are you doing out here?"

Joseph: "Ma'am, I get up at this time for morning exercises. What are you doing, may I ask?"

She looked at him. "Yes, you can. I am doing an investigation. You will learn in time. You have to do the same for your job."

Orka walked up to them. "Hello, Ma'am."

Joseph pointed. "You have the lamp I broke."

Camille: "I thought Freyja broke this."

Joseph: "No, I did."

Camille: "How, Joseph?"

Joseph: "Freyja is a nice man. I helped him move food to his car. Trust me you, wanted this food to go. I dropped a can and it hit the lamp. It broke. I hope he is not in trouble."

Camille: "No, he is not. I know everyone takes food. We order a lot of it and a small amount spoils. Well, I have it now. The lamp. I will see you two around and have a nice day. Oh, I was not here."

Joseph: "Yes, Ma'am." Captain Davis walked away as their friends came. Camille turned off her jammer and picked up her phone as she walked into the main building. General Tatius just got up and sounded groggy. "Yes?!"

Camille: "This is Captain Davis. General, you need to get to your office now."

Tatius: "You found something?"

Camile: "General, I found more than something. I found a lot. I am having the main building scanned now."

Tatius: "Do so. I will be there shortly."

After morning exercises.

Thomas walked to Alice. "I am not talking to you. You are acting crazy."

Ion walked over. "She always acts like that. We are going for the run in the woods."

Alice: "I am allowed to be crazy. We need to get our things for the run."

Orka looked at them. "We can take our NAV test. It will be easy. We just have to run to each point and scan the bar code and hit the button. The camera scans us and tells the computer we were there. The navigations teacher looks at it and we pass. All we have to do is use the compass and read the map, then get to each point. Easy as that."

Alice: "How do you know what bar code? There are hundreds of them."

Orka: "They give you a bar code with numbers. What happened? Left your brain on off?"

Alice: "Do not go there."

Orka: "I will go there."

Thomas raised his hands. "Ladies. Let's go."

Ion looked at them. "You two want to act crazy and love each other. Do it on your own time. Joseph, how do you deal with them?"

Joseph shrugged his shoulders. "I do not know."

Orka touched his hand. "See you later."

Alice ran over a grabbed Joseph's hand. "I will see you later." Joseph looked at her weirdly. Orka looked at her letting go of his hand slowly so she could see.

Orka: "Oh, you."

Ion: "Stop, what's got into you two? Let's go." Alice stuck her tongue out at her. Orka did the same, but she waited as Alice stuck her tongue out. She went to grab her tongue but missed.

Alice: "You missed."

Thomas rolled his eyes. "What the? Let's go."

Joseph saw the rest of his squad run to the barracks to get their things to run in the woods. Orka: "Well, we will be the last ones."

General's office.

Tatius: "Captain, this is going to be good."

Camille looked at him. "Well, this building is scanned and clean. We did find some listening devices aimed at the windows. We are lucky, the meeting rooms are in the middle of the building. We have twenty-four hours for cleanup of all spy equipment. MP stands and patrols around the building and roof. We also have what I believe to be some traitors amongst us."

General Tatius drank his morning coffee. "This coffee you humans make is a good scent. Now I can jam this whole base, but it will not help. They are using closed in receivers. That means someone is driving by or walking. They are also bouncing the message from each device. We have to find them and stop them. I will talk to the Admiral. Keep looking. We will leave everything where it is."

The head of the Military Police walked in. "Sir, you called."

Tatius pointed at the Colonel. "This is Colonel Aodh. There is a special forces team here?"

Aodh "Yes, Sir. You mean the Elementals?" Camille smiled because she had only heard of operations like this. She always wanted to be part of something like this.

Tatius: "Colonel, you will work with Captain Davis. We will get these spies and find these traitors." The window was open, and they heard screams coming from the training woods.

Tatius: "Colonel, get out there and get that team into my office."

Camille stood up. "We will find them, or we will hear more of that."

At the gate.

The military police looked at Joseph. "You have to take the longer run. Private, that is what it says here."

Orka looked at him. "Good for you. You passed all your NAV classes. We are going now. See you on the other side." His friends went running through the gate.

MP: "You can start running. Your equipment checks out. You run fast enough and you can cross their trail." Joseph ran through the gate.

Woods

Effie looked at the group running into the woods and picked up the data phone. Hunter: "She is in the run. There are pointy eared, a human and a slave trooper running with her. The human they want dead is running alone. I know what they said, but we can get him. He is a human boy."

Effie looked at her phone. "Do it fast, I am going to help the others get the girl."

Orka looked into the woods as she ran. Alice was first in the group through the gate, and she looked like she never touched the ground as she ran. She was next through the gate, and she looked back. Ion was behind her some meters and was having fun with the run. Thomas was in the back taking his time and looking around at the scenery. Orka's mind was on Joseph's run, and she hoped he was having fun. Orka glanced at the map tied on her forearm. She saw they will cross paths. She watched Alice run around the bend and the forest came to life. The four elite hunters stood up and charged at Orka. Ion charged forward, but one of the hunters turned and was ready for him. The elite tackled Ion to the floor and held him down. One of the hunters grabbed Orka and pinned her against a large tree.

Thomas jumped on the back of the hunter pinning Ion to the floor and forced his knife through the back of the hunter and it came out his chest. The other hunter jumped on the back of Thomas, but Ion already rolled out from under the dead hunter and jumped on the back of the hunter. He stabbed him multiple times. Someone threw a knife into the hunter's neck that was pinning Orka. The last elite hunter charged Alice, but never made it to her. Orka through her knife and hit the hunter in the back of his neck. They looked at each other, then they heard a scream in the distance. A military police truck drove up to them and a five-man MP squad jumped out fully armed.

Effie heard a scream behind her. She turned and saw Joseph looking at her a quarter mile away. He was standing over the bodies of two hunters. He had a hunter's decapitated head in his hand. She took a step back and was surprised. "What are you?! No human is that strong or can move or run that fast!" He was now only one hundred feet from her. Joseph looked into her eyes. Effie felt fear run through her soul. Her body could not move. She looked quickly at her data phone and saw it was being jammed.

"You are Death!" Joseph moved so fast she could hardly see him. He was thirty feet from her. "You are the monster from M793! I remember you! You're the boy! We all think you are still on that planet but here you are!" Effie tried to raise her pistol, but Joseph dodged side to side as she fired wildly, trying to hit him. The last thing she heard from behind her was, "Death!" The military police heard another scream. "Okay, you Privates stay here. We will check that out. There are more MPs on the way." Joseph came running down the road. Alice looked at Orka. "See. There he is. He is fine."

General's office.

Tatius looked at Captain Davis and put down the phone. "That was the MPs. No mangled bodies but one head was off a hunter. The privates killed the elite hunters. Your boy killed more. The only reason I am not taking this higher up is because the higher ups want this too. The hunter crime boss is out of control. Emperor Xona wants them dead. He wants to hold the peace." Camille looked up as Luthien walked in and Tatius raised his hand.

Tatius: "Before you say anything. We heard the screams too. The privates killed the hunters. They were in training. They are doing their end of the basic infantry training. The privates killed six hunters."

Luthien shook her head. "Your boy again, but cleaner. I do not know. The hunters are not allowed on this world. They are dying. I have to call the High Ambassador."

Camille had a grin on her face. Camille: "Call the High Ambassador. Tell him to call her. She will not like the news. Tell him we will build him that house he was joking about."

On the planet Searrun.

High Ambassador Tara slammed all four of her fists into the desk. She then grabbed the largest book next to her and threw it into the wall. "That High Ambassador Ishton!" She flipped a table. "He asked me! Asked me! When will I come to the planet?! He is crazy!" She threw a glass across the room. "He wants me to get the dead! He is asking me to do this personally!" Tara walked to a window. "You are making us look like fools! The hunters are rushing in and not looking. How many hunters are dead now?! The last ones did not scout out the area! We still have the spies. Get out and get me smarter hunters. The ones that ask for a lot of money."

Dorock stood up. "I will make a call out for my finest."

Tara: "You better!"

On the planet Kallos.

A team of marines walked into a shopping store. Thomas looked at everyone. "It is nice the Admiral let us use the truck. Now the list. Get what is on it. Thank you for your help."

Luke: "This will be fun. Karg you with me."

Karg looked at Thomas. "Why did you put me with this human?"

Thomas: "Karg, you want to escort Joseph?"

Karg: "No."

Thomas: "Then go with Luke."

Karg: "He is human."

Thomas: "Go!"

Thomas looked around the store. "Joseph, what will you get her? Orka likes Flowers."

Joseph: "Remember, she likes flowers, and she eats them."

Thomas: "Well, she loves eating chocolates."

Joseph: "Do you know she loves chocolates, but her people get a little high from it. I am going to get her underwater flowers. She loves drinking the water that surrounds the plant." He walked to the fish section.

Joseph: "Shrimp and mackerel with chocolates. Oh, and the other sea life she likes. She likes that." Thomas looked about and got Orka flowers and chocolate.

Joseph looked at David. "No balloons. The General said no balloons on base. We can get one saying happy birthday, but it has to be empty. The General is giving us time so we can do this."

Ion called out to Joseph and the squad came running to see what he found. Ion: "Joseph, you want to woo my sister?"

Thomas jumped in the way and raised his hands as the squad laughed. Thomas: "No, no, no! They are not ready for that. Humans get married in their twenties. They do not want to get thrown out of the military. They want a military career. They got strict rules to follow."

Joseph looked at Thomas. "What is woo?"

Thomas: "Ion get those water flowers."

Ion looked at him. "Why are you acting like Alice, crazy? Well, the women of my world like these flowers. I did that to my mate."

Thomas raised his hands. "We have to get this ready. No more of this wooing!"

The morning exercises.

Joseph and Orka met that morning and trained hard. They went to their classes to learn proper etiquette. Orka went to her tech class and Joseph went to his morning class. She went to the medical bay to work before lunch. A doctor grabbed a medical scanner from the table and ran to the emergency room. Orka looked about for her new scanner that Alice and she were testing. A doctor walked to her. Doctor: "Is this yours? It is not the normal scanner they give us."

Orka looked at him. "Yes, Sir. It is one I made. Alice and I am testing this. We made that scanner." The doctor gave the medical scanner to her.

Doctor: "I have some people that can help."

She smiled. "Sir, that would be greatly appreciated."

Doctor: "Oh, one other thing. That scanner just made my life easier, and it saved lives. It can detect more, and it works quicker. It also gives more information that is needed at the time of any science, rescue, emergency, and hospital or medical center. I will get you some people to help with it." The doctor walked away and she looked around. Orka jumped up and smiled.

She walked to the mess hall and found Alice and some of her friends. Orka: "Alice, I have to tell you something, but I have a question."

Alice grabbed her hand. "Look, they got seaweed."

Orka looked at her. "Where are the guys?"

Alice looked at the other ladies of the medical bay and then at Orka. "Oh, I forgot. They are in training."

The Lance Corporal walked to them. "You will see him later for dinner."

Orka looked at Alice. "We are all in the same squad. We all train together. We are one team."

Alice: "Well, forget that. They have them doing something."

Orka: "What something? We have to be there. That is our squad."

Alice: "Forget that. They just wanted them." Orka: "Oh, a doctor used our scanner we are working on, and it works. He said he will get us some help and it saved lives in the hospital. It works."

Alice hugged her. "That is good. That is very good." They had lunch together and talked about their work on the new scanner. Orka looked about wondering what they had the guys doing.

Hospital

Orka worked at the medical bay and all her friends disappeared. She looked around and saw no one. Leonova walked to her. "We are going to the beach. The General is letting us eat on the beach." Then Orka saw Tomy. "Come on Orka, you will like this." They walked out of the hospital into the night. Tomy escorted Orka through the dimly lit field of the forest. As they got closer to the beach, they saw fire pits placed about to light the darkness of the night. Ion joined them and they saw a circle of people. Orka now saw all her friends. They escorted Orka to the circle. She stopped, but Ion pushed her to the center of the circle.

Ion: "Orka, I know you do not understand but you will learn." Ion left her there in the center.

Luthien walked to her. "I must say it is nice to get to know you."

Captain Davis walked to Orka. "This is a nice party in your honor, Orka. I know you read about surprise parties and birthday parties. This is your Happy first birthday for you being fifteen." Orka was surprised and cried tears of joy. The squad came out of the dark with a beautifully made cake. Orka was ecstatic. They placed the cake down on a well decorated table. Ion walked in front of Orka and kneeled down. "I know you are learning your species' customs. We bow to the persons with their special day, like birthdays, then we dance around them." Ion jumped up and began dancing around Orka. As he did so, he grabbed Joseph, and they danced around her. Then, others joined in with the fun. Everyone was dancing around Orka, and she laughed and cried for joy.

Then, they were rudely interrupted by Gesa as he walked out of the dark with his staff. "How dare you?! This is illegal and not permitted." Two of his men came out from behind him. The military police reacted quickly and stood in their way. General Tatius walked past Gesa and walked to Luthien. "There is no such law or rule."

Gesa looked at her. "I will bring this to the Admiral. I want this disbanded."

Rear Admiral Trey walked past him. "I approved of this, and it was asked for some time ago."

Gesa looked at Admiral Trey. "I tried to meet with you. All I got was the Captain or the General or their staff."

Trey looked at him. "How did you get on this beach?"

Gesa looked about. "We walked across the beach. I will bring this to my Ambassador."

He heard a strange voice from his left. "The Admiral is busy with us."

Gesa looked at Ambassador Tyshdish walking by him. "You happened to walk past the military police without talking to them. As we walked here, we watched your shuttle land."

He heard another voice from his right as Gesa looked and saw Ambassador Dugor. "Last time I checked you could only be here for inspection. You are breaking the peace accords. Your Emperor will not be happy about the news. You have an out-of-control crime lord. I will personally talk to your Head Ambassador about this hunter problem on this world. No hunters are to work on any of our worlds. You ITS! Oh, you cannot be on any of the Nanos worlds. The Ittors people do not want Nanos on their world because the Ittors lost the war. You have to stay in orbit. So, leave!" Ambassador Zev walked past them.

High Ambassador Ishton walked up to Gesa. "I see all I need to know." Gesa turned and walked to his shuttle, and they watched him leave.

Admiral Trey walked over to a box and pushed a button. Modern music came from the radio. Trey: "Okay everyone let's have fun. That is an order." Alice ran and grabbed Orka and danced with her. Thomas and Tomy got Joseph and Orka to dance together. They taught them how to dance.

Ambassador Zev walked over to Admiral Trey. "Is it true, the spies?"

Trey looked around. "Yes, but we are removing all the spy equipment from the fields first. There will be multiple arrests soon. We almost know where they have their base."

Zev: "Is that him and is that her?"

Trey: "Yes, that is."

Zev: "I hear a lot about her, but I am interested in him. I am happy he is on our side."

Ambassador Dugor looked at them. "Tell me about him. His history."

Trey watched the cadets dancing with some of the officers and staff. "Well, I got to planet M793, and the archaeologist reported he was there. We watched him and M793 was his playground. There are ancient cities there. He got one of the cities working. I got there as an Ittors ship left. We landed a building for the scientist. We use it from time to time. We tried hard to get him off, but we had to wait. Now he is here."

Ambassador Tyshdish looked at everyone having fun at the party. "Before I get into this fun, as I will tell the rest of you to do as well, more than half the government is against the Emperor. His own people do not like him wanting to free these slaves. I do not know why all the secrets for what is happening now. Those control chips and spying on their allies. This is a cold war. We must get ready for what comes tomorrow."

The morning exercises.

0400 (4AM) came and they saw the new cadets running around and in the next mess hall. They said their goodbyes to some of their friends. Thomas looked at Orka. "I will be at the academy ten minutes away and I will be working in that medical bay and hospital." They said their goodbyes and watched Tomy and Thomas leave. A lot of their boot camp friends were shipped out. The new people came onto the base. Joseph walked onto the floor of the barracks. A Sergeant stopped him. "Private, who are you?"

Joseph stood: "Sergeant, I am Private Joseph Ramiro. Sergeant."

Sergeant: "Okay, you are with me for advanced infantry training. We still have a month, but I want to be ready now. What are you doing now?"

Joseph: "Sergeant, I have etiquette class and other classes."

The Sergeant looked at his data tablet. "Okay, after that meet with me in the mess hall. I have to go to medical. I have some people over there that I have to get."

Joseph: "Yes, Sergeant." Joseph went to his classes.

Hospital

The Sergeant walked to the hospital and asked around for the Privates. He walked up to Alice and Orka. "Privates, I need both of your names."

Alice: "Private Alice Oakwing, Sergeant."

Orka: "Private Orka, Sergeant."

The Sergeant looked at Orka. "I need numbers and letters from your helmet. Your species does not have last names."

Orka looked down. "Micky is on my helmet, Sergeant."

The Sergeant looked at her. "It is okay kid, look up. Micky it is. Privates you have classes?" Alice/ Orka: "Yes, Sergeant."

Sergeant: "Okay, come meet me after the classes at the mess hall."

Alice watched the Sergeant walk out of the hospital. She looked at Orka. "Micky!" Orka: "Alice do not start." Alice: "Micky! Micky!"

Orka looked at her. "We got work to do."

Alice: "Micky!" As Alice turned Orka slapped her bottom. She jumped.

Alice: "Ouch, what?"

Orka: "Go away."

Orka turned and Alice slapped her bottom. Orka: "Ouch." Orka turned as Alice walked up to the doctor. Orka: "Alice, I will get you."

Mess hall.

After classes, Joseph walked into the empty mess hall. He walked into the second hall and saw cadets working on the tables of the cafeteria, then he walked into the next hall. The Sergeant was there with other marines. Joseph recognized everyone there, but there were new marines there. The Sergeant looked at him. "We were waiting for you."

Joseph: "Sergeant, I had class on the other side of the base."

Sergeant: "I know." The Sergeant motioned for Joseph to sit on the floor with the others. "Okay, I have thirty marines. After lunch all of you will pack and move to the new barracks. After the move in and settle in, you will start getting everything you need. We will be out in the field for seven weeks and classes will be in the field. Two of you have to see the General for rank up. Do the move." He walked to Orka and Joseph. "Go see the General. He is waiting for you."

The Sergeant got up and walked away. They went to lunch and found that they had changed the floors. There were new tables and chairs. Orka and Joseph walked out of the mess hall and saw engineering teams with hand-held minesweepers. They were looking for something in the ground. They would pull it out and throw it into the back of the truck. Military police were everywhere. Ten officers were standing over the new civilian boss of the cafeteria. He was hand cuffed and on the floor. He screamed out. "I did not do anything!" They put him in a van. Tatius watched Joseph and Orka walk into the office. He waved at them to come over to him. They walked to the General. "Congratulations, you both are now Private First Class. Good luck both of you." General Tatius shook their hands and went on his way.

They ran to the barracks and packed their things. A truck drove up and they loaded it up and climbed on. The truck drove them to the new barracks. They walked onto the floor and found it was divided into two parts. Two Sergeants met them on the floor. One sergeant walked forward. "We are your training,

Sergeants. The ladies to the left and the guys are to the right. The bathroom is in the middle of the floor and the showers are at the end of the barracks." The thirty marines got their places in the barracks.

Orka was putting her things away. Sergeant Karen Beau walked up to her. "You got flowers."

Alice smiled. "Yes, Sergeant. It was her birthday last week."

Then the sergeant saw the pictures. "He is on the other side."

Orka: "Yes, Sergeant. He is. Sergeant." She saw a picture of Joseph in uniform and saw the dark green, black, and gray tag. She saw the clear tag on Orka. Karen knew not to ask, and she knew why the two of them got ranked up.

Karen: "Happy birthday and congratulations on the rank up." The Sergeant walked away and saw the other Sergeant.

The Sergeant looked at her. "You have a minute, Karen?"

Karen: "Yes."

He looked at her and whispered, "Remember, you wanted someone in your group to have a black and gray tag. This one has a dark green, black, and gray tag. He is in your group."

Karen looked at him. "I got off that shuttle and I found many people with black and gray tags, but then I saw some other people with dark green, black, and gray tags. The base I came from, I found two. I went home to Earth and saw my family. I saw someone there with one of those tags."

Sergeant: "You have to tell me how he shoots and fights."

She looked around. "Well, we will see." The Sergeant walked into the male section. He saw Joseph putting his things away and then he saw the tag and a picture. "That lady is on the other side."

Ion walked forward. "Yes, she is my sister."

Joseph put his things in the closet. "Yes, Sergeant. Most of us here went through boot together." The Sergeant heard someone walk up behind him.

He turned and saw Captain Davis. She walked to Joseph. "The Admiral wants to talk to you and Orka."

Camille looked at the Sergeant. "Sergeants, meet me outside."

He walked outside and saw Sergeant Beau standing there waiting. Camille: "Sergeants you are in training and new at this. I overheard you both. Stop looking for the black and gray tags. Many of them took theirs off their uniforms, like I did. So, you do not know who they are. Do not ask, do not tell. Have a good day." Captain Davis walked away. Joseph and Orka walked out of the barracks and to the main building.

The Sergeant looked at Karen. "There is a sea of them here. No more talk of this." She shook her head yes. She knew what the color matches mean, but this one was new to her. She did not know what the dark green with the black and gray tag meant.

After the meeting with the Admiral

Orka looked at Joseph and he had a leather bag. Orka: "You know I hate that thing."

He looked at her as they walked to the barracks. "It is a copy, and they want me to put it in the closet."

Orka: "No, you do not understand, I hate that thing."

He looked at her. "You tell me all the time. Stop, you are free now. No one can take you back. They want this thing in the closet, and that is it." They ran to the barracks.

On the planet Searrun.

Thal walked in with Dorock. "Ma'am. He is here."

Ambassador Tara looked at Thal. "I know you. I am very happy to see you."

Thal: "Ma'am, Let's talk business. I know your problem. I told Dorock. Your hunters are in a rush. There are some large dangerous animals there. Forget the animals. The Marines are the problem. You send hunters to the marines. I have the crew that can get that girl. The spies, they have been found."

She looked at him. "How do you know? I do not have that information."

Thal: "Ma'am, the upper government. Then you know."

Tara looked at him. "I am fifth!"

Thal looked out the window. "The minister knows."

She got up from her desk and walked to the window where Thal stood. "The minister is third. Dorock, you did me good. Now what do you suggest Thal?"

Thal: "Let them get the spies. I will use their work and get the girl and the boy. Dorock knows I am the special forces hunter of our people."

On the planet Kallos.

Thomas walked into Tomy's new apartment and greeted him. "Hi, how are you. Look at this new apartment. I was surprised how much this place is. Oh, I was thinking and talking to my mother and sister. We want to adopt Orka and Joseph."

Thomas closed the front door. "My father wants to adopt them. My mother thinks it would be nice if you and I adopt them."

Tomy smiled. "Yes, I say yes, but tell me about Joseph."

Thomas looked at him. "I cannot answer that question and I will not."

Tomy: "Come on Thomas. I know Joseph is human and he ended up on some horrifying planet. Orka got on some shuttle that ended up on his planet. Then, Joseph and Orka found each other."

Thomas: "Tomy, that is all you need to know, okay? Let us help them have a normal life. I have to get up early and get to the academy. I need to get my uniform, schedule, and books ready. Help me."

Tomy: "Oh, you know I will. I found this nice place to eat. Let's go."

On base.

Captain Davis looked at the night sky and walked into the main building. She walked into the meeting room. The holographic table was on. Admiral Trey, General Tatius, and Colonel Aodh stood around the table. Camille studied the table. "Hello, everyone. What we are looking at is an apartment building. The Elementals teams are moving in with Special Reaction Teams of the military police and the other MPs are on the ground to prevent any of the spies from escaping. We have ID'd all of the spies and their guards."

Ambassador Ishton walked in. "Hello, good I did not miss anything. The green and blue are our men or personnel."

Captain Davis pointed. "These are the guards and spies in red. We know everything about them, and we have already taken their basement strong hold. There was no one in there and it was unguarded. You can see our officers in the base, cleaning it out."

Ishton raised his hand. "I know this is happening in the dead of night or early morning. How fast and how quiet is this happening?"

Trey: "The United Planets have right of privacy laws. We can break that law for terrorist acts or spying on government from a foreign act. We first had to prove this to the high court. We had to get court approvals to do this operation. We have thermal on, and the teams are going into the spy's apartment. You can see the neighbors are still sleeping. They are the ones in white. The neighbors will wake in the morning and not know what happened." Ishton watched a team quietly open a door and turn off the alarms. They walked in and grabbed the spy. The spy was gagged, and they were shackled and given to the reaction team.

Ishton: "How did you deal with the dogs?"

General Tatius pointed. "The dogs are not well trained. We have dogs too. We send our dog in, and it brings out their dog. That is one way we get their animals. The other is the teams attract the animal and stun it, then they cage the animal and remove it. The animals will wake up in the pound."

Ishton watched them move the spy's equipment. "This is impressive. Their guards are being arrested quietly by the teams."

The morning exercises.

Alice walked up to Joseph. "We are going to be in the same squad. Ion and Orka are on the other one."

Ion looked at Alice. "You mean fire teams. There are four in a fire team. We are a fifteen personnel squad."

Alice was imagining and acted as if she was loading a big gun with a heavy round. "Yes, I mean fire team."

Joseph looked at her. "You are going to like what we do now."

Orka looked at Alice. "You want to shoot the big guns and blow things up? I want to do that too."

Alice: "Yes, I want to blow things up and shoot the big guns. This is going to be fun." They walked to the mess hall. Alice acted as if she had a missile launcher.

Ion looked at Joseph. "What is wrong with her?"

Joseph: "I do not know, but it is okay."

Orka laughed. "She dropped herself too much on her head."

Alice looked at them. "Hay, I am right here! Look, the Army is in town. They are walking through again."

Ion: "They always walk through. We walk through their area."

They watched the Army platoon walk down the street. One of the army guys hit his pal on the shoulder and walked straight to Joseph. "What are you doing here?!"

Joseph looked at him. "I joined the Marines. It is good to see you to brother."

"What happened to your eyes? Why didn't you come home?" He grabbed his little brother Joseph. "I want an answer."

Joseph: "Well, there are laws now on runaways. That is how I got here, and you?"

"I joined like your other brother."

Alice moved over to them. "Let him go." His brother went to push Alice, but he felt Joseph grab him. He was amazed at the strength Joseph had. He could not move.

Joseph: "Oliver, no. This is between you and I, brother."

Oliver: "I am a Corporal of the army. Let me go."

Orka looked at him. "Corporal, your platoon leader is looking for you."

Oliver: "Quiet you alien."

Joseph: "Do not talk to her like that."

"What is going on here Corporal?! Let go of him." Everyone looked back at the Army Lieutenant.

Joseph: "Sir, yes, Sir."

Joseph let go of his brother and saw Captain Davis. The Army Lieutenant looked at Oliver. "I want an explanation. Now! The Navy Captain brought my attention to this action of yours. You, Corporal. Are you part of this?"

Oliver's friend: "No, Sir."

Lieutenant: "Then get back to your platoon." Oliver's friend ran back to the platoon waiting.

Lieutenant: "I want an answer."

Oliver: "Sir, he is my brother."

Lieutenant: "And!"

Oliver: "Sir, I just wanted to talk to him."

Lieutenant: "Do you see his tag?"

Oliver: "Yes, Sir. What does it mean?"

Captain Davis walked over. "Corporal! It means none of your business, like I told your Lieutenant. You lost someone. So, you are brothers. I will give you time to talk. Show some respect. You are the alien on this world, Corporal."

Oliver: "Sorry Ma'am."

Lieutenant: "Sorry, Ma'am. I will not let this happen again. Corporal get back to the platoon. You want to talk to him, we will give you time to talk, but now is my time and you are wasting my time!"

Oliver ran back to his platoon and the Sergeant jumped on him. He screamed at Oliver. "The Marines do not take kindly to someone trying to abuse one of their own. If you want, I will hand feed you to them. You are lucky. The Marine was about to stomp you into next year. The Army is defenders and Marines is special forces of the Navy. They are Marines and they are all special assault teams. Think before you act. You went after his friends. Oh man. We need to talk down the Marines. Call the President. You are crazy. We are in the middle of Leatherneck city, look around. They are all just waiting for you." The Lieutenant walked over. "Corporal, you are not that smart. Let's go. Move out platoon. Marines, we are just passing through." The army platoon walked away. Camille looked around at the people watching. "Navy and Marines, get back to your task. I will have a word with the General and he will call the army. Let them walk through like we always do."

In the main building.

Captain Davis rubbed her exhausted eyes, and she drank coffee. She waited in the security room. A Captain of the Space Navy walked into his office in the morning. Camille walked in behind him. He turned and said, "Hi, how can I help you?" He saw her gun in her hand and slowly reached for his. Then, he saw Colonel Aodh walking in with the MPs.

Aodh: "Please go for your gun traitor! The Major General killed himself this morning. He was going to leave the planet, but he saw us coming." The Captain sat down then quickly grabbed his gun and shot himself in the head. Camille looked at the body on the ground.

Camille: "We already have everything. You just made our job easier."

On planet Searrun.

Dorock kneeled and bowed his head. High Ambassador Tara walked into her office and the doors closed behind her. Tara: "What is going on?"

Dorock looked down. "It is harder to get on Kallos. They are holding up the inspection. They brought in Ambassadors."

She walked to the window and looked out into the night sky. "It sounds like they have started a secret war."

Dorock: "Ma'am, there is no information coming from the planet. They will not let Gesa on the planet until the inspection."

Tara: "What happened to our spy network."

Dorock: "They were found, and all were captured."

Tara looked at Dorock. "They are sending them to the field, then the inspections. That is smart, the young ones will have heavy weapons in the field. It will be harder to get them. Tell Gesa to do everything covertly. Put teams on the ground."

Dorock: "And Thal?"

Tara: "He is always doing things covertly. He plays in the shadows. That is why I like him."

Over Kallos.

Gesa picked up the data phone. "Yes, Dorock."

Dorock: "I need everything done under the table." Gesa put the phone down as he was seated on the bridge. Gesa got up and walked off the bridge as he stroked his beard and smiled. He walked to the middle of the ship and interrupted a card game. "Colonel, I need a three-man team to gather information and a team of ten for support. Wait, make it a team of twenty. Water operations."

The Colonel looked at him. "And."

Gesa: "Colonel, they will be out in the field and their barracks will be locked. Only the military police will be walking around. The officers there will be training cadets or Sergeants. We need this information."

The base.

Orka looked out at the ocean from the beach as she touched her wet hair. Ion and Joseph walked out of the ocean, followed by Alice and her friends. Sergeant Karen Beau walked up to them. She knew they had this time off, but she needed to ask some questions. Karen: "Orka, you did your classes and did your work in medical?"

Orka: "Yes, Sergeant and got seventy five percent of my gear ready, Sergeant."

Karen looked at the ocean. "How about everyone else?"

Orka: "Sergeant, I can only talk for myself, Sergeant."

She looked at her. "The truth, and you will not get anyone in trouble. Just want to know who needs help."

Orka smiled "Okay, Sergeant, Joseph is at eighty five percent, Ion seventy percent, Alice eighty percent, and the others are at a sixty-nine to sixty seven percent ready. We are helping each other."

Karen smiled. "That sounds good. Teamwork is very good. Tell everyone they need to be one hundred percent by tomorrow. We still have one week till training. We are going to be a medical team, but it will be learning advanced infantry training. Have fun." The Sergeant walked away from Orka. Orka saw Joseph throwing Alice and Ion into the water. She ran and tackled Joseph into the water. Sergeant Beau walked back to the trail, then she saw First Sergeant Calup waiting for her.

Calup: "Sergeant, congratulations on becoming Sergeant."

Karen: "Thank you, First Sergeant."

Calup: "You asked about Joseph. General Tatius cleared you. He is taking a lot of classes. Dark green, black, and gray tag, and the black-gray lines on his belt. He is very special and take this advice, when the sun looks as if it is setting in combat, call Joseph and watch the sunrise. Good luck, and train them well."

The barracks.

Sergeant Beau got up to use the bathroom and saw it was 0255 or 2:55AM. She walked out and saw Joseph walk by the military police. Karen walked to the officer. "Did someone leave?"

The officer smiled. "Everyone's still here. No one left." She looked down on the MP uniform as she turned. She saw a black and gray tag. She walked away and walked into the female bunk area. She looked out the window and saw Joseph running to one of the school buildings. The lights started to turn on in the school. There were others running there as well. She thought to herself, *I never knew there were classes at this time. Wait, I saw him come to the barracks late one night. The MP said the same thing. I know why they are lying. No more questions.* She walked into the bathroom and saw Orka.

Orka: "Hello sergeant."

Karen: "Hi, you, okay?"

Orka: "Yes, Sergeant."

Karen: "You okay, you can talk to me off record."

Orka: "Ma'am."

Karen: "Yes."

Orka: "Well, I watch Joseph leave every morning and come back every night to go to training. I just worry about him."

Karen: "He is doing the best thing. You know that."

Orka: "Yes, I know. We make sacrifices so others can live in peace."

Karen: "Yes, that is it. You know freedom is not free. People have to pay for it with their lives so others can live in peace and freedom."

Orka: "Yes, I know. Someone has to stand on that wall."

The young academy.

Kor sat in a tall chair and waved his feet under him. Novear walked to him. The nurse looked at her and smiled. "It is nice they found many families."

Kor: "She is my sister and is the marine coming."

Novear: "My husband is coming. We are going to take you to the computer training."

She looked at the nurse. "Yes, it is nice. They are finding many families through their DNA. I have more family now. Kor, what are you thinking of eating?"

He looked up at her. "Humans make this thing called cheeseburgers and French fries. That is good."

Novear: "Okay, that was easy. Let's go get cheeseburgers. My husband will be with us for one more week. You like trying foods?" Kor shook his head yes.

Novear: "We will try seal tomorrow. I have to take you to my father's farm. He raises them there. You would like it there. There are a lot of animals there. You need to meet my sisters and brothers. Let's go."

The barracks.

The end of the week came. The fifteen-personnel squad started their thirty-mile march to the field to start their advance infantry training. They started in the early morning and met other marines doing the same thing. It was foggy and misty out that morning. They marched all day till the sun set. In the middle of the night, the MP walked with his partner. Both officers knew they were breaking the rules. He checked the doors on one side of the street and his partner checked the other side of the street. They were supposed to check inside all the buildings, but there was no one in the buildings. The military police were down the street and too far to see the Ittors commando team watching them from the roof.

They opened the roof hatch and climbed into the barracks. The commandos found Orka's section and looked around. They looked through everyone's things and found Ion's section. One walked to the data pad on the wall and hit the button. He saw it said Private First-Class Joseph Ramiro. The commando pointed at the section. They opened his closet and saw Orka's dirty slave helmet and collar. The commandos picked the locks of Joseph's private lockers. They found her dirty slave dress and a file that said M793. They read the file and saw the boy was still on the planet. The commando team took pictures and put everything back.

They walked to the ground floor and walked out the barracks. The commandos moved as quickly and quietly as they could. They left the base through the beach and never knew they were being watched. Captain Davis pointed at the view screen. Luthien looked at General Tatius. Luthien: "I have a question. Why put it all on Joseph?"

Tatius: "Well, the story goes the cadet found the collar and the helmet. He took it because he liked how it looked. He was at the embassy, and he walked into the park and found it. He thought he was doing the right thing by saving her dress for her. The dress was destroyed. We had to get one made."

Luthien looked at the screen. "So, no one can blame the government or the military."

Tatius: "The file we left them. We want them to think the boy is still on the planet. We want no one to think we got him off." Tatius pushed a button to change the view screen.

She turned and looked at him. "Smart General, and if they go after Joseph?"

He smiled. "Then they meet the monster."

Out in the fields in the early morning.

They prepared for another day march in heavy rains. The inspection started on the base with many different alien species. They walked into the barracks of Orka and Joseph. Gesa knew exactly what closet to open.

Gesa: "Who is this person?"

Admiral Trey took his time walking over to Gesa. He hit a button. "Private first class. I remember him. He found a helmet and a collar. If I remember he was on your world at the embassy. He walked out into the park. How I remember it is the look of that helmet."

Gesa looked at Trey. "This is not the original one. Do you know where it may be?"

Trey looked at the helmet. "I do not know."

Gesa: "But Admiral."

Admiral Trey raised his hand. "I do not know. I do not know where or what everyone on this base does on their time off. I know he found that collar and a helmet of one of them. One got on without them on." Gesa took a step back in surprise.

Trey: "What is wrong? The private does not know your laws or customs." Trey walked away and Ambassador Zev looked at Gesa.

Zev: "You look as if you lost something very valuable." Gesa looked down and walked away. He made it to his luxurious quarters on his ship.

He grabbed the data phone. "Dorock, we have a problem."

On the planet Searrun.

Dorock kneeled and looked at the High Ambassador Tara behind her desk. "Dorock, that boy does not know the customs of our people. I do not have to get the humans involved. I do not care, there are exceptions to the rules. Question the boy and get me the helmet and the collar. Find her and get the child from the academy. No more delays." She stood up from her desk. "This is taking too long. How can one human boy be a massive problem? You have the money, manpower, and men. Get me the girl and boy. And kill that monster that is killing the hunters. I am tired of these meetings! Get this done now!"

On the planet Kallos.

They trained extra hard in the field. They learned heavy weapons, advanced tactics, and joint operations. They learned how to work with other branches of the military. The new marines learned communications, and they called in planetary barrage, air support, bombing runs, artillery, missile strikes, and rocket attacks. The marines learned about their new tactical combat suits. They also learned nuclear, biological, and chemical warfare. They learned advanced warfare and urban warfare. They learned history, strategy, and tactics. The marines took classes on old and new equipment. The squad laughed at themselves as they talked about embarrassing and crazy stories they went through.

Ion laughed at Joseph. "You had Alice, and she drove you crazy. I feel bad Zor."

Zor looked at them. "I was on fire and Joseph's face was black."

Mar pointed at Ion. "You had Orka."

Ion laughed. "She is just as bad." Orka and Alice laughed at the fun they had.

Sergeant Karen Beau talked to the Sergeant by her tent. "He is impressive in everything. He moved a military jeep by hand. Well, picked up half of it to get something that rolled under it."

The Sergeant put his finger over his mouth and walked away. They did their ten weeks and two weeks were added on. Sergeant Beau got them a ride on one of the small tactical shuttles. The large side doors were open. Orka had her legs hanging out with Alice and Ion. Joseph was at the other door. She remembered what they told her. When the transport is landing raise your legs. This is because if the landing gear fails, her legs do not get crushed. They flew low over the trees or between them. It was better than walking back sixty miles. They all had new bags that carried their new books and data pads. The marines enjoyed the wind in their faces. They flew over the barracks, watching cadets and marines training.

The shuttle came down for a landing in the empty parade field. Sergeant Beau tapped them on their helmets for them to raise their legs. The pilot was so good they never landed. The landing gear never touched the ground and it hovered. Its landing gear was one inch off the ground. The fifteen-personnel squad jumped out. The pilot double checked to see everyone was out. The second pilot gave a thumbs up for all clear. The transport lifted up and flew away. Sergeant Beau gave hand signals and the squad walked to the vault building where the marines stored the small arms (rifles and pistols). Everyone signed their weapons back, but the weapons specialist told the squad to hold their tactical knives. The squad walked back to the barracks. Sergeant Beau called everyone to her. "Okay, you have a week off, but some only have two days off. If I see you in the mess hall, I see you. Get cleaned up and get sleep. Dismissed." All of them walked to their bunks.

Joseph put his things down on his bunk and asked Ion and Zarn. "I am taking a backpack. You guys want something from the store? Only fruit drinks." They both asked him to get them drinks. Joseph walked to the middle of the barracks. The MP looked at him.

Joseph: "Hello, officer. Can I knock, I am going to the store and just want to ask."

MP: "Go ahead private. Knock." He knocked on the ladies' section of the barracks. Alice came out with half her combat suit off. Alice: "Hi Joseph, what do you want?" She smiled and he looked at her.

Joseph: "Okay, ask Orka if she wants something from the store, and do you want something?"

Alice: "Oh, I want a drink." He looked at her and waited. She looked up for a second.

Alice: "Okay, okay, I know no drinking, no kissing, and no smoking. Yes, get me that human strawberry drink. Thanks. I am going to get Orka. Oh, I know she is going for one of those sea drinks." Alice ran back into the ladies' section.

Orka came out with a smile. "You know what drink I like." He looked at her. "Yes, you want the tree root with seaweed and fruit juices. That one you like."

Orka: "Yes, that one. Get two of them for me. Thank you. You still got your helmet, and you did not change."

Joseph: "No, Micky, I want to get out, then come back."

They hugged each other. Orka: "Come back fast and be careful." Joseph ran down the stairs and then outside. He looked up at the night sky.

Joseph walked to the last checkpoint. "Hello, Sir."

Colonel Aodh walked to Joseph. "So, where are you going?"

Joseph took out his ID and stood at attention. The MP looked at him. "Private First Class. Empty bag."

Joseph: "Sir, I am going to get some juice drinks. I am just crossing the street and then I will return, Sir."

Aodh: "Okay but wait one minute. Is your suit tracker on?"

Joseph: "Yes, Sir, I have not turned it off, Sir." Aodh: "Okay private. Do not turn it off until you get back to the barracks."

Joseph: "Sir, Yes, Sir." He began to cross the huge six-way street. Colonel Aodh looked at the military police in the booth. "I know you are new at this, and I scanned him. I want you to track him and it will be good training for you." MP looked at the computer at the desk: "Sir, I have the private." Aodh: "We track them from time to time to keep the soldiers out of trouble."

Joseph walked across the median of the road, when an MP outside saw something flying low over the road. The officer looked at the head military police officer teaching the new MP. "Sir, Colonel! Do you see that?!" The MP pointed at the very low flying cargo shuttle. Joseph never saw or heard the low flying shuttle over the traffic. He saw five shadows moving at him at the last minute. Joseph was hit by four electrical nets, and he hit the ground. The alarms on the base were now sounding. He was thrown into the shuttle and the commando team jumped in. The cargo shuttle lifted off the ground. They closed the door as the MP stormed across the road. They watched the shuttle accelerate into the sky.

Colonel Aodh looked at the new officer. "You have him! Tell me you have him?"

MP watch the computer screen carefully: "Sir, we are tracking him!"

Aodh: "Send that to Star Base Admiral One Priority One! I want my marine brother back. Get me a strike team and call the General. Hit the alarm."

The alarms sounded throughout the base. Sergeant Beau screamed out. "You got one minute to get your combat gear on and get your weapons." The sergeants ran into their offices and opened the emergency arms locker and gave out weapons to the marines on the floor. There was a banging on the walls from the MP. The sergeant ran out. MP looked at the sergeants: "Command wants a count."

Karen: "Sergeant Karen Beau. MP, I am missing one. Private First-Class Joseph Ramiro. Missing. He went to the store."

. The MP picked up the phone. "Sir, like I said, I saw him leave the building to the store. He is ours. Sending information now, Sir."

The officer put the phone down. "Order is to defend this building."

Star Base.

Brigadier General Tatius called Admiral Ryder on Star Base 17. "Ma'am, we are tracking him, you should have it now."

She looked at her intelligence officer. "Tell me good news." Intel officer: "Admiral! We have him. He is alive. I do not think they know his tracker is on. We also have the shuttle on radar and scanners. The sky is clear in front of the shuttle. There is a beacon going off, the cargo shuttle is stolen. The shuttle's tracker is on, and the shuttle's computer is talking to our computer. The shuttle is up for maintenance, it only has sub warp and ion drive. Ma'am, they can still fly to a ship and jump to warp. A small fleet is on an intercept course. That shuttle is going straight to the Ittors ship. There is a United Planets cruiser near that ship. It is an Avenger class. It is 19 kilometers or 11.8 miles out from that ship."

Annie saw the red phone light come on. She pushed the button and picked up the phone. "Go!"

"Hello Admiral Ryder, this is Rear Admiral Trey. There is a cruiser on a watch eye mission. It is called Independence. We did not know they were going to do this. The cruiser Captain is waiting for your call." The line went dead.

She looked at her comms officer. "Call the Independence cruiser Captain!"

Comms officer: "Captain on the line."

Ryder: "Captain! Tell me good news."

Captain: "Admiral, the shuttle landed on the Ittors ship. We are locking weapons on that ship and calling them."

Admiral Ryder's data phone came on and she read a message, *Received information and waiting for intelligence.* It was from Fleet Admiral Shar. The Captain of the Independence moved his ship in front of the Ittors ship.

Ittors ship.

Gesa sat on the bridge of his ship. His eyes widened and he jumped to his feet. Gesa pointed at the view screen. "Colonel! What is going on? That cruiser has all its weapons locked on us. Raise shields! They are ready to fire on us!"

Colonel: "You wanted the boy right and you wanted him questioned."

Gesa looked at the view screen then at him. "You should have questioned him on the planet! You question him on the planet! What do I tell them now?! We have a warship ready for a fight and more on the way! Where are you taking him?!"

Colonel: "To the Brig on the ship."

Gesa: "Do not close that door." Gesa looked at the view screen.

The comms officer looked at him. "We are being hailed by the warship. They are warning us not to move or we will be fired upon."

Gesa watched the warship move in front of the view screen. The warship was now face to face with his ship. Gesa: "Comms officer, hold them up. Tell them I am trying to find out what is going on."

Comms: "Sir, they are demanding answers. We have twenty fighter wings and other wars ships coming at us. We have fifty marine boarding ships coming from the star base. Sir, the United Planets is saying they will not negotiate with terrorists. They will board us when the marines get here. Look, I did not sign up for this."

Gesa looked at the Colonel. "Everyone, calm down. Take the boy to the brig Colonel, and do not close that door. Not a thing should happen to him. Tell me about the shuttle."

The Colonel looked at him. "We did not buy it."

Gesa: "You fool, that shuttle was for cargo and that is what it was for! They got a tracker on it." Gesa waved his hand and sat down with his hands over his face.

Hanger.

The cargo shuttle doors opened and the commander of the commandos touched his ear mic. "Change of orders. We are still going to the brig." They took Joseph out of the nets and carried him to the interrogation room. The commando team opened the door and put him in a chair.

One of the commandos pointed at the floor. "I will watch the kid in this cell. He is a human boy. He cannot give me trouble and I have my armor on. Too bad we have to leave the door open." The four other commandos walked down the hall. They were looking for the security in charge of the brig. The commando team heard a loud thump coming from the brig. Something heavy hit the ground.

The commander pointed at the brig. "One of you check it out."

One of the commandos replied, "I will be back." He walked back to the cell and found the other commando dead on the floor. He took a closer look and saw something had crushed his neck. He saw two vents' doors open and saw Joseph under the table looking up at the vents. "What happened?"

Joseph pointed. "I do not know what it is, but it came out of the vent and then went back into the vent. Get me out of here."

Commando: "Stay there human, do not move." The commando put his head into one of the vents. The last thing he felt was someone kick the back of his head. Blood sprayed everywhere as the lifeless body fell from the vent. The three-man commando team heard a loud bang in the vent from the brig. They ran back to the brig to find out what had happened.

Bridge

Gesa looked at the view screen. "What is wrong with the cameras in the brig? Send a maintenance team to check it out. Someone, call the commandos. Tell them to check in. I need to know what to tell that Captain. When you talk with the commandos tell them to take the boy to medical."

Comms officer: "Sir, Ambassador is calling."

Gesa: "Hold him up. Tell them we have a gas leak."

Brig

Two of the ship's security walked to the brig. They saw Joseph running from the interrogation room. They watched him turn the corner and they ran after him. Two other security officers ran to the brig and ran into the interrogation room. Everything was destroyed in the room and blood was everywhere.

The commando team was dead. One of the guards pointed and they saw someone's legs at the end of the hall. They turned the corner and saw two dead. They walked down the hall and found four more dead. They found a body hanging from the overhead vent and another man was embedded into the wall. Some of the walls were ripped open and air lock doors were ripped apart. There was blood and body parts everywhere. They picked up a data phone to call the bridge and went to hit the alarm. The alarm never sounded. They heard horrifying screaming down the hall.

Bridge

Gesa had the captain of the warship on the screen. "Please, please. I want no problems, Captain. Those fools thought they had a runaway slave. They did not follow orders. I promise you. I told them to stay off the planet. I do not want to start a war. You can put the weapons away. My ship is going nowhere. They are not that smart."

Captain: "We want our marine back now! Or we will board you!"

Gesa: "Oh, you need something, like something from my government or something like that."

Captain: "We do not care! We will board you! They can talk later!" The comms officer jumped from his seat and his headphones landed on the floor, with screams for help coming from the other side. The captain of the Independent saw Gesa jump as he heard the screams.

Captain: "What is going on aboard that ship?!"

The old man helped up the comms officer. "Get up! Get up! Captain, I do not know, but I will." He looked at the security officers. "Where is the head of security and the Colonel?" The officers looked at each other.

The Captain tapped on the camera. "Gesa, what is going on?!"

Gesa: "Please, give me some time. The head of security and the Colonel went down to get your marine. Please, I beg you."

The navigation officer looked at his computer screen. "Twelve more warships are coming out of warp. They are not playing around."

Gesa looked at everyone. "Now guards, where is the head of security and the Colonel? Find them and find out what that screaming was about." The science officer tapped his computer screen.

Gesa: "What is it? Why are you tapping the screen?"

Science officer: "The head of security is dead. There is a weird report here. It says the human is running from something. This is not right."

Gesa looked at the science officer. "What?!"

Science officer: "There is something wrong here. Fifteen were reported dead and now twenty dead. There is something on the ship."

Gesa: "Shut down the bridge. Lock down the bridge!" The bridge doors closed.

Gesa: "Captain, please give me a minute." The view screen went dead.

Gesa: "What happened comms officer?!"

Comms officer: "They terminated the signal from their end."

Gesa: "I do not want them shooting holes in my ship! Get him back! Send a message to him! Tell him that we will find out what is happening, and the marine will be returned safely. Keep trying to get him back, I love this ship and I love my body. I am allergic to weapons fire." Gesa looked at the science officer. "Twenty dead! What decks?!"

Science officer: "Deck fourteen and fifteen. All over deck fourteen. There are now twenty-five dead."

Gesa: "That is the decks that go straight to the shuttle bay. Where the hell did, they get the shuttle? Ask the shuttle pilot."

Science officer: "The pilot is one of the ones dead. Deck sixteen now. Three more dead."

Gesa: "Arm everyone. I want ten-men teams."

Cruiser Independent.

The Captain sat in the captain's chair and looked at the three hundred and sixty all around view screens on the bridge. The Commander walked to the back of the bridge to the holographic table and turned it on. Commander: "Captain, Sir. Their computer core is sending us information." The Captain studied the ten view screens in front of the bridge.

Captain: "Comms, tell marine transport to slow down. I want to get this information. I wonder when they gave him that computer hacker device."

The commander looked at the intelligence officer. "Send it to the star base."

Captain: "Call Admiral Trey. Tell the marines to stop there. Something is happening on that ship. Back us away from that ship. Intel officer, you got anything?"

Intel officer: "Sir, I got one of their radios. I just hear screaming and shooting."

Captain: "Comms, get me Admiral Trey on a private line."

Star Base 17.

The intelligence officer called over to Admiral Ryder, and she ran to him. Intel officer: "Ma'am, we are getting information from the Ittors ship now."

Ryder: "Send it straight down to command."

Commander: "Ma'am, the Independent is moving away. The Super Carriers Gorbachev and Reagan is moving in but staying away. I am getting something from an open radio on the Ittors ship."

Ryder: "Well, let's hear it." Commodore: "Ma'am, you do not want to hear this."

Ryder: "Put it on the small mic here." Commodore: "Okay, I warned you."

Ryder: "Wait, give me your headset."

Intel officer: "Here Ma'am."

The Admiral listened in to the screams of horror. "Oh, take that back. What is on that ship? They need to be rescued."

Commadore: "Ma'am, Command just said no one on that ship. Let it play out."

Ryder: "Command knows. Can anyone else hear this?"

Commodore: "No, they need our military equipment, and they need to be nearby."

The Ittors Ship.

Gesa heard the engineering crew screaming for help as they died. The death toll slowly climbed. Gesa: "Close more doors to deck eight. Close the doors. Hell, close all doors, personnel only, open code. I want to see what is happening in engineering, give me cameras."

Science officer: "We have no cameras. That creature is giving off some kind of electrical discharge. We sent a crew down to check the computer core and they have not come back."

Gesa: "No word from them?"

Science officer: "Not one. Wait, I hear a team on deck 15. There is a team down there shooting at something. I hear a rocket launcher and missile fire."

Gesa looked at the science officer. "What?! Tell me!"

Science officer: "There is screaming, and someone said what is that. Another said let's get out of here and one of them said it is too dark to see. There it is. Look, you can see its eyes, then they are dead. I hear grenades and grenade launchers going off."

Gesa threw a cup across the bridge. "It goes up to ten, then turns around and goes back down to fifteen. Send a team of a hundred to the computer core. Now! So, we can unlock the lifeboats and get off this ship. How many dead?" Science officer: "Hundred."

Engineering

Joseph ripped a metal bar from the wall and jammed it in the gears of the door to engineering and the fusion core. He remembered what Orka taught him about how to read the Ittors language.

Cruiser Independent.

The Captain looked at the Commander. "Report!"

Commander: "Captain, we hear a lot of screaming on that ship. Gunfire and explosions. Something is killing them. They are using heavy weapon fire to defend themselves. They are shooting everything in their armory at something. A timer came on the screen and it says fusion core emergency ejection! Sir, no gases was ejected out first. That is no normal ejection!"

The Captain screamed. "Helm, Get us away from that ship! Now! Comms, call the fleet and tell them to get away from that ship."

The Captain picked up the phone. "Admiral Trey."

The Ittors ship

Gesa screamed as the engineering screen turned red across the board and alarms sounded. "Brace yourselves! Raise shields inside the ship! Now!"

Engine room

An engineer jumped at Joseph, but he was too slow. Joseph grabbed the back of his head and crashed it into the wall with force. The engineer fell to the ground dead. Joseph climbed into the vent as the security teams showed up. A makeshift bomb exploded. The security teams looked at each other as they heard a small bomb go off. The emergency core doors to space exploded open, and the escaping gasses sounded like air being forced through a tunnel. The massive fusion core ripped itself free with force destroying the large emergency doors and ripping out large decks as it flew into space. The power in the fusion core built itself up and the core exploded in space. The shock wave ripped the engineering department apart. The shockwave shot out hitting the Ittors' ship and the cruiser Independent. Both ships shook violently. It bounced off the Independent shields. The Ittors personnel that were still in the area were forced out the jammed opened emergency doors and secondary emergency doors. They flew into space and suffocated, cooked, and froze at the same time. New explosions erupted and three engines launched into space, taking with three security teams and ship personnel. More decks and ship hull ripped off as the eight small fusion cores were ripped off the ship. They exploded and more of the ship was ripped off. The warships outside felt the shock waves. The shock waves ripped massive holes in the ship. The ship's crew and soldiers were sucked into space. The shields on the Ittors ship collapsed, and the hull was cracked and vented gases and air.

Bridge

Gesa screamed at the comms officer as he climbed off the ground. "I am missing engineering decks! I am missing a quarter of my ship! The back end of the ship is gone. Call on the troops, arm everyone! What is going on with my ship? What is on this ship? I need a damage report!"

Helm: "Sir, we have red lights all over engineering and the ship."

Gesa turned on the screen. "Captain, your marine is somewhere on this ship. I need help. I need you to board my ship. I am requesting rescue. I have three hundred five dead. There is something on this ship. We need help."

The Captain looked at Gesa on the view screen. "You have small weapons fire. You have fires all around your ship. I can help if your ship was not spinning on all four accesses. You need to get control of that ship." One of the bridge doors opened, the guard ran in, and the door was quickly closed. Screams came from down the hall.

Captain: "What was that?"

Gesa: "Captain, I do not know. Please! There is something here. These fools brought something up here with them."

Captain: "I called in a tug. It will be here shortly."

Somewhere on the Ittors ship deck30

Two teams of ten troops of fully armed soldiers walked by each other in the dimly lit hall. Smoke grenades flew out of the vent. Joseph came out of the vent into the thick smoke and stayed low to the ground. He had guns in both hands and shot at both teams. The teams ended up shooting at each other. Joseph found a weapons locker and smiled. The lights on the ship began to turn off. A guard ran down the hall in time to see one of the soldiers being dragged into the dark. The soldier was screaming and clawing at the ground. The guard looked around and ran for his life. He saw a man in front of him waving at him to come to him. Something ripped him into the dark. The guard stopped and turned. He looked at the ceiling and saw something looking at him.

A three-man team saw Joseph running at them. The guards raised their guns and aimed past Joseph. The third guard pointed. "Something is chasing him. Ready yourselves and fire at it." The guards watched Joseph run at them, then they knew something was wrong. It was too late. Joseph ran onto the wall and across the wall and onto the ceiling. The guards looked in horror as Joseph began killing them. The last guard began shooting wildly at him and the hall lights went off. The last guard screamed out in horror as he died. A five-man team ran to the hall, looked into the dark hallway and turned on their flashlights. They saw the three dead guards but they never saw Joseph behind them hanging on the wall next to the ceiling.

Upper decks

Joseph opened hatches to the lower decks. The three-man team of guards did not see him in the dark. Joseph pulled one through the floor to the deck below and threw smoke grenades down and up. The guard hit the lower deck and fired. The two squads at the ends of the halls fired their weapons in panic. They fired rockets and missiles at each other. The guards who just lost a man shot down the hatch as another guard team below them fired up in panic. Smoke filled the hallways and people panicked. They fired their weapons as someone fired their weapons in the smoke. Chaos began to take over the ship as no one knew what was happening in the ship.

Bridge

Gesa looked at the lights. "Helm, tell me something?"

Helm: "I have nothing. I have no controls. Engineering is gone, controls is gone. We are dead in space. Computer core is gone. We have a quarter of a ship. Emergency power is struggling. Life support is barely on." Comms officer through off his headset. Cries of help and screams were erupting all over the ship. The noise of guns and heavy gun fighting erupted all over the ship. People were using heavy weapons and it sounded like a war broke out all over. No one knew where the monster was. There was gun fighting on all the decks and grenade explosions on the ship. The bridge crew heard missiles and rockets being fired throughout the ship. The ship was slowly going dark. Hatches were blown open to space. The venting air took more troops and personnel into space. They heard someone using a heavy machine gun outside the bridge doors, then they heard missiles and rockets firing.

Gesa turned on the data phone. "Dorock! What am I up against?!"

Dorock could hear the gun battles and the screaming on the other side of the phone. "Self-destruct your ship and kill it!"

Gesa: "That is no longer an option." Gesa heard the call end. He threw the phone into the wall. Someone hit the door to the bridge in a panic. The person screamed and white blood sprayed through the door. The lights went off on the bridge. The light came from emergency lights, the view screens and the computer consoles.

Gesa: "Everyone, arm yourselves. Close secondary doors. Comms get me the Colonel or anyone in his command group."

Comms officer looked at Gesa and pointed at his computer screen. "We are jamming our own comms. We can only talk to the outside world."

Gesa looked around the bridge. "Then stop us from jamming ourselves. Call for help. Damn, where is that tug boat to get us under control?"

Helm: "Sir, it is on its way. Marine boarding party stopped and is waiting."

Hanger

Joseph jumped through a hatch to the shuttle hanger. He saw the Major looking at him. "Good, you are still alive." He looked around and saw the Colonel was dead. The Captain was bleeding out and the Major was wounded. Joseph heard gunfire down the hall. The Ittors were shooting at each other and killing themselves. He looked behind the Major. The shuttle bay crew walked in front of him. A metal wagon was next to Joseph. He grabbed the thousand-pound wagon and swung it at the crew, crushing all of them beneath it. The Major jumped back and looked at Joseph. "It is you!" The lights went out in the hanger and horrifying screams cried out.

Bridge

The gunfire and screaming stopped. The ship was dead quiet and dark. The science officer looked at their computer screen. "Emergency power is gone. They are all dead. We are left."

Gesa looked at the view screen. "Captain, help us."

Captain: "We have a tugboat trying to connect to your ship now."

Gesa looked at the emergency lights as they went off. Light came from the view screen and computers. Gesa looked at the view screen: "We have no time. That thing is trying to get in here."

Captain: "Try your best to stay alive. How many did you have on that ship?"

Gesa watched the computer consoles go dead. "I had one thousand two hundred and twenty-five on board this ship. There are twenty-five working on their own on the planet."

Two Ittors put their guns to their heads and pulled the trigger. Gesa screamed, "No! Stop!" They heard one of the bridge doors get forced open. It was too dark to see the doors.

Gesa looked around the dark in panic: "That thing is in here with us!" Gesa turned in time to see the navigation officer's chest explode and his lifeless body hit the ground.

The security officer looked around wildly with his weapon in his hand. "Where did the other guard go?! He was here a second ago. The overhead vent is open." The science officer was pulled into the darkness but there were no screams.

They turned when something smashed into the wall. It was too dark, and they saw the communication officer was missing. Then, they heard a crushing noise and saw the helm driver missing. The Guard stopped looking around and saw the horror in Gesa's face. It was behind him, and he could feel it. The guard's head was crushed and what was behind him went into the darkness. Gesa was so scared he dropped his gun. He breathed hard and shook in fear. He was the last one alive and that thing was playing with him. Gesa could barely make out the monster's golden green eyes looking at him from the darkness. It was just waiting and looking at him. He thought and screamed at it, "What are you?!" The creature jumped on a computer console and sat down. Gesa jumped when someone cleared their throat behind him.

Gesa turned to look at the view screen to see Admiral Tray looking at him. "Admiral, what is it?" Trey: "The boy from M793. What did you do to him? The M9 system. Ittors people and you had a chance to save him, but you left him there to die. Taking the girl away you promised him he will be free and be kept free."

Gesa: "This is about revenge!"

Trey: "No, not at all. You got them involved in something they do not want to be part of. It Is about leaving them alone and free. Let them live their lives. Oh, one other thing. I held up everyone. We could have been on your ship at any time."

Gesa: "Admiral, he is behind me!"

Trey smiled: "Yes, he is."

The view screen went dead and now there was no power or air. Gravity and all life support were failing. Gesa turned slowly. The light that came from a port window showed Joseph's silhouette. The phone came to life and Dorock picked up the phone. "Did you kill it?! Gesa!" He heard the ripping, crushing and braking of Gesa's body. He heard Gesa's screaming in torturous pain, then, the gargling of blood and silence. Dorock shrieked, then he heard, "Death!" The phone went dead.

Cruiser Independent.

The tug stopped the Ittors ship from spinning. Commander: "Captain, everyone is dead on the ship but one. It is our marine. He is in the cargo shuttle. There is no life support or oxygen. It stopped working on that ship."

The Captain looked at his Commander. "What is the name of that ship?"

Commander: "Sir, it is the Ta z da, it means Superior." A special troop carrier came up to the ship Ta z da. Tactical shuttles came out of the amphibious assault carrier. All of the ship's systems were dead with no power at all. The marines dropped on the hull of the ship. Their main mission was to get their marine back. Fire teams slowly walked into the shuttle bay. Bodies, body parts, and blood were floating in zero gravity. Marine First Lieutenant: "Marines, check every corner and look out for boobytraps. Keep your eyes open and head on a swivel." One marine raised his arm as they walked to a closed cargo shuttle.

"Staff Sergeant, he is inside." The marines took control of the shuttle bay and the hanger. The marines were entering the ship through the blown-out hatches and torn open hull. The hallways were full of bodies, body parts, and blood. Private: "Gunnery Sergeant, it looks like they just painted the walls." Sergeant: "Corporal, watch your corners and that scanner." The combat medic looked into the shuttle and then down at the scanner. "Gunnery, the marine is wounded, and you clearly see he used the bio foam. He is alive. The shuttle is pressurized. We will have to enter through the air lock. There is no gravity in the shuttle as well." The marines walked, climbed, and crawled through every deck and vent on the ship.

The entire ship was now taken, except the bridge. The marines slowly walked onto the deck of the bridge. The hall looked freshly painted. The walls, floor, ceiling, and doors was drenched in Ittors blood. A marine captain walked onto the shuttle bay deck and looked at his watch. "This whole ordeal lasted for over ten hours. Get our brother out of the shuttle and back to the base. The medics are waiting on him." The combat medic went into the air lock and gave a thumps up that their brother had pressurized his suit. The marines depressurized the cargo shuttle and opened its doors. They stormed onto the shuttle. They put Joseph into the clear case gurney and pressurized it. The rescue shuttle backed into the shuttle bay. The rear ramp lowered, and they put the case with Joseph on the ship. The ramp closed.

The medical personnel on the shuttle opened the case and put Joseph on the medical bed. They tied him to the bed and the medical team stabilized him. The head medic gave a thumps up for the pilot, and the medical team sat down and strapped in. The rescue shuttle lifted off the deck and flew out of the shuttle bay. The pilot of the rescue shuttle nosedived and accelerated to the planet below. The marines pried the doors open to the bridge. The bodies laid about. Gesa's body was mangled, and his face was ripped from his head and placed on the view screen.

The base.

Orka put her things away. A different alarm sounded on the base. It was the medical alert. Orka turned to run to medical. Alice and Ion grabbed her.

Orka: "Let me go! I need to know! It is over twelve hours."

Sergeant Beau looked at her. "Brigadier General Tatius ordered you to stay away from medical. The orders are for you to stay on the base. No waterways."

Orka looked at her. "I need to know. Sergeant."

Karen walked over: "Orka, go to the beach and wait there. I will find out what I can."

Orka looked down. "Thank you, Sergeant."

Ion: "Will she be safe there, Sergeant?"

Karen: "There are marines in those waters and on the beach twenty-four. You can go with her. The squad can go with her. We got the stand down order."

Alice hugged Orka. "He is okay. Let's get this gear off and stored away. Then we will go to the beach."

The main building.

Rear Admiral Trey looked at General Tatius walking into his office. Trey: "Yes?"

Tatius: "Admiral, why are you not worried about the twenty-five hunters on this planet?"

Trey: "General, you think I am not worried. I am. Did you read their history? They call Orka's species the Alpha predator of their planet. They have always been dangerous to the Ittors. It is Orka. She never had the surgeries. We undid the surgeries. Her species started to work more efficiently when we took out the control chips. Just think about it. Joseph trained her in the old ways."

Tatius: "There is nothing to think about. Old ways. What does that mean? I am doubling up the guard."

Trey: "General."

Tatius: "What? Old ways. She knows hand to hand combat better. She knows how to swing a blade. They got guns, laser guns, pulse guns, plasma guns, and the other guns. The other guns phaser array or disruptor array guns. Pick one."

Trey: "You made your point."

Tatius: "Good, armor is on the way and air cover."

The beach.

Orka sat at the beach and waited. Her friends watched over her. Orka looked out at the ocean: "You guys do not have to guard me."

Ion walked up to her. "We are not guarding you. We are helping you. I care for him and honor him. Sister, he helped you and our people. I care for him."

Orka: "You hated him."

Ion: "Forget the past and live for the here and now. He is a good man."

Alice hugged Orka as their friends surrounded them. Lance Corporal Zarn walked to her. "I just met the man, but I think he is amazing and a strong man."

Corporal Valda looked at Orka. "The Sergeant is coming. I just met him, and he will be okay, don't you worry. He is awesome."

Sergeant Beau walked on the beach. "Okay, everyone's eyes and ears on me. Joseph is going to be okay. We can all go to see him." Orka got up and the squad walked to the medical bay. They walked into Joseph's hospital room and found him asleep.

The doctor walked into the room. "All of you cannot be here. He needs his rest." The squad went to walk out, but Ion stopped Orka.

Ion: "You stay with him."

The doctor looked at Ion. "She is not his family."

Ion: "Sir, Doctor, they are family. She chose him and he chose her. They are bonded. It is the bonding custom of my species. They are family, Sir."

The doctor took a step back. "Well, it is your custom and I respect that. As long as she is not on duty or working and she gets rest, she can stay." Orka took a chair and moved it to Joseph's bedside. She crossed her arms on the bed and laid her head down on the bed. Orka closed her eyes and prayed for her hero."

On Searrun.

Dorock kneeled out of the way to the camera of the view screen. The view screen came to life. High Ambassador Tara kneeled then stood up. She looked down. "Yes, Emperor Xona. What a privilege for your call."

Emperor Xona looked at her carefully. "Did you hear what happened with the inspector?"

She was first going to say no, then changed her answer. "Yes, Sir. I did, but I did not know how to tell you, my Emperor."

Xona: "So, you were going to lie to me?"

Tarra: "No, Sir. Please. I changed the inspector. That is what I have done."

Xona: "What did you hear? What happened to him?"

Tara: "Sir, what I heard is that he brought his personal ship, and it has been confiscated. This whole situation is under investigation."

Xona: "You did change the inspectors and he brought his ship. Any more information?!" The emperor slammed his fist into the desk. "Anything?!" Xona looked at her. "Any orders you gave?"

Tara: "No, Sir."

Xona: "I was just schooled by military Command and Ambassadors! If you do not know what military command is, that is twenty people from the military and ten ambassadors."

She looked up from looking at the floor. "My Emperor."

Xona: "What I want to know is did you order the kidnapping of a United Planet Marine!"

She had a shocked look on her face. "No, never. I never gave an order such as that. Sir, he asked if he could ask questions to someone. I never knew he went that far."

Xona: "Did you know he also had one thousand troops on board his ship? Why did he need one thousand troops and twenty-five elite hunters? There's something you are not telling me! Twenty-five elite hunters are now on the planet of Kallos. Why?!"

Tara looked down. She knew at any time Emperor Xona could have her killed. She knew the history of the emperors and how quickly they killed those they mistrust. Tara shook with fear and tears came to her eyes. "Please, Sir. My Emperor. I had no idea."

Xona: "Do you know his ship is in a dry dock?"

Tarra: "No Sir. My Emperor. What happened to the crew and the troops?"

The emperor could see the fear in her face. "One thousand two hundred personnel killed by some beast. In the conflict the marine was shot, and the marine still lives. The twenty-five on the planet. I asked for them to be hunted down and killed. They are the enemy."

Tara looked at the screen. "My Emperor. What do you want from me?"

Xona: "You will call and express your deepest apologies. Our people are almost at war with the United Planets. A war I do not want. A war we will never win. The people are sick and tired of all this war the old emperors and their children love to get into. My people are happier now with more money and food in them. They are happy they have had over fifty years of peace. They are happy they are not sending loved ones to war. I want peace. I sent a heavy cruiser to the planet Kallos to assist. The United Planets Navy almost blew up the cruiser when it came out of warp. The captain of the cruiser called me, and I ordered him to let them board the ship. Our captain lowered the shields and let them board. The United Planets took and impounded our heavy cruiser. They took the crew captive. Get them to understand we had no knowledge and no control over his actions."

Tarra: "Yes Sir."

Xona: "I have to go to the United Planets headquarters. I personally have to clean this up." She looked at him about to turn off the view screen, then he stopped. "How many dead now? What is the death count at? Over hundred? I know of that crime lord sending hunters there. Find Dor whatever his name is! Bring him to me for questioning. I want no more of our people going to that world."

Tara bowed her head. "Yes, my Emperor."

Xona: "Okay, I want a meeting tomorrow, that is it. Have a good night." The view screen went dead. Ambassador Tara walked to her desk and sat down. She looked at Dorock. "Get your elite hunters off the planet for now. Let things calm down. Then we will do it like Thal said, covertly."

Luxury farmhouse.

The mother looked at Dorock. "So, what do you have?"

Dorock looked at her. "We still have someone on the inside. I got you vials of her blood and others with the same blood." He put a five-gallon container made of special materials on the floor in front of her. She sat down on the couch.

Her son walked in and sat down at the desk. "And the twenty-five elite hunters?"

Dorock looked at him. "They are on the planet, and I was told to have them removed."

Prince Korien walked in. "No. They will finish their mission on that planet. We need more blood, and we want our property. She is making a new product chain. We can clone the blood, but we need more."

The Prince looked at Dorock. "Do not worry about my father. His health will decline."

On Kallos.

Orka felt someone running their fingers through her hair. "I like your hair and how you can move it."

She smiled at Joseph. "You, okay?"

He smiled. "Yes, the doctor said the suit did its job and the bio foam. I should be out of here in a week."

Orka: "Good. You hungry?"

Joseph: "No, Orka, but you should go back to the barracks and get rest. You look tired."

She smiled. "I need to watch over you."

Joseph: "I am okay. I am in the hospital. Go get rest."

Orka: "Okay, I will be back after breakfast."

Joseph: "See you then." Orka got up and hugged Joseph. Then, she closed the door behind her as she walked out. Orka walked down the stairs and saw

Ion sleeping on the stairs. She tapped him on the shoulder and he opened his eyes. "Yes, Orka."

Orka: "You should go to the barracks."

Ion: "I wanted to see Joseph."

She pointed. "Go see him, he is up. I am going to the barracks." Ion watched her walk out of the hospital and run across the street. She ran into a dark field toward the barracks. He walked up the stairs and heard physical fighting in the hall. He looked down the hall and saw a hunter fighting with the hospital staff. The heavy door to Joseph's room was closed. Ion pulled his knife from his belt. He ran at top speed toward the hunter. The anger of the hunters hunting his family drove Ion forward to save Joseph. The hunter never saw Ion leap through the air. At that last second, the hunter saw Ion in the air with both hands on his knife. The hunter had no time to react. Ion put his whole-body weight behind the strike. The seven-inch blade pierced into the hunter's body. The hunter hit the ground, lifeless. The doctor got up from the ground and helped a nurse up. Doctor: "Marine, stand guard. Nurse, call the MPs. I am going to hit the button for general alert."

The alarm sounded.

In the barracks, Sergeant Karen gave out the rifles and weapons. She called on her marines. "We have orders to save our own. We are to locate Orka. Marines! Move out!"

The field.

Orka walked through the darkness. She heard something coming up behind her. She looked behind her and saw two hunters running into the darkness. She dropped to one knee and remembered what Joseph taught her. She pulled her tactical cleaver from the back of the belt. Orka looked around quickly. Four hunters were trying to be silent. Orka looked for the closest hunter. The hunter to her left jumped out first. She swung the twelve-inch blade twice and the hunter came apart in the air. He hit the ground lifeless. Orka heard two hunters coming behind her fast. She rolled backward, Cutting the hand off one and the leg off the other. The hunter with no hand felt Orka's claws ripping through his face as her blade sliced through half his neck and his body hit the ground. The other hunter felt her claws rip into his chin. She pulled his chin up and sliced his neck open.

Orka jumped into the darkness as the last hunter got to her. The hunter stood in horror and felt her claws rip into his neck. Orka did not let the body hit the ground as she ran into the dark field. She was on the hunt. Orka's people are the top predators on her home world. Sergeant Karen Beau and her squad made it to the medical bay. The Corporal handed a rifle to Ion. The marines started their hunt into the darkness for Orka.

Field.

Orka saw hunters coming from the beach. They were running into the woods and the field where she had just killed the other hunters. One of the hunters stopped by the large tree and he looked into the darkness. He heard a windy noise. The cleaver flew through the air hitting the hunter squarely in the head. As the hunter collapsed, Orka retrieved her cleaver and cut the hunter's neck. The other hunter heard the hunter's body hit the ground. The hunter had enough time to see Orka swing her 12-inch tactical cleaver at his neck. She landed behind him as his head rolled on the ground. The marines found the bodies in the field. Sergeant Beau looked at Ion.

Ion: "Sergeant, these are elites. Orka is on the hunt."

Alice pointed in the direction of the beach. "Orka is going to the beach."

Karen keyed her radio. Command: "Report."

Karen: "Sir, the fight is going to the beach. She is on the hunt now, as her brother said." The radio came to life. "Armored columns on the way. Air support if needed. Drone eyes in the sky." The Sergeant gave the hand signal to move out.

Woods

Orka put her blade through the back of a hunter, and it came out of his chest. She pulled the blade out and saw he had two seven inch knives. A hunter saw her and charged at Orka. He fell to the ground lifeless with a knife in his chest. A hunter looked around a tree and his lifeless body hit the ground with a knife in his neck. A hunter ran around the tree, and he hit the ground lifeless as his head rolled away. Another hunter ran to see what happened and was cut down by the darkness.

Shots rang out wildly. Orka rolled and unarmed a hunter and cut him down. A six-man team of hunters was now barreling down on her as she jumped behind a tree. Orka took a deep breath. The first two came around the tree on either side. They never saw the gunshots that ripped through them. The last four stormed around the tree and looked around, but Orka was not there. Shots rang out above them. She put her cleaver back in its sheath as she ran out on the beach. Orka looked and saw six hunters on a deck. Four jumped into the ocean. She then heard something behind her. Orka looked back and could barely see her squad some distance in the dark woods. Behind the marine squad were armed units. Armored personnel carriers letting their marine infantries out.

She took off at top speed to the docks. One of the hunters turned in time to get shot point blank range in the face. Orka threw down the gun and jumped over the collapsing body. The last hunter on the dock felt her claws rip into his chest as he grabbed her. They both fell into the ocean.

Alice made it to the end of the dock and ran back to the squad. "Sergeant, white blood is coming up where they went into the water." Karen looked at Ion.

Ion looked out into the water: "Ittors blood, sergeant." Everyone saw one of the hunters trying to climb out of the water onto the dock. Orka swam out of the water onto his back and ripped into his back with her two-inch claws. She used her massively strong legs to pull him back into the water.

The hunter let out a horrifying scream of pain and a cry out for anyone to help. The last thing anyone saw was his hands going down as his blood rose to the surface of the water. Ion and his people stood by the water's edge. They crossed their arms and looked down at the water. Then, they turned, and all their eyes turned black. They made whale noises to each other.

General Tatius ordered them to their squads. "Ion, is it safe to go in the water to help Orka?"

Ion looked at the ocean and then at the General as his eyes changed back to normal. "Sir, it is highly unwise, Sir. The great hunt is on, and she has the taste of the blood of her enemies. My species now see Orka as the Goddess of war and Joseph as the God of war. The only ones that can tame each other. Beneath the Great master of all the universes and Great living God above all."

The General walked back and whispered to himself. "Great, we take the computer chip out of them, and they need more evolutionary advances from the cave man. Great, I have Achilles and his wife." He looked at the Captain. "Get me a radio operator and get me the Admiral!" One of the hunters tried climbing out of the water onto the dock. Orka's hands came out of the water and grabbed his head. She pulled him back down into the depths of the ocean. The last two hunters climbed out of the water. One stood on a metal buoy and the other climbed onto the deck holding his bleeding stomach. The hunter was missing his chest armor. Orka jumped out of the water over the deck and pulled the hunter into the water by his head. The ocean was full of the blood of the hunters.

A hunter looked at the marines on the beach. "Help me! Help me get off this buoy! Come on help me!" The marines waited for orders that never came. The hunter felt something jump onto the buoy. He slowly turned and saw Orka. Her eyes were as black as night. She was eating something, and white blood came from it. The hunter was horrified. She was eating the hunters she had killed. The hunter screamed in horror as he threw two knives at her. "OH, GOD! HELP ME! SOMEONE!" Orka easily smacked the knives away. The hunter pulled his pistol, and she smacked it out of his hand.

She growled and jumped at the hunter's upper body. They both fell into the ocean and white blood rose to the surface. A shuttle flew out of the water and a missile slammed into it. The shuttle immediately exploded and crashed into the ground. Fighters flew overhead and the water was full of the elite hunter's blood. Orka walked out of the water.

Orka: "Hello, Sergeant." Everyone saw she was drenched.

Tatius looked at Sergeant Beau. "Sergeant, get her too medical." The squad escorted Orka back to the medical bay. Her eyes slowly changed back to her cat purple eyes.

Ion looked at her. "It will be okay. No one has hunted like that in a long time. You are at the age for a hunt. Your people are happy. Now we will take you to Med Bay. They will get you cleaned up."

Star Base 17 dry dock.

Captain Davis walked around Gesa's ship with her space suit. She looked around with her flashlight and looked down using the scanner.

Camille: "Admiral Trey, the inside of this ship is a mess. Like you said, a war was fought here. Three decks up and two decks to the side blew up. The missile came from inside the maintenance vent. There was a rocket fired from inside the elevator shaft. Command wants a report. Well, he used darkness, smoke grenades with grenades. I found where he got wounded. It appears a lot of them panicked and they shot at the shadows of their friends. You see, he jumped from one vent to the other across a hall. Sir, what will happen to the ship?"

Trey: "Captain, the ship will be destroyed after you do your investigation. There will be no evidence. Need to know only."

Camille: "Whoa, I almost fell in a hole in the wall. I am almost at Gesa's quarters. The marines went through this ship, Sir."

Trey: "Yes, they did. They scanned everywhere and found nothing of interest. They took the computer core with them."

Camille: "Sir, I am in his room and found something disgusting. I do not want to talk about it. I thought they cleaned this ship up."

Trey: "They did not have enough time. Their emperor wants this ship destroyed after our investigation."

Camille: "Found something, a ledger and a map of star systems. I was in the Captain's office, and it was blown up. On my way out."

Trey: "Captain, how did it get blown up?"

Camille: "Sir, someone fired a rocket through the vent and that is how it got blown up. I found wildfires that burned the crew and troops. Special gas pipes exploded making some of the halls like fire tubes. I am getting out of here. There is nothing here. On my way out."

The base.

The next morning. Admiral Trey looked at General Tatius. "Emperor Xona said there will be no more attacks."

Tatius: "Sir, we will have to see."

Trey: "We deployed a fleet to their system and there are three fleets here."

Captain Davis hit a button and the view screen came to life. High Ambassador Tara looked at them. "I must say sorry and my deepest regret. I never knew the inspector's intentions. I changed the inspectors because he requested to do his inspections there and early. I am severely sorry."

Trey looked at her. "Do you know anything that played out here last night on the base?"

Tarra: "I have no knowledge of anything that happened there last night." The puzzled look on her face told Trey she had no clue of the incident.

Trey: "There was an attack here last night of twenty-five hunters. They were quickly dispatched."

Tarra: "Admiral, I have no knowledge of this. The Emperor has posted strict laws to find anyone sending hunters there or ordering them to go there will be killed. Anyone wanting to go to Kallos now must get permission from the Magistrate and the United Planets."

Admiral Trey studied her. "Your Emperor is at the Council. I know he is talking. He has no clue, and he is requesting a full investigation."

Mess hall.

Ion sat down for lunch next to Alice. Karen sat down with Zarn and Valda. Karen: "Alice, you saw Orka and Joseph last. How are they?"

Alice: "Well, Sergeant, they got them in medical tanks. You know the tanks that help you heal faster. I saw them get moved, but I do not know where."

Ion drank water from his cup. "I saw them as well."

The planet Searrun.

The mother walked through the luxury farmhouse. The sun was setting, and she walked into the office. Her son was watching the sunset. She put the wine cup down on the desk and walked to her son. "Dorock is coming here after his meeting. So, son, what do you think are his plans? I do not mean Dorock. He is just a piece in the game."

Son: "Mother, I do not care what his plans are. Father supported him and I will support him. He will help our people more than his father. They say this will be the darkest night of the year."

The mother looked out the open doors. "It is a beautiful sunset."

"Yes, it is. Is it not?" The voice came from behind them. "Hello."

They both turned and saw Orka sitting at the desk sipping wine from the mother's wine cup. Orka smiled. "Hi, looking for me?" She tossed the cup. "That does taste good, but I cannot have that." The mother quickly pulled a remote from her pocket and hit the button.

Orka: "Oh, that did hurt at one time." Orka easily took off the collar. "Oh, this does not work. I do not have a helmet." She put the collar on the desk.

The mother looked at her angrily. "You beast!" Her son took a step toward Orka. Orka immediately opened the top right drawer to the desk and pulled the pistol out.

Orka: "No! And why does everyone put their gun in the same place? Oh, I do know my way around this house." She put the pistol on top of the desk and made sure it was loaded.

The son looked at her. "I have thirty guards."

Orka smiled. "Dead guards. You did not hear us kill them and it is daylight. Some are hanging from trees, stapled to walls, embedded, or implanted into walls or the ground, and some drowned. Heads and body parts are missing. Some are clawed and one has a shovel through his chest and he is nailed to a tree. I said ripped apart, that too." Orka picked up the wooden sheath for the small, crystal, bronze sword.

Orka: "Oh, I left this." She put the crystal bronze sword into the wooden sheath.

Orka stood up and broke a glass case. She pulled out her doll that her mother made her. A mother she will never know. She put it in her combat suit. Orka: "The doll belongs to me!" The son looked at her.

Mother: "You are my property."

Orka: "I am no one's property. No living intelligent person should be property. I am a free person. Order of your Emperor."

Orka walked between them. "Your Emperor Xona sends his regards." They looked at her with shock and horror. Orka pulled the crystal sword from its wooden sheath. She spun, slicing first through their necks then flipping the sword in midair stabbing them in their chest. Orka put the sword back in the sheath as the bodies hit the ground. She walked into the field where Joseph waited for her.

Joseph: "Come, Micky."

The High Ambassador's palace.

The sun fully set, and the night got dark. Not even a shadow could be found. Dorock kneeled and High Ambassador Tara walked in. She sat at her desk. "What do you have for me? I want more hunters for the covert operation. Now give me a report." Tara had placed extra guards around her office for that night. Two guards died instantly by the river, other guards had blades ripped into their chest, others walked to the wood line by the river.

Two drowned while three others received head traumas. Guards had their heads removed from their bodies and others had blades ripped through their backs and out of their chest. Others had their throats cut and some were pulled into the darkness. Four others had their chests crushed and some guards were hung by steel cables. Knives were thrown into guards' chests and backs. Some were pulled down from off the rear wall to their deaths. Guards tried to scream but it was too late, and they drowned in the pond. Others was embedded in the walls. A ten-man squad was hacked to death by a tactical axe and short sword. Some of them had a tactical spear ripped through their chest and thrown into them. Guards were stapled to trees and walls.

As one guard looked over a balcony, the guard behind him was choked to death. Before he could turn around his head was lobbed off. As a sixteen-man team ran out looking for three missing guards, they ran into the darkness and their bodies would not be found till morning. Guards were hanging from trees, and inside the building they were grabbed and killed. Bodies littered the courtyard, backyard, and pool. Inside, the guards died silently by the water fountain. Many died by being grabbed from the back of their heads as a blade was thrusted into them. High Ambassador Tara heard something happening in the hallway behind the closed doors. She stood up and walked over to the center of the room. They both jumped as the secret door opened slowly and she walked closer to Dorock. He now had his pistol in his upper right hand. The loyal General to the High Ambassador walked out of the secret door slowly looking down at the spear sticking out of his chest. Someone thrusted the spear through his body. The General collapsed dead.

Ambassador Tara screamed out in horror. The doors to the main hallway flew open but there was no one there. They saw bodies and blood in the hallway. Tara hit the button on her belt. They heard alarms sounding around the building, but no guards came to them. She screamed out, "I have a one thousand men army on the way, and I have six hundred armed men on the grounds!" They both wondered where the guards were. Dorock looked at the opened doors and got up. He walked to the doors, slowly aiming his pistol at the open doorway. They heard someone at the desk and looked quickly at the desk. Orka sat at the desk with the spear she removed from the General's corpse.

Orka looked at Tara: "You have no more guards."

Ambassador Tara took a step back and looked at Dorock. "Shoot her!" Dorock had a look of horror on his face as he looked at Tara. Three of his hands had something held tightly in the dark. A shadow stood in front of him. All Tara could see was the shadow and its golden green eyes.

They heard Orka say the words they most feared. "Your Emperor Xona sends his regards. He does not need your services anymore."

Dorock slowly turned his head toward the shadow. He let out a horrifying scream as the shadow used one hand to crush his hand that held the gun. Tara could hear the gun and Dorock's bones breaking in his hand. She screamed in horror and the shadow kicked Dorock thirty feet from the doorway. Dorock slid across the marble floor in her office, and he dropped the crushed gun he held in his broken hand. The Ambassador went to run but was grabbed by Orka and thrown to the ground. She turned the Ambassador over. Joseph walked out of the shadows toward Dorock: "You remember me Dorock!" Dorock screamed out. "Joseph, Please Have Mercy!" Joseph "You gave me none on M793! I will show you the same hospitality!" Tara looked up at Orka, but her head was forced to look at Dorock.

Orka: "You should have left me on planet M793. All we wanted was to love each other and be free. Now watch and look at the monsters you help make. You left him in a pool of his blood. You and the others. All of you beat him and threw him around. You hunted him for trying to free me. The only thing he wanted was to free me and get off the planet."

Tarra: "Joseph, He is a human boy, but how?"

Orka: "Planet M793 makes nightmarish creatures. They call it the Hell planet. Give the planet time, and it changes anything that can change. Humans do have the body for that, but you have to have the mind for it too, or you go mad."

The Ambassador watched in horror as Joseph punched and kicked Dorock as he screamed for death. Tara heard the horrifying noise of Dorock's bones breaking and being crushed to dust. Dorock begged for death, and he began to gargle on his blood as he begged. Joseph took his time. Dorock was now bleeding through his skin and had problems breathing. Tara was screaming and crying as she watched. She tried to get loose, but Orka's training with the marines made her too strong for Tara to fight. She begged to see no more and begged to be let loose. She remembered what they did to Joseph. How bad they beat him and she watched and helped. Tara knew she would be next. Joseph walked behind Dorock and made him look at Ambassador Tara. He grabbed his head and slowly crushed it.

Dorock screamed to his death and kept screaming until there was no more air in his lungs. Ambassador Tara watched Dorock's body hit the ground. She could see the sun had risen. Orka picked Tara up and slammed her into the ground. Orka ran out of the office and picked up a large bag. She ran down the hall. Joseph walked over to Ambassador Tara. She could hear the emergency vehicles coming to her aid, but Tara knew they would be too late. Joseph opened a window so all could hear. The Ambassador knew Orka was placing traps around the building, and she heard doors closing.

Tara closed her eyes and remembered they all had their fun with him. She remembered she threw Joseph around as he begged Ambassador Tara to stop. She remembered she laughed at the boy as she threw him out the shuttle rear ramp. Tara looked up at him and saw Joseph grabbing her. "Please, I am sorry for what I did to you. I will give you anything or tell you anything." Joseph looked into her eyes. She saw the think she now feared most. The golden green eyes of a predator up close. She felt the strength of a thousand men in his hands.

Joseph snarled at her as he looked into her terrified eyes: "The people with you said Death and I am Death! Let me help you with your flight. Is that what you told me?" Tara screamed in horror as she soared hundreds of feet through the air. She flew a hundred feet and hit the ground hard. Joseph was on her fast and threw the Ambassador through the wall. She screamed in horror as she went through the wall.

He moved fast and grabbed Tara in midair. Joseph threw the Ambassador through the floor. Tara felt herself break and she spit blood out of her mouth as she flew through the ceiling. The Ittors people heard High Ambassador Tara screaming in horror and for mercy. All Tara's bones shattered and broke as she went flying through the marble walls and floors. The armored vehicles got to the High Ambassador's Palace as Tara screamed and her lifeless body hit the ground in her office. The armed guards got themselves ready to storm into the building. The Emperor's shuttle landed, and the door slid opened. Emperor Xona walked out of the shuttle looking for the Chief Guard. Everyone saluted their Emperor.

Xona: "Everyone put your weapons down or away. I am going in."

The Chief Guard bowed his head. "Sir, my Emperor. That is not wise, Sir."

Xona looked at him. "I brought them here." The Emperor walked past the vehicles to the front gate. He looked at all the dead bodies in the front court-yard and walked to the front door. Xona knocked on the door with his cane.

Orka opened the door and the Emperor walked in. "Oh my! You two had fun. Hi, Joseph. I am so happy to see you again my old friend. Orka, Joseph and I go way back. We met on M793. I helped him and always went back to see him. Joseph, I got that candy you like. You can share it with Orka. Thank you for your help taking care of this problem. I am the informer. There is one last problem. He is on the planet Kallos. He killed a good friend of mine and he is after the young boy. He is now on Kallos. My personal guard and a very good friend. Make him suffer. You have to save the young boy. Now to get you out of here. Come, we are going to the roof." They walked to the roof and a United Planets shuttle landed.

Farmhouse

Prince Korien watched the shuttle leave into space. One of his staff looked at him. Aid: "Sir, you think it is wise to let them go?"

The Prince looked at Orka's dead masters. "It is the best thing my father did. Is my war going to start on time?"

Aid: "Yes, Sir."

Korien: "Good."

United Planets Frigate.

Joseph looked at Orka who was looking at a box. Joseph: "What is that?"

She looked at him. "The Emperor put this box in my bag, but before he did he showed me what it is. It is beauty products that are not good for me. It works only for a specific species." She opened the box, and they looked in it.

Orka: "It is beauty products. A whole line. He did know I was into medicine and science. He did say study and break the rules. Go to the academy. He said study this as he held the box. I will put it away until I can. That candy is good. I like it." They hugged each other as the ship went to warp. Okra looked into Joseph's eyes. "You know we are not allowed to kiss. There is no one here." Joseph looked around and smiled. Orka smiles as he looked into her eyes and they embraced.

The End For Now!   Counter ?

Death Count 2